PRAISE FOR *IF YOU LIE*

"Strap in. This thriller is as twisted, gripping, and bingeworthy as they come!"

———Noelle W. Ihli, author of *Ask for Andrea*

"*If You Lie* is jam-packed with suspense and tension. It's a twisty roller coaster ride of a thriller that left me breathless."

———Steph Nelson, Author of *The Final Scene*

"An addictive, action-packed thriller with gasp-worthy twists and a shocking conclusion. Grab your popcorn and settle in—you won't be putting this book down until it's done."

———Faith Gardner, author of *Like It Never Was*

"Set course for suspense! A tidal wave of twists and turns await you in the latest thriller from Caleb Stephens. *If You Lie* is one cruise you don't want to miss."

———C.B. Jones, author of *Crybaby Bridge* and *The Rules of the Road*

ALSO BY CALEB STEPHENS

The Girls in the Cabin
Feeders
Soul Couriers
If Only a Heart and Other Tales of Terror

IF YOU LIE

A PSYCHOLOGICAL THRILLER

CALEB STEPHENS

THRILLERSCAPE PRESS

Copyright © 2024 by Caleb Stephens
https://www.calebstephensauthor.com/

Published in the United States by Thrillerscape Press.

All rights reserved. No part of this publication may be reproduced, distributed, or transmitted in any form or by any means, including photocopying, recording, or other electronic or mechanical methods, without the prior written permission of the author, except in the case of brief quotations embodied in critical reviews and certain other noncommercial uses permitted by copyright law.

Any references to historical events, real people, or real places are used fictitiously. Names, characters, and places are products of the author's imagination.

Formatting by Molly Halstead.

First printing edition 2024.

ISBN: 979-8-9914610-0-9

Content advisory: This book includes references to infertility, domestic abuse, suicide, abduction, gun violence, and assault.

*For all the wonderful women in my life—you know who you are.
And for Bodhi, the naughtiest dog I know.*

CHAPTER ONE

Sounds came.

The steady ping of rain drumming against steel.

The muted whoosh of wind. The high whine of rubber kissing asphalt.

I was moving.

Why am I moving?

Air clawed up my throat and slid back down again—slowly, painfully—my lungs pulling harder than my esophagus would allow, my chest rising and falling in uneven shifts. I couldn't breathe.

I should be able to—

My eyelids snapped open to darkness. Pure black. I tried to scream and couldn't. My voice was gone, lost in my burning throat. Another sound came instead—this one closer, directly overhead.

Clack. Clack. Clack.

I raised my hands and brushed a loose rod, then pushed past it and felt cool metal press against my palm. I followed it lower, the metal curving behind my head until it terminated in a rubber seal.

A car, I thought. *I'm in a trunk.*

Oh, God ...

Oh, fuck.

It's why my knees were jammed in a fetal position, why a rough pad of carpet burned against my cheek and scratched my neck. A shot of cold panic swam down my spine. Time stuttered, and I wheezed for oxygen. It felt like I was breathing through a straw. I was going to pass out if I didn't get it together and fast.

Focus, Olivia. Stay calm.

And then: *He thinks I'm dead.*

It's why my hands weren't bound, why my mouth wasn't gagged. It's why my ankles weren't slung in an interstate of knots. The man who'd done this to me thought I was dead. I could still feel his fingers squeezing, digging into my neck, could still hear his voice burning hot in my ear.

Fucking die, already!

Those words pouring over me in a shower of sour breath.

Clack. C-Clack. Clack.

Think, Olivia! You have to think!

I slowed my breathing and forced my mind to calm. There had to be a way to open the trunk or signal another car. A wire to rip free from the brake lights or a latch to pop. Didn't all the newer cars have those specifically for situations like this? For women who, like me, simply disappeared?

And I *would* disappear if I didn't find a way to get out.

My heart sloshed in my chest, and I rolled to my right, toward the sidewall of the trunk, and extended an arm. My fingers brushed over objects I recognized. Jumper cables, and a can of gas. Coiled rope and boxes. A hard plastic case. Duct tape. Nothing else.

Jesus, no latch.

I tried the other side, muttering a prayer as my hands crawled through a graveyard of clinking bottles, my fingers scraping over the dry brush of cardboard and through the crinkle of plastic sacks. Dust tickled the back of my nose, and I nearly unleashed a sneeze before I bit it off. *Don't! He'll hear you.* Then I tried again, moving slower this time, feeling for what *had* to be there.

And it was—nestled a few inches above the floor of the trunk. A trunk release. A lever to pull.

Reality wobbled. My heart fluttered and crashed.

Work, I thought. *Please, God, work.*

I pulled.

There came a click, and the world exploded into a fireball of light. A gray sky moved above me, swollen with thunderheads, trees sweeping past on either side. Headlights coasted behind the car in a sea of rushing metal. Cold rain lashed against my neck. I forced myself upright, and the brakes slammed and sent me hurtling backward as the car screeched to a stop.

Move! Move! Move!

I scrambled from the trunk.

One foot connected with the ground. The other slipped. I crashed to the road, and the sound of rain filled my ears along with the heavy thunk of a door opening. Two boots hit asphalt.

His boots.

Air scabbed over my lips. The world swam.

Go! I pushed myself upright—and I ran. Across the white line on the shoulder of the road and into traffic with brakes shrieking all around me. Horns tearing past. Rain pelting my face. Wind hissing in my ears. Behind me came a full-throat roar.

"Stop, you fucking bitch!"

My lungs burned for air, everything smearing to a blur.

"I said, stop!" Louder this time. Closer.

But I didn't stop, *couldn't* stop. I kept running—pushing through the fire in my chest, ignoring the pain in my throat—until I stumbled off the road and tumbled down a grass-slicked descent.

Rolling now. Everything spinning. Gasping for air.

I splashed into a pool of muddy water and came up coughing, wiping my eyes to a sight that filled me with terror. The man stood above me on the hill, looking down with one hand balled into a fist and the other holding a knife.

You're dead, I thought. *He's going to kill you.*

A cloud of blue and red light rose behind him followed by a voice. "Remain where you are! Drop the knife!"

But the man didn't. He just stared down at me with his breath turning to mist.

And took a step. Took another.

Then the gunshots rang out.

CHAPTER TWO

Seven years later

I woke with a start, my eyelids snapping open without warning or hesitation; a flashing, *Bang! Hello, Olivia, welcome back!* Outside the plane's window, a wet slice of jungle flashed past. Palm trees interlaced with deep pockets of shadow.

My phone buzzed on my lap. I knuckled the sleep from my eyes and grabbed it, scrolling past the unread text messages and news alerts flooding the screen in favor of the envelope icon at the bottom. An email I'd already read at least two dozen times since it hit my inbox two weeks earlier. The email that had me sitting on this plane now.

My thumb hovered over it—and clicked.

To: **SurvivorPodmail; livmiller;**
From: **QMiller@gmail.com**
Subject: **I'M GETTING MARRIED!!!**

Via — Hi! How are you? Doing well, I hope? It's been far too long. Look, I'm not really sure how to start, other than to get right to it—I'm sorry for how everything ended with us. We both said a lot of cruel things we didn't mean. *I* said a lot of cruel things. I didn't know how to deal with my life back then. I couldn't make sense of it. I couldn't cope.

Which is why I ran ...

I paused and thought of Quinn. I hadn't laid eyes on my sister in what, four years now? Five? I pictured the last time I saw her, the Las Vegas scarecrow, throwing me out of her Section 8 house with her cheekbones sawing beneath her skin like knife points, her voice leaking out in a tight rasp.

You're dead to me, Olivia! I don't ever want to talk to you again!

Then she'd slammed the door in my face, leaving my plea for her to return to Columbus with me and get her life together rotting in my throat. And now here she was, diving straight out of the blue, bomb-shelling me with an engagement announcement and an invitation.

I sighed and continued to read.

I needed some space to heal, you know? I just needed time. But that doesn't make what I did right. I'm sorry for vanishing like that. It was an awful thing to do. I can see that now.

I've met the best group of people, Via. The *best*. I've grown in so many ways because of them. The past only controls us if we let it. And I'm done living in the past. I'm ready to move on, and I hope you are, too.

Which is why I'm writing ...

I'm getting married! My fiancé's name is Bryce. He's intelligent, kind, hot, and *very* funny. We have so much in common. He proposed last month, in St. Martin. Of course, I said yes! (In a place like that, coming from that man, how could I not?) And you know who I wanted to tell first?

You, Via. I wanted to tell *you*.

Listen, I think it's time we patch things up. Bryce has scheduled a cruise, and I want you to come. It's going to be amazing. Please say you will. Call me, and I'll fill you in on the details. I can't wait to hear your voice.

Love, Q.

I slipped the phone back into my pocket. It didn't even sound like Quinn, the letter written with the cotton-candy cadence of a sixteen-year-old. I could practically hear her sing-song pitch dancing up from the letters. *I said yes! How could I not? Let's go on a cruise!*

"First time to Puerto Rico?" The question came from the guy in the seat to my left. He sported a heavily veined nose and the watery gaze of a functional alcoholic.

"Yes," I mumbled.

"You have to try the pernil," the man added. "It's delicious."

"Mm," I replied, glancing out the window again, telling myself, *do not engage.*

Something about my face invites conversation: With wide eyes, and an easy smile, I'm approachable—no resting bitch face here!—which made men like this one think they actually stood a chance. Honestly though, even if he looked like Ryan Gosling, I wouldn't be interested. After what happened to me, I had issues with men. Being strangled and stuffed in a trunk will do that to you.

A tinny voice announced our arrival through the speaker and I returned my attention to the phone. At first, I thought the email was a joke. A cruel hoax by someone in the media looking to make a few bucks off an emotional response. A quick, *fuck off, asshole,* they could splash over the gossip sites, or sell to some B-level media outlet. It had happened before, especially after my autobiography dropped. But *Fighting for Air: The Olivia Miller Story* released years ago, and I couldn't remember the last time someone reached out for an interview. Besides, tragedy has a short shelf life in America, and mine was long past the expiration date.

A sudden *ding!* extinguished the seatbelt light, and fifteen minutes later I stood near the baggage belt, waiting for my suitcase with a cup of dark roast. I took a sip and closed my eyes. The Quinn I'd left in Vegas five years ago was the definition of a hot mess. What would she look like now? She'd long ago obliterated all of her social media accounts, so I had to imagine her face—a perfect pair of lips drowning in a nest of frown lines. Nostrils scabbed pink from drugs. Eyes cupped in dark circles. Hair pulled back into a tight ponytail greased with neglect. My sister, the burnout. How she fit with Bryce Cullen was beyond me.

Finding her fiancé online wasn't hard. A quick Google search after my call with Quinn revealed a diamond-handed finance bro with pearl-white teeth and a body that looked like it had never ingested a single gram of sugar. Polo shirts without a single wrinkle. Olive skin and dimples. A cleft chin. Sandy blond hair thick with product. Hot was an understatement because Bryce was beyond perfect. Which, I guess, was the other reason I'd decided to come. Simple curiosity. How the hell had she snagged this guy?

I trashed the coffee and retrieved my suitcase, then wheeled it to the doors and took a deep breath. *You can do this, Olivia. You can do hard things.* It was my father's favorite expression, one I'd adopted long ago, thinking it would give me courage, but it never did. It only made me feel worse; he'd never been great at doing hard things.

Outside, the humidity hit me like a fist, instantly teasing beads of sweat from my pores. People rushed past, *way* too many people, Ubers and taxis and bodies mixing into one big wall of noise and light and sound.

And no Quinn.

"You want a ride?" a man with silver teeth called through an open window. "I take you where you wanna go."

"Thank you. No, I'm fine."

"Oye. Get in. I'll cut you a deal, mami."

"No, really I'm—"

"Via?"

I turned toward the voice. A woman stood behind me, wearing a sleek black skirt and a white fitted top. A waterfall of strawberry-blonde hair fell over her shoulders and pulled my gaze lower toward a set of bronzed legs and toned calves. She tilted a pair of oversized sunglasses toward the bridge of her nose and stared at me with eyes the color of spring grass, eyes I'd recognize anywhere.

My mouth fell open. "Quinn?"

Her smile widened and she closed the distance between us.

"Oh my god, it *is* you," she said, enveloping me in a rib-crushing hug. I hung slack in the embrace, limp. This woman looked nothing like the shuffling zombie I remembered, staring out at the world through a pair of filmy, pill-addled eyes. This woman was vibrant and gorgeous. This woman was *alive*, looking like the A-list actress Quinn had always aspired to be. And she was hugging me—not exactly the welcome I'd expected.

I slithered from her grip. "You look great, Quinn. Really."

"Thank you." She set her hands on her hips and appraised me, her head tilting to the side. A diamond the size of a beetle winked from her ring finger; I guessed three carats. "And you haven't changed a bit."

I peered down at my frayed jeans, scuffed Converse, and vintage Nirvana shirt which clashed aggressively with her dress. My cheeks flared. An apology crept onto my tongue but I wouldn't let it out. What did I have to apologize for? Still, I wanted to. It's what felt natural in the moment. A way to break the ice. *I'm sorry, Quinn. For everything.*

"God, it's good to see you, Via! So good."

"It's good to see you, too."

"C'mon. I can't wait for you to meet Bryce."

I reached for my suitcase, but Quinn took my hand and tugged me forward before I could grab the handle. "Don't bother. Javier's got it."

A man with sand-colored skin I hadn't noticed until that moment stepped past me and took the bag with a curt nod. I stared at him, confused. *Quinn has staff now?*

"It's fine, Via. Let him do his job."

"Olivia," I corrected.

"What?"

"I go by Olivia now." I hated my nickname—Via. Only two people had ever called me Via: Quinn and my father. And my father was dead. Via died with him.

Quinn frowned. "Okay, I'll try to remember that. Come on."

I followed her in a daze, watching her walk, still attempting to connect this Quinn to the hollow-cheeked version who lived rent-free in my mind. I couldn't reconcile the two people—it looked like she'd aged in reverse.

She came to a stop in front of a white stretch limo parked a few feet from the curb.

"We're taking *that*?" I asked.

Quinn's forehead bunched like it was a stupid question, like everyone in Puerto Rico took Maserati stretch limos from the airport.

"I told you this trip was going to be amazing." The tone of her voice rose on the last word, matching the flowery cadence of her email. My sister, who'd communicated in monotone for as long as I could remember, was now speaking in uptalk. When did it happen? When had she changed?

I hesitated and she cocked her head. "Hey, are you okay?"

I blinked. "Yeah, fine." My throat constricted. I couldn't move. Being here, with this new version of Quinn, after so many years apart, suddenly felt overwhelming. I didn't know if I had it in me to wade back into our past.

"Quinn, I—"

"Listen, Olivia," she interrupted, "before you say anything, hear me out. I know this is a lot for you. It is for me, too. I must have rewritten the email I sent you at least thirty times. I almost didn't send it at all. But I meant what I said. I want you in my life, and I think you want the same. Let's give it a chance, okay?"

For some reason I couldn't pin down, I wanted to say no. I wanted to dash back into the airport while I still had the chance. But the way she was looking at me, with so much sincerity in her eyes, so much need, prevented me from replying with anything other than, "Okay."

"Good. And truly, this is going to be so much fun. Just wait. Bryce has so many activities lined up for us. You're going to love every minute of this trip, I swear." She held up her little finger in an echo of our long-ago childhood ritual: *Pinkie swear?* My hand moved on its own, and I watched my finger twine with hers.

"Promise?" I heard myself say.

Quinn smiled. "On my life."

CHAPTER THREE

My vision was sun-bleached as I entered the limo, the contrast off, like a television spitting static. When it cleared, I found myself staring at a row of strangers sitting across from me, watching my every movement. Heat stung my cheeks. *What the hell?* Quinn hadn't said anything about other people coming along. On the phone, she'd only mentioned Bryce.

A hand jutted forward, followed by a voice coated in smooth tenor. "Hello, Olivia. It's nice to finally meet you. I'm Bryce." I took his hand and shook it, his grip that of a businessman, firm with passive-aggressive dominance. "Quinn's told me so much about you."

I wish I could say the same, I nearly spat, but instead managed a weak, "Nice to meet you, too."

"Hey, everyone, this is my sister, Olivia," Quinn chirped next to me, proudly.

My hand rose in a timid wave as the limo eased from the curb.

"Oh my god, I can't believe you *actually* came," said a man sporting a headful of coiled brown hair. "You're really her, right?"

I stared at him, trying to make sense of his statement, of *him*.

The way he leaned forward and planted his elbows on his knees reminded me of a child's stick-figure drawing of a human come to life. He wore a red Rolling Stones T-shirt and appraised me through a pair of thick-rimmed glasses, grinning as he waited for me to answer.

"I'm sorry?" I said.

"I'm such a fan of your podcast. It's so exciting to meet you!"

The tumblers clicked into place, and I felt my entire body unclench. It still took me by surprise when people recognized me in public, even though I'd been doing my true-crime podcast for years now. I'd started it shortly after waking up in the hospital with a partially crushed trachea ringed in a necklace of burst blood vessels. I couldn't talk very well for the better part of a year, and when I finally could (and still with some rasp), I wanted my words to matter, to mean something. A near-death experience has a way of clarifying your purpose in life, even if it comes from a random act of violence.

It turned out my purpose was putting sadistic assholes like Sean Grieves, the man who attempted to kill me, behind bars. With the aid of my research assistant, Nina DeSouza, and our nearly one-million listeners, *Still Living with Olivia* has helped solve over two dozen murders and disappearances. It's not enough—but it's a good start.

I forced my mouth into my standard fan smile—a three-quarter turn of the lips with no matching wrinkle of the eyes. "The one and only."

Quinn set a hand on my knee. "Via ... sorry, I mean, Olivia.

This is Alex. He hasn't stopped talking about your show since I mentioned you were coming." His grin widened, and I decided I liked him. "And this is his boyfriend, Liam."

"Hello," Liam said, offering a casual wave. He wore a cheetah-print tank top and a pair of purple shorts that did little to conceal his milky white thighs. His brown hair was lighter than Alex's, more acorn than walnut, and he stared at me with decidedly less interest.

Quinn continued: "Next to him are the Strouds. Tim, Kerry, and their son Darren."

"Hello," they said in tandem. The parents had the hollow-faced look of marathoners who woke at five a.m. every morning to pound out the daily ten. Their son's warm brown skin and shoulder-length black hair didn't match. *Adopted?* He had to be. He was probably about my age, late twenties or early thirties. Good looking.

Maybe this trip wouldn't be so bad, after all.

"And last but not least," Quinn said, gesturing to her left, "are Caprice and Chaz Hanson."

Caprice ran a hand through a mane of poorly dyed blonde hair and then tugged at the ends, which were highlighted bright pink. "Hiya!" she chirped. "Have you thought about influencing? You definitely have the look. You're so pretty. That smile! Wow!" The compliments came in rapid fire, too fast for my brain to process. I gawked at her without saying a word.

"Hey," Chaz said. He had dark hair that stood in stark contrast to Caprice's, gelled into spikes. But the shape of his nose matched hers, as did his eyes. They couldn't be married. They looked too much alike.

"They're twins," Quinn said, reading my mind.

"She's the older one," Chaz added.

Caprice grinned, like it was an accomplishment. "By all of nine minutes!"

Quinn swept an arm around the cab. "Everyone here is an entrepreneur. Tim and Kerry run a regional health and supplement franchise, Star Fitness, that's—"

"Spark, actually," Tim said, leaning in.

"Sorry. *Spark* Fitness," Quinn corrected, "which is killing it. And Liam is in tech. He recently launched a lifestyle productivity app—what's it called again?"

"ListKiller, not that anyone's heard of it," Liam said.

Alex stiffened next to him, then put his hand on Liam's knee. "What are you talking about, babe? You have over a thousand downloads!"

Liam shrugged. "It's a start, I guess."

Alex took his hand and gave it a squeeze. "It's more than a start. That's a lot of people."

Quinn looked my way. "And as you've probably guessed, Caprice and Chaz are influencers. They both have massive followings."

"Mine's bigger," Chaz said.

Caprice rolled her eyes. "Only on Instagram. And, besides, I get way better engagement."

Chaz snorted. "Whatever. I have more sponsors."

I pinned a smile on my face. My nerves were fraying already.

Quinn gave an awkward laugh and moved on. "And Bryce runs one of the most successful green-energy hedge funds on Wall Street. Vitreous Energy."

That, I already knew. In addition to my own research, I'd had Nina run the traps on Bryce. Vitreous Energy, a fund focused on sustainable investing, had produced eye-popping returns for the last two years. After minting his fortune, Bryce funneled a substantial chunk into philanthropic pursuits, mostly nonprofits focused on cancer research and climate change. He'd even funded a mission trip to Haiti, bringing an army of contractors to rebuild a small village after it was leveled by a hurricane.

A charitable donation here.

A day on the soup line there.

Activist debates and articles championing the pros of green energy and carbon control. On and on it went. By all accounts, the man was an angel. A saint. Neither Nina or I had uncovered a single negative remark about the guy anywhere. Just endless praise and adoration, which made me uncomfortable. Everyone has skeletons squirreled away somewhere, especially people with money. Everyone but Bryce, apparently.

The fog of small talk filled the limo as the ocean swept past in a smooth cobalt arc. Long strips of beach outlined the water, salted in umbrellas and towels. People moved between them with drinks in hand, looking tanned and happy. The image sparked a vague memory of Quinn and I as kids, Quinn leading me over a belt of sugary sand toward the ocean.

"Come on, Via! Let's go for a swim!"

She was there with me one moment, pulling me deeper, the waves crashing down all around us, and gone the next. Then there was water everywhere—in my mouth, flooding down my throat, that harsh salt sting invading my lungs until I blacked out. When I came awake, it was to a lifeguard giving me CPR, shouting for me to, *Breathe, goddammit!* It's how I felt right now—like I couldn't breathe.

"Ever been on a cruise before?" Bryce asked, and it took me a second to realize he was talking to me.

I nodded. "Once, sort of."

"How do you 'sort of' go on a cruise?" he asked.

"Our dad—" I waved at Quinn as if it weren't clear we were sisters "—took us to Seattle when we were little, but we had some bad tacos, and—"

"We were supposed to go to Alaska," Quinn interjected. "Everyone got sick in the hotel room, so we bailed. It's a terrible story. No one wants to hear it." She barked a laugh, and I flushed with embarrassment. Growing up, Quinn never liked to appear less than perfect. Before she fell apart, a ketchup stain on her dress was cause for crisis. Apparently, that was one thing that hadn't changed.

"So, how's the podcast going, Olivia?" she asked.

The question felt physical—like a slap to the face. Was she serious? She looked serious, like she actually wanted to know the answer. Her face flickered, and I saw the Quinn I remembered from years earlier flash to life, hollow-eyed and ranting after I told her I planned to discuss more than just my attempted murder on the show.

"Like what?" she'd asked.

"Like ... our past."

"Olivia, please tell me you aren't going to talk about Dad."

"I have to."

"You can't."

"Quinn, I need to be authentic."

As soon as I'd said it, she was on me, her fingernail slamming into my sternum in time with her questions. *"How dare you do this to me, Via!"* (Stab.) *"How dare you air* my *trauma to the entire world!"* (Stab. Stab.) *"How dare* you *try to build a fucking career from* my *pain!"* (Stab! Stab! Stab!) Her saying, *my* trauma, like his death wasn't *our* trauma, like I hadn't been through the same shit, too.

My hand rose to my chest and hovered there. Nausea boiled thick at the base of my throat. Being here with Quinn, with *this* Quinn, and our lifetime of unresolved issues suddenly felt like too much. I needed light, needed air, needed out of this car packed full of strange faces that were patiently waiting for me to answer my sister's bizarre question.

Quinn's brow crimped. "Olivia, are you okay? You don't look so good."

I closed my eyes and pulled in a long, slow breath. "I'm fine."

"I think we should stop the car," Quinn said.

I ran a hand over my face, took in another gulp of air, and shook my head. "No ... no, I'm good."

"You're not good. You're turning white. Stop the car!"

"I'm fine, Jesus!" I snapped, barking back at her with more intensity than I meant. She blinked at me like I'd lost my mind, her mouth opening and shutting like a fish out of water. I realized every face in the limo held the same expression as Quinn—eyes wide, brows stretched, mouths open—my outburst splattered across their features in a mash of shocked confusion. My cheeks burned, and I started to apologize, but Bryce spoke before I could.

"We're here."

CHAPTER FOUR

A mountain of shipping containers surrounded us, steel rectangles piled nine high, coated in dull reds and oxidized blues. Above them, a metal crane swayed back and forth, picking through the stacks, looking like the fossil of some long-dead creature.

"*This* is the port?" I asked.

"Yes," Bryce answered.

"Where are all the people?"

"What people?"

"Everyone taking the cruise. The other tourists."

"Oh, Olivia," Quinn said, setting her hand on my knee like she was a doctor about to deliver a terminal diagnosis. "Did you think we were going on one of the big ships?"

"Yes ... no, I mean ..." I stopped, suddenly unsure of what I thought. Quinn insisted on taking care of all the details of this trip. She'd used the term cruise over and over again in the single phone conversation we'd had leading up to it. *Don't worry about a thing, Via. The cruise will be great. I've got it all covered. Just bring your passport.* Sure, I'd thought it was strange there weren't any forms to fill out or waivers to sign. But what personal information could my sister need beyond my birthday and social security number that she didn't already know? I suddenly felt like an idiot.

"Don't worry," Quinn continued, "this will be so much better than a trip on one of those tourist traps."

I smiled and said nothing, taking in the industrial dump of a port with a growing dread. It reminded me of a human trafficking case I'd worked involving a shipping container stuffed with women intended to be sold to the highest bidder. A port worker discovered them after hearing their muffled cries. Two of them were dead by the time he got it open, both of them mothers. I'd had trouble looking at shipping containers with anything but suspicion since.

The limo swung left, and a yacht appeared through the windshield, a gleaming white beacon moored to the end of a long pier. It looked severely out of place among all the rust, large, but nowhere close to the floating city of a ship I'd expected.

"You own a yacht?" I asked Bryce, annoyed with the awe I heard creeping into my voice.

He laughed and shook his head. "Me? No, maybe someday if I play my cards right. This one belongs to Xclivity."

Xclivity? I turned the word over in my mind. It sounded corporate, but not too corporate—one of those purposefully vague entity names. A nutrition lifestyle brand or a spa franchise offering specialty massages with à la carte upgrades, like salt scrubs and facial peels. Was Xclivity another one of his companies? I made a mental note to have Nina look into it as soon as I got the chance.

"The last time I took a commercial cruise ship, I got Covid," Kerry said, brushing her palms over her shorts as though the mere mention of the ship had coated her hands in germs. "The fatigue lasted for weeks."

"Right?" Liam said. "Those things are floating cesspools. It's impossible *not* to get sick on them. I don't know how anyone can handle being trapped at sea with so many strangers, either. They treat you like cattle. And the food ... so gross."

Trapped at sea on a trip with strangers. Exactly what I was doing. *Great*.

"The big ships are so disgusting," Quinn said. "Especially after traveling on *The Athena*."

I narrowed my eyes. Growing up, back before our relationship went to hell, Quinn and I had enjoyed the finer things in life. Nice dinners and custom dresses, toys other kids couldn't afford. Enrollment in private schools. But Quinn acting like a vacation most people were lucky to experience once in their lifetime was beneath her felt like a one-percenter mentality. Despite the thought, I couldn't help but feel a tinge of excitement. The yacht *did* look incredible. I could already picture myself soaking in the sun on the upper deck, drink in hand.

Caprice nodded. "Totally gross."

"But why is the ship here?" I asked. "At this dock?"

"It's cheaper than a slip at one of the yacht clubs," Bryce said. "We try to save money where we can."

I nodded like it made sense, like I was a seasoned sailor myself. "The ship looks nice."

"Oh, it's more than nice," Quinn said as the limo came to a

stop. "It's magnificent. Trust me. It's even more impressive up close. Let's go."

I clambered from the limo and trailed after the others. Gulls wheeled overhead, singing to one another in high, stinging squawks. Through the pier slats, the ocean lapped against the wooden pilings in a hypnotic slosh, kicking up wafts of industrial chemicals mixed with the scent of wood rot; an acidic musk that slid up my sinuses and coated the back of my throat. Ahead, Quinn took Bryce's elbow and leaned her head against his broad shoulder, and it struck me again how different she seemed, how at ease. She no longer looked like someone wading through a foot of wet cement with every step, struggling to remain upright. It was jarring, to say the least.

I was still watching her when a loose board struck my toe and sent me pitching toward the water. A hand seized my wrist before I plunged over the side and brought me whirling back onto the pier, and I found myself staring at Darren, the fitness couple's son. He stood in front of me with his hair pulled into a man bun, which only added to his forehead-stretched look of shock. I peered down at his fingers wrapped around my wrist. A star-shaped birthmark flashed beneath his thumb. "Am I under arrest?"

His fingers uncurled and he shoved the hand into his pocket. "Sorry about that."

"I'm totally kidding! You just saved me from taking a bath."

He smiled and looked over my shoulder. "I thought it was a cruise liner, too, if it makes you feel any better."

"Really? You didn't know it was a yacht?"

"Nope, no clue. Same as you. My parents didn't mention a thing."

"Don't you think this is all—" I waved a hand "—I don't know, a little weird?"

"You mean docking a yacht like this in the middle of a dump? Yeah, I'd say so. But weird doesn't even begin to describe my parents. They're always doing shit like this. Taking random trips with Xclivity. Trying all these bizarre diets. Attending self-improvement courses. They made me read *The Secret* so many times growing up, I thought it was the Bible."

I laughed. I'd read the book once myself, a fluffy bit of self-help literature about the law of attraction. Simply focus on your desires hard enough, while visualizing positive outcomes, and the universe will hand them to you on a silver platter, no questions asked. If only life were so easy.

"But whatever," Darren continued, "I don't really care what I have to do if it means I get to tag along on a free trip or two."

"So, you've been on one of these things before, then?"

"No, this is the first. But I've heard my parents rave about them for years. If nothing else, rich people know how to have a good time."

Rich people. Money. Most people think money will solve all their problems if they can just get enough, that it will somehow make them a better person. It doesn't.

Money is what destroyed my relationship with Quinn.

We continued toward the ship, and I watched Darren's parents stride purposefully in front of us, looking nothing like their son.

The question leaped from my mouth before I could stop it. "So, are you adopted?"

Darren frowned. "Me? Nope. Believe it or not, I have a rare genetic condition that darkens my skin. It gets more intense every year."

"Seriously?"

His eyes crinkled, and he laughed—a full, warm sound that set my face on fire.

"You're joking."

"Yeah, I'm adopted."

"So is my sister," I said, trying to hide my embarrassment.

"Really?" Darren asked. "That's cool. How old was she when she was adopted?"

"Just a baby. It happened before I was born."

Darren glanced at his parents. "I don't remember much about my adoption, but I guess Tim and Kerry pulled me out of a pretty bad situation when I was younger. I owe them a lot."

"They seem nice."

"My dad is," Darren said. "My mom's … tough."

"How so?"

"She's very focused. Very entrepreneurial. I'm nothing like her and it drives her crazy." We reached the ramp to the yacht, and he waved me forward. "After you."

I didn't move. I just stood there paralyzed instead, staring up at the boat with icy fingers of dread weaving through my chest once more. I had no logical reason to feel this way. *The Athena* looked lavish. Beyond magnificent. But it didn't stop the voice in my head from whispering, *This is it, Olivia. Last chance to turn around.*

Shaken, I took a step back, pulled my phone from my pocket, thumbed Nina's number, then tossed Darren a quick, I'm-fine-just-fine smile. "I'll be right up. I have to make a quick call first."

He shrugged and strode up the ramp as I hit the call button. Nina answered on the third ring. "Hey," she said. "I started digging into Sutherland. You were right. The guy is guilty as hell. Wait, why are you calling me? Shouldn't you be drunk by now?" Nina was always doing that, always on, launching into our last conversation like it never stopped, a movie on pause for hours just waiting for you to hit play and resume.

"Soon, hopefully," I said.

"How's everything with Quinn? As awkward as you were expecting?"

"Sort of, but not how I imagined."

"How so?"

"Well, she looks way better than I thought she would for starters. I almost didn't recognize her."

"And that's a problem because ..."

"It's not. It's just ... the way she talks is different, how she moves, and what she says. I mean, it's probably nothing, but she seems *off*."

Nina laughed. "Do you think Bryce Stepford Wifed her or something?"

"No, I wish it was that. There's this organization everyone

keeps mentioning, Xclivity. I've never heard of it before. We're actually taking their yacht, *The Athena*, if you can believe that."

"Cool name, but I thought you were going on Royal Caribbean."

"That makes two of us."

She sighed, heavy and hard. "You want me to look into them, don't you?"

"You know me too well."

Nina, a bespectacled whirlwind of a data analyst, found me somewhere during the second season of my podcast and demanded I let her join the show. I told her I didn't need the extra help, which was true—or at least that's what I'd told myself—though that wasn't the real reason I'd turned her down. After Sean, I didn't trust anyone, especially strangers. But when Nina emailed me a file stuffed with documents on the Bronson case a week later, one that laid everything out in chronological order right down to a timeline of Megan Bronson's disappearance, I knew she was someone special. I made her an offer on the spot.

It wasn't until two years later that I discovered why Nina wanted to join the show so badly. Her mother had been murdered—stabbed to death—when Nina was just seven years old. The authorities discovered her body in a ditch in southern New Mexico, wrapped in a sheet, missing her tongue. They never found her killer. Like me, Nina wanted justice, even if it wasn't her own. If there's one thing I've learned about true-crime podcasters, it's this—we all have axes to grind, and Nina's is as sharp as any. I don't know how I ever did the show without her.

"Okay," she said. "I'll pull the formation documents and bank accounts, look into the money. All the things."

"Olivia, what are you doing?" I cupped a hand to my forehead and spotted Quinn perched above me, leaning over the railing. "You need to board. We're about to shove off."

I waved at her, then turned away and whispered, "I don't know if I can handle this."

"You've been talking about reuniting with your sister for how long now?" Nina asked, her tone sharpening.

"Awhile."

"Then stop trying to sabotage things. And go enjoy yourself for once. Forget the podcast for a few days. I'll hold down the fort."

She had a point. After all the cases we'd worked this year, I needed a break. "That's not the worst idea."

"My ideas never are. Seriously, Olivia. I want you to promise me that you'll leave work behind. You need to relax."

"I will."

"Nope, I know you. That's not good enough. I need to hear it."

"Fine," I huffed. "I promise. I'll relax." But even as I said it, I knew it was a lie.

CHAPTER FIVE

From a distance, the yacht looked amazing—like something staged for a television commercial—but standing on it stole my breath. Deck after shining deck stretched away in a series of sublime curves. The ship was all sparkling glass and white siding the color of cake fondant or freshly fallen snow. Outdoor couches and chairs with plush cushions were artfully arranged on the cinnamon-colored wood. Above me, the sky crackled a perfect cerulean blue.

"Just wait until you see your room," Quinn said with a grin.

I tore my gaze from the boat. "It's gorgeous. How many trips have you taken on this thing?"

Quinn pulled her lower lip between her teeth and sawed gently at it as she considered the question. "I don't know, three, maybe? No wait, four if you include the trip to the Dominican last month." The way she said it bothered me, flippant, like the islands were a ten-minute errand to the corner gas station for a quart of milk. *I'm off to the Dominican, be back in a few.* And exactly how long had she been dating Bryce to go on so many trips? Did she even work anymore? These questions testified to how little I knew my sister. Questions for which I now wanted answers.

"How about a quick tour?" Quinn said.

"That would be great."

I followed her through a sliding glass door and into an oval lobby furnished with cream-colored carpet and more plush seating. Circular sofas were layered throughout the room, surrounded by groups of lounge chairs and chaises angled outward toward floor-to-ceiling windows. Beyond them, the ocean looked surreal, like an endless sheet of beveled glass.

"Welcome to *The Athena*, ma'am. Something to drink?"

I glanced down at a woman in a crisp white uniform standing before me, holding a tray peppered in brightly colored cocktails. "Um, sure, yes." I selected a pomegranate-hued concoction in a martini glass and took a sip, hoping for mostly vodka only to be disappointed by a refreshing combination of lime and cranberry juice. The woman watched me expectantly, awaiting my reaction. "Delicious, thank you." I forced a smile and hoped she didn't notice my disappointment in the lack of booze.

"Right?" Quinn replied, taking a glass for herself. "Carmela makes the best fresh-squeezed juices I've ever had. Everything is organic. What's this one called again? It's my favorite."

"Ocean bliss," Carmela said with a polite smile. A *sad* smile, betrayed by a pair of marionette lines curving down toward her chin. I tried to guess her age—a favorite game of mine. Would I look this good in my sixties? Would my features be as smooth and dignified as Carmela's? Or as sad? Because this woman with the light brown skin and ebony curls was fucking sad. I could sense it wafting off her like smoke, could feel her resignation in the way she stood with her shoulders slumped, her eyes distant. A woman, I guessed, who carried a lot of scars.

"I'm glad you enjoy it, Miss Miller."

"It's wonderful. Thank you, Carmela."

"You're welcome. Let me know if you need anything else." I watched her go and my gaze settled on a massive, burnished metal sign mounted behind the bar. There it was again, that name—Xclivity—stenciled in luminous white letters set below a looping infinity symbol.

"Are you coming?" Quinn asked, pausing halfway across the room. Her voice startled me. I hadn't realized she'd moved.

"What is that?" I said, inclining my head toward the sign.

"What? Xclivity?"

I nodded. Quinn crossed her arms and looked at it, looked at me, then flattened her lips in thought. "It's a wonderful organization. Very philanthropic. Very ethical. They're actually sponsoring this trip."

"Yeah, Bryce mentioned that. But what do they actually *do?*"

"Oh, Olivia, *so* much."

I tried not to clench my jaw at her condescension.

"Wellness. Self-improvement. Proper nutrition. Ways to attain spiritual focus and realize your potential. Achieve what you want to achieve. So many people limit themselves. It's truly sad. It's a disease."

"*Oh*-kay," I said, flatly, trying not to laugh.

"But there will be plenty of time to talk about Xclivity later. Right now, I want to show you the rest of the—oh, shoot." She scanned her watch. "We don't have time. Dinner's at six-thirty. The tour will have to wait. Come on."

Quinn spun and strode from the room. I followed her, rounding the corner into the hall and very nearly colliding with a bald man heading in the opposite direction. A big man, heavily muscled, with thighs that were as round as tree trunks and arms that threatened to burst through the sleeves of his jacket. But they weren't what gave me pause. It was his eyes that sent a shiver all the way to the base of my spine. In the muted light of the hall, they looked like buttons sewn on either side of his nose—dull and flat. I'd seen eyes like that before. The eyes of a killer.

"Pardon me," he said with a slight smile.

I tried to speak, to say, *excuse me, or sorry about that,* but all I could do was stand there and try to make sense of him and how he fit here, nestled among all this opulence. He finally nodded and stepped past me, leaving a trail of cigarette smoke hanging in his wake. Acid bubbled in my stomach, and I hurried after Quinn, fast-walking down the long, carpeted hallway, past a slew of staterooms before catching up with her as she came to a stop in front of a door marked #202.

"This is you," she said.

"Who was that?" I asked, ignoring her.

"Who?"

"The big guy. The giant." *Who else?*

"Oh," Quinn replied, like she hadn't seen him. "That's Marco. Don't worry about him. I know he looks scary, but he's a big puppy. He's Julianna's security detail. You'll love him."

"Who's Julianna?" I asked. *And why does she need security?*

"You'll meet her tonight. She's wonderful." Quinn opened the door and waved me in.

I stepped past her and was immediately encompassed in a sense of wonder. High-gloss wood paneling covered the walls. An artificial skylight bathed the teak floors in a waterfall of honeyed light. Potted plants were stationed in the corners—ferns spouting lush green fronds placed next to a scatter of orchids. Across the room, an oil painting of an oak tree with leaves splashed in fall color hung centered on the wall. The branches seemed to rustle as I moved closer.

"What do you think?" Quinn asked.

"It's stunning."

Quinn laughed. "And it's all yours. Anyway, like I said, dinner's at six-thirty. You'll have plenty of time to wash up. Your dinner clothes are on the bed."

Dinner clothes? I rotated, half-expecting to see the contents of my suitcase stacked neatly on the duvet. Instead, a silver dress glittered up at me like a star. I stared at it and massaged the back of my neck, confused. And then Quinn's meaning hit. I gawked at her. "Wait, you want me to wear *that?*"

"Yes, of course. Why? Don't you like it?"

No, and you know I don't. I took a breath and tried to measure my response. "I do—it's just, I brought another outfit, and this isn't really my style."

"Olivia, please. I know you, and I can't have you showing up to dinner in a sweater dress and flip-flops. This isn't a college frat party. These people matter to me. They're my friends. Besides, you deserve to look your best."

I set my hands on my hips and surveyed the dress with a clinical eye, assessing it like it had crawled onto the comforter and died there. "Thanks, but there's no way I'm wearing that."

Quinn crossed her arms. "Olivia ..."

"What? Even if I wanted to, I'd never fit into that thing. It's way too tight."

"You will. It's your size."

"How would you know? You and I haven't talked for ..." I stopped as Quinn's face darkened. She opened her mouth and shut it, her eyes going pink at the corners. I recognized the look from our childhood—that brief moment before the ice cracked and the tears started to fall.

Her gaze fell to her feet, and she blinked.

Jesus, is she actually going to cry?

"Quinn." I took a step forward, about to cup her arm when it flew up in response, knocking my outstretched hand aside.

"Wear whatever you want! I don't care. I was only trying to do something nice." Her face hardened, and I played out the rest of the night in a terrible array of flashing images: Quinn firing clipped, one-word replies at me whenever I spoke—*fine* or *okay* or a shrugged *whatever*. Me attempting to smooth things over. Quinn rolling her eyes every time I did: *You couldn't do this for me, Olivia? After everything you put me through, you couldn't wear a simple dress?*

"Wait." I snatched the dress from the bed and held it to my

shoulders. It hung high and tight. A size too small, at least, but I could squeeze into it if I tried hard enough. *Maybe.* "I didn't mean to be rude. I'll wear it, okay?"

"Really?"

"Yes. I shouldn't have reacted that way. It was a nice gesture. I'm sorry."

Quinn tapped her chin with a finger and assessed the fit. Her eyes brightened. "It's perfect. You'll look gorgeous, I promise. The bathroom's over there." She nodded. "Why don't you take a quick shower and clean up? And make sure to use the deep conditioner. It's amazing. Oh, and we're disembarking soon, so if you feel a sudden movement, don't panic, okay? It's just the ship pushing off." She flashed a final bright smile, and then she was gone, marching back through the door as a parade of questions leaped up my throat, only to log-jam in my mouth unanswered:

Where do I go for dinner?

Why the formal dress code? Why didn't you tell me to bring something nice?

What happened to you, Quinn?

Who are you?

Who have you become?

CHAPTER SIX

I showered, let the water grow hot and stream over my face, let it pelt my back and legs as Quinn's voice purred away in my head like a Pantene commercial. *I want you to look nice for my friends, so make sure to use the deep conditioner. It's amaaazing.* Since when did Quinn say shit like that? She never cared what I looked like before, so why did she care about it now? All she'd ever cared about was herself.

And she had reason to, didn't she?

An image of my father's face flashed to mind—his cheeks flushed cherry red in his casket, his hands clasped peacefully at his waist, all his demons gone, washed away in a cloud of carbon monoxide.

Stop, Olivia, don't go there. Now isn't the time.

There's another version of myself I keep trapped inside my skull. An older, wiser me who speaks with the voice of my therapist when I'm about to do something stupid or spend too much time wallowing in the graveyard of my past, rooting for skeletons I'd worked long and hard to bury. It's a favorite pastime of mine, a way to distract myself when I feel insecure or unsettled; a subconscious reminder that I'd been through worse and somehow survived. That I could get through this, too, whatever *this* was.

I killed the water and toweled off, then fetched the dress from the bed and stared at it, the constellations of tiny silver beads chilling my hands as I searched for the zipper. It took a moment, but I found it hidden in a nearly invisible seam and then wiggled my way into it with a sigh. Thankfully, the dress fit better than I'd feared, the stitching clean, the lines smooth. But it *was* too tight and short, leaving most of my thighs painfully exposed.

I studied them in the mirror, two bleached slabs of flesh cutting down toward a pair of round knees, and a set of too-large calves ending just above the ankles. They weren't the legs of a model, but to me, they were perfect. I treasured the shape of my body. My looks were all I had left of my mother. I'd killed her, after all. My first breath was her last.

When I was younger, I'd often catch myself gazing at my reflection, trying to find her staring back at me, buried in the features of my face. Like hers, mine hung slightly out of proportion, evidenced in the nose that skewed a few degrees to the left, and the lips that curled a couple millimeters higher on one side when I smiled. I had her freckles, and her ears and chin. I had her thick brown hair and dimpled cheeks. I was, as they said, my mother's daughter through and through.

Quinn saw it, too. I would sometimes wake to her staring at me. *You look just like her,* she'd whisper in amazement with the tips of her fingers grazing my cheek. *I wish I did.* Quinn, who would have traded her full lips and high cheekbones for mine, who would have gladly given me the graceful curve of her neck if it meant she could take my place. I felt a brief flicker of pride in those moments. Quinn had been lucky enough to know our mother, and love our mother, but I *was* our mother. She'd given a part of herself to me. It was a truth I was only too happy to own until I recognized it for the curse that it was; all Quinn and my father saw when they looked at me was everything I'd taken away.

Feeling wistful, I trailed over to the shoe box lying open on the bed next to the dress. A note rested on top, printed in Quinn's looping font. *Make sure to wear these, too. They make the dress.* Q. The Louboutins were another gift I wanted nothing to do with. The antithesis of everything I looked for in a shoe; a ski-slope heel leading to a red sole with zero ankle support. An elegant fracture waiting to happen. A wobble or a crack. It wouldn't take much.

A vibration rattled the floor as I put them on, a sudden shudder that brought the ocean to life through the balcony door in a spray of golden-peach light. The water's movement was hypnotic, the motion soothing. I watched the rippling blue plane for a moment, then turned my attention to the full-length mirror on the wall and assessed my hair. It *did* feel softer after the conditioner. It looked smoother, too.

"A French braid, perhaps?" I asked my reflection as I applied some light makeup. She nodded, looking like a stranger to me in her cocktail dress and designer heels. I blew my hair dry, then tipped my head to the side and wound thick strands of it around my fingers, weaving them in and out, in and out, until the braid was complete.

And then I waited.

Watching the clock on the wall tick closer to six-thirty.

Glancing nervously at the ocean.

Chewing my fingernails to the cuticles.

Wondering what the evening would bring while simultaneously wishing it wouldn't bring anything at all. I wanted to lie down and go to sleep. At exactly six-thirty, a polite *tap, tap, tap* brought me off the bed and to the door, where I hesitated. Formal attire didn't suit me. I felt like a little girl playing dress-up. The knock came again, and I steeled myself—*you can do hard things, Olivia, you really can*—then opened the door.

Darren stood on the other side.

He wore a fitted charcoal blazer and a pair of wool dress pants, his hair slicked back behind his ears. His irises were a warm brown, and his face seemed more defined this close, not perfect, somewhat asymmetrical with a slightly crooked smile that only added to the charm. In other words, he looked incredible. His eyes flicked down toward the hem of my dress and then dropped lower to my ankles before rising again, coming to rest on my face. I felt naked beneath his gaze. Bare. My cheeks were flaming.

"Wow, you look amazing," he said.

"I—thank you, so do you," I managed. "Where's Quinn?"

"She sent me to get you. Apparently, I'm your escort for the evening." He offered his elbow. "Ready?"

No, I thought. *Not at all.* But I linked my arm with his anyway—I could barely stand upright in the stilettos. "You know where to go?"

"Not exactly. But your sister said the dining room is the next level up, toward the front of the ship. Said we couldn't miss it."

I nodded. "Lead the way."

We strolled down the hallway together in awkward silence, Darren's cologne filling my nose with the scent of sage and citrus. It reminded me of how long it had been since I was this close to a man without panicking. It had been seven years since I'd pulled myself half-dead from the trunk of the psychopath who tried to kill me then sprinted across the highway, only to wind up gasping for air in the bottom of a ditch.

I never found out why he'd done it.

Sean Grieves died that day, cut down in a hail of gunfire, but I still carried the weight of his ghost in my bones. I sensed his footsteps when someone trailed behind me a little too close. I heard his voice in the timbre of a harshly uttered word. It was his face I saw in the dark of my room when I woke, sick and gasping for air. And it was Sean who sat across from me when I last pushed myself to go on a date. I started hyperventilating when he pulled me close and tried to kiss me.

That was five years ago, and I hadn't touched a man since.

"I think it's up these stairs," Darren said as we strolled into a well-lit mezzanine. A spiral staircase rose from the center with white pearlescent marble steps, the spindles chrome, the structure rising toward a hand-blown glass chandelier dangling from the vaulted ceiling, spilling rainbows of light.

"Wow," I mumbled.

"Amazing," Darren echoed.

"Oh. My. God," a voice screeched. "Aren't you two the *cutest!* Caprice materialized from the hall behind us, along with Chaz, who made a box of his fingers and mimed taking our picture.

"Where's her corsage, D?" he said with a laugh before slapping him on the shoulder. "Don't tell me you forgot it."

Caprice rolled her eyes. "You're such an ass, Chaz. Ignore him. You both look gorgeous."

"So do you," I lied, eyeing Caprice's dress, which looked not unlike a cupcake, frosted in layers of blue and violet tulle. She wore her hair in braids, her eyelids raccooned in a pink eyeshadow that matched the highlights in her hair, and she bounced in place like a piston firing with too much energy. If I didn't know otherwise, I'd think the woman had downed a few Red Bulls in preparation for eighties night at the club.

Chaz stepped past her, clad in a white blazer with a black lapel. A pair of silver chains hung from his neck, and he'd further sharpened the gel spikes in his hair. The guy looked like a porcupine. "I don't know about you all," he said, starting up the steps, "but I could really use a drink."

"He has a point," Caprice said, following behind, pausing as she passed to whisper, "He's cute," into my ear in a voice loud enough for Darren to hear.

Needles of heat stung my cheeks, and I started after them before he could see me blush.

CHAPTER SEVEN

Guests and waitstaff milled near a massive formal dining table decorated with vases full of lush pink blossoms as we entered the dining room. A wet bar chimed with activity to my right—the hum of a blender followed by the clink of ice on metal. Couches topped with deep white cushions clung to the edges of the room and spilled onto an open-air deck, giving view to the bow as it rocked gently toward a tangerine horizon. The scene looked like a postcard, a vacationer's dream. I had no reason to be anxious, to feel the way I did. From the second I boarded the plane my nerves had been on overdrive. I needed a drink.

"Would you like a glass of wine?"

I nearly jumped. Carmela stood before me. The woman moved like a cat.

"Please," I said, taking a white.

Carmela rotated the tray toward Darren. "Sir?"

"Thank you, yes," he said, nabbing a red, which he promptly raised in response to Tim calling him over from across the room with a wave of his hand. "You okay for a moment by yourself?" Darren said, glancing my way.

"Totally." I took a sip and made a shooing motion with my hand. "Go."

"Great. I'll save you a seat."

I watched him go and then faced Carmela. "So, how long have you been with Xclivity?"

She bit her lip in thought. "I'm ... not exactly sure. Many years."

I squinted, paying attention now. The *how-long-have-you-worked-here* question was standard small talk. One most people knew the answer to instantly. "Do you like it?"

"Absolutely." She gave me a hollow smile. "They're a very nice group. I get to travel to many wonderful places."

"I bet. Do you ever get to bring anyone along? Friends? Family?"

Her smile wilted, her eyes flicking over my shoulder before coming back again. "No, unfortunately not."

"I'm sorry," I said. "That must be hard. Do you have children?"

"I ... do, yes. A boy and a girl." Her face flushed. "They're ..." She hesitated. "They're adults. I haven't seen either of them in a very long time." The way she said it, with her voice wavering, made me wonder if I'd pushed her too far, too fast. And I didn't even know what I was pushing for, but my instincts were picking at me, blaring that I was about to uncover something important. Still, I didn't want to traumatize this poor woman—she looked like she was close to passing out.

I placed my hand on her shoulder. "Hey, are you okay?"

"I'm fine." She leaned closer, her voice dropping to a whisper. "But you need to be—"

"Carmela, please attend to the rest of the guests."

I jolted at the voice and turned to find Marco standing behind me, surveying Carmela with his arms crossed. What had she been about to tell me? I needed to be what? Careful? It was the only thing that made sense, not that I'd find out now.

Carmela blinked and swallowed, her face firming, snapping back from wherever it was she'd been. "Yes, sir. Right away." Then she was gone. Marco watched her go before turning his attention toward me. "Are you finding everything to your liking so far?"

"Yes, it's all very ... nice."

"Excellent."

He stared at me and said nothing else. In the fading evening light, his eyes looked sinister. Gruesome. My insides squirmed. I wanted to get away from this man. But I also knew better than to judge a book by its cover. I'd met more than my fair share of people on the podcast who looked like murderers and were anything but. The opposite often held true. When you spend as much time studying criminals as I do, you quickly realize looks don't have a lot to do with it. Anyone can do bad shit given the right circumstances.

Despite the thought, I couldn't shake the feeling Marco already had.

A gentle *ting, ting, ting* sounded from across the room. Bryce clinking a knife against a water glass near the table.

"Please, everyone, gather 'round and find a seat. Dinner is about to be served."

Here we go, I thought, crossing the room, feeling like I'd somehow time-warped back to my high school years, once more the weirdo with acne and bad bangs and nowhere to sit. A sliver of panic wedged in my throat when I noticed Darren had already planted himself between his parents. I scanned the table and aimed for an open chair next to Liam, nearly colliding with Alex in the process.

"Sorry, go ahead," I said, nodding at the chair.

"No, please," he said, "you were here first."

"I think you were, actually."

"It's fine, I can—"

"Oh, for Chrissake!" Liam said. He leaned back and seized Alex by the wrist, then jerked him toward the free chair on his other side. "Just sit, already!"

I stared at Liam, stunned. Was this how he usually treated Alex? He hadn't seemed like the type in the limo, but maybe I'd misjudged him.

Liam popped an eyebrow and waved me toward the empty chair. "Well? Are you going to sit, or what?"

Was I? I certainly didn't want to. Not next to this guy. But Quinn had already settled in across from me, along with Bryce, who was busy draining his Old Fashioned. Chaz plopped down next to him, followed by Caprice, and every seat was full except for the one at the head of the table. I wasn't about to take that one.

"Who are you wearing?" Liam asked as I sat. His eyes were busy roving the landscape of my body, analyzing it with cold precision. Was he being nice now? The guy was giving me whiplash.

"What?"

"Your dress. Who's the designer?"

A band of heat enveloped my neck. My tongue thickened. "I don't know. My sister—"

"Dolce," Quinn answered for me. "Though I almost went with a Dior. Their spring collection is to die for."

Liam massaged the corners of his mouth with his forefinger and thumb. "Mm, that's what I thought. You chose well."

Quinn beamed. "Right? Thank you."

I studied my sister from across the table. She wore a red velvet dress with a plunging neckline, and her hair had been artfully styled, pulled into a perfectly curated messy bun spilling wispy golden strands. And were those diamond earrings?

"Yo, waitress!" Liam shouted with a toggle of his empty wine glass. "Bring me another."

Carmela spun his way, and I saw it before it happened—her toe catching the fold in the rug beneath the table and the single lurching step she took after, the wine glasses swaying on the tray. She fought for balance and came to an abrupt stop next to Liam. A single bright red splash of wine slopped over the lip of the closest glass and onto his shirt.

He pushed back from the table and padded his chest frantically with his napkin. "Oh my god! You clumsy bitch!"

Carmela's face turned as red as the stain spreading across Liam's chest. "I'm sorry, sir."

I stiffened, every muscle in my body flexing tight. "Hey, what's the matter with you? It was an accident!"

"Do you know how much this cost?" Liam spurted, still dabbing away, his bow tie trembling. "It's a *Brioni!*"

"I don't care what it cost," I snapped. "You don't treat people that way. Who raised you?" I reached over and set my hand on Carmela's. The tray trembled in her grip. "Ignore him. Seriously, you're doing a great job."

Liam paused his frantic wiping and cocked his head at me, the look on his face a hot spotlight searing my skin.

"What?" I asked, the word hanging between us until Alex dipped his napkin in a glass of water and joined Liam's dabbing.

"Calm down, babe. Look, it's coming out."

"No, it's not. It's ..." Liam peered over my shoulder and his eyes went wide. "Oh, *here* we go."

I turned. A tall, slender woman stood in the doorway in a vintage-looking bohemian dress. She was beautiful, with dark hair and eyes so brown they bordered on black. Her face held a timeless quality, almost lavish, with high cheekbones that rounded into a narrow jaw. Wide, full lips. Pale skin. She looked familiar in a way I couldn't place, like I'd seen her somewhere before, even though I knew I hadn't. A starlet from a different time who surveyed the room from behind an expressionless mask.

Chairs scraped.

Silverware clattered.

Half the table came to their feet: Bryce and Quinn, Liam and Caprice, Kerry and Tim—all with a fist pressed to their chest, looking like they were about to recite some twisted pledge of allegiance.

I eyed Darren and mouthed a nervous, *What's going on?*

He shrugged in response and then stood. Chaz did the same,

his knee bumping the underside of the table with a bang that made me jump. Alex rose next. I moved to join them and stopped when I noticed the woman gazing at me. The weight of her look was like gravity. It pinned me to my chair.

"Stand up," Liam hissed.

I did, and the woman's face relaxed. She returned her attention to the rest of the group and brought her palms together before pressing the tips of her fingers to her forehead. The others mimed the action, everybody looking as if they were deep in prayer. I briefly wondered if I was hallucinating. The woman raised her head and smiled.

Everyone took their seats, chatting again like they hadn't jumped to their feet to welcome this woman with some bizarre ritual.

I retook my seat in a daze and watched her glide across the floor toward the empty chair at the head of the table. She moved like a ghost. "Who is that?" I asked.

"That," Liam said, "is Julianna Nadar. The Architect. You're in the presence of royalty."

The Architect of what? I waited for him to elaborate, but instead, he gulped the rest of his wine in a loud swallow. "God where is that waitress?" he moaned. "Hey, over here!"

Carmela scurried to refill his glass, her hands trembling as she poured.

"Careful," Liam said.

I shot him a withering look. "It's okay, Carmela."

She surveyed me with something close to warmth in her eyes, finished the pour, and then retreated to the bar. I wanted to rush after her and tell her not to let Liam get to her, that he wasn't worth her energy or her time. I've come to the conclusion after conducting hundreds of interviews for *Still Living*—with both the criminal and the innocent—that there are two types of people; decent human beings who care about others and generally do the right thing, and those who only care about themselves. Liam belonged squarely in the second camp. The guy was a Grade-A asshole.

"So, Olivia, what case are you working on?" Quinn asked from across the table.

I turned toward her, feeling on edge. Another question about my podcast. I didn't get it. Five years ago, after the first episode aired, Quinn told me—point blank—that she'd never speak to me again if I didn't pull it off the air. She said I'd taken advantage of her by discussing the death of our parents, and in particular of our father. Quinn considered losing him her exclusive trauma, something not to be shared. Ever. My father meant everything to Quinn. Besides me, he was all she had.

And sure, I knew his suicide marked the day our lives diverged and took two very different paths, but what was I supposed to do? Preach the virtues of building a true-crime platform based on honesty and transparency while lying about where I came from and what I'd been through? Hell no. I had as much right to talk about what happened that day as she did. Which is exactly what I'd told her. When I did, Quinn cut me out of her life like a malignant tumor. So, her asking me a question about my podcast—*again*—was beyond bizarre.

I set my glass down. "It relates to an infant hot-car death in

Texas. The father claimed he forgot the baby was in the back seat. My co-host, Nina, and I have evidence that suggests otherwise."

"That's awful. I've listened to every episode, you know. You must be so proud of yourself. You and Nina make an excellent team." She leaned forward and laced her fingers together beneath her chin. "What you've done for all those people is amazing."

Every episode? What the fuck? I couldn't tell if she was being sarcastic or serious.

"It really is," Bryce echoed. "To help so many victims find closure is an incredible achievement." He gave me a wry half grin and raised his glass. "Cheers."

I returned the motion, unsure if he was mocking me. I had no clue what to say next. Luckily, Liam interjected and droned on about his productivity app until the appetizers arrived. The waitstaff set platters of canapé crackers garnished with quail eggs and asparagus on the table along with trays of salmon and cream cheese puffs that looked like sugar-dusted mushrooms.

"Try one," Bryce said, still watching me. "They're delightful."

I popped it into my mouth. *Delightful* indeed.

Salads were served next, the leaves so green, the tomatoes and cucumbers so fresh, I wondered if they'd been harvested from some hidden rooftop garden. Dinner followed shortly after. Platters of caramelized chicken and shish kabobs of skewered meat. Bowls of pasta and bread drenched in butter. Blackened mahi-mahi delicately fileted on tender beds of lettuce.

I ate in silence, smiled when appropriate, and laughed when everyone else did. I nodded and shook my head like I was part of the conversation—*Yes, housing prices are out of control. No, I'm afraid I haven't invested in crypto yet.*

I had no interest in anything other than Quinn.

I studied her swanlike features, watched as she tucked her hair behind her ear with a coy movement and picked daintily at her food. I listened to her speak in her new and unfamiliar lilting fairytale cadence. *Do tell me more. Are you serious? Stop it, you're kidding me!* She giggled and stroked Bryce's arm, like a princess fawning over her prince. It felt like I was staring at a caricature of my sister; a child's sketch of what an adult should act like. So easy-going. So carefree. So proper. So *not* Quinn.

And I needed to find out why.

CHAPTER EIGHT

After the plates were cleared, Julianna stood. "Thank you for coming, everyone. My name is Julianna Nadar. For those of you I haven't yet met, hello, and for those of you I have, it's good to see you again." She parted her hands and swept her arms wide. "For the next few days, I want you to consider *The Athena* your home away from home. Spend time reveling in the natural beauty of the ocean and soak up the sun. Eat, drink, and relax. Go jet-skiing. Get a massage and get to know each other." She smiled, something about the shape so natural and fluid, her voice so warm, it startled me; I'd been expecting something decidedly colder. "But please remember why you are here. Do not forget The Work."

I frowned. *The Work?*

Julianna continued: "To be selected for the Transcension, this trip you are now on, is one of the greatest honors Xclivity can bestow on its members. It's a testament to the fact that you've abandoned the scarcity mindset and reoriented your focus toward the Law of Plenty. Know that each and every one of you are here for a reason. Believe it."

The Transcension? The Law of Plenty? What were these terms?

53

Tim raised his glass. "Hear, hear!"

"And to our guests," Julianna said, eyeing the rest of the table, "who likely have no idea what I'm talking about—"

"Yeah, that would be me," Chaz said, barking out a laugh.

Caprice slapped his shoulder and issued a pissed-off, "Shh!"

"It's okay," Julianna said, fixing her with a beatific grin before turning back to Chaz. "When we select a member of our family for the Transcension, they may bring a single guest. Only one. A person they consider instrumental to their life and future wellbeing. Caprice has chosen you, Chaz. To her, you are that person. Do not make light of it." She turned her attention to the rest of us. "Darren, Alex, and Via, welcome. You were chosen as well. You mean a great deal to those who brought you, and it's our privilege to have you with us on our voyage to Elysium."

Great, I thought dimly. *Quinn told her my nickname.* And then: *the others are guests like me?* I knew Darren was, but I hadn't connected the dots that Chaz and Alex were as well. And what the hell was Elysium? I glanced at Quinn, who stared at Julianna with the same rapt attention as the others.

Julianna's smile broadened. "Our relationships represent the very core of who we are. At their best, they fulfill us and enhance our spiritual and emotional wellbeing. At their worst, they leave us bitter husks of our former selves, hollow and dry. They keep us mired in the past without the ability to move forward. They keep us stuck."

I risked another glance at Quinn—who was now gazing right back at me, her eyes two green suns boring through my skull, her jaw set.

My skin buzzed. My lips went numb.

I looked back toward Julianna. She opened a black jewelry case and pulled out a forest-green band—a bracelet—which she handed to Chaz. He took it and pinched it between two fingers like an entomologist studying some kind of rare and deadly insect. "What do I do with this?"

"Put it on, of course."

He moved to but dropped it when Julianna spoke again, the bracelet clattering onto his plate.

"But *only* if you are truly willing to open yourself to your sister over the next few days and prioritize repairing the cracks in your relationship." Julianna surveyed the rest of the table. "This bracelet, an unbroken circle, is a symbol of unity, of family. And like a circle, when we are linked, we do not easily break."

Oh, God. I didn't want one of these things on my wrist, didn't want to enter into whatever cultish pact it symbolized. And what was that exactly? A willingness to partake in some bizarre self-improvement cruise? Some weird-ass bougie psychotherapy trip where Quinn and I would magically work out all of our differences?

Chaz scooped up the bracelet and eyed it again with a grin. "I mean, it looks more like an oval to me."

Darren laughed.

"Humor is your mask, I see," Julianna said.

Chaz leaned back in his chair. "What?"

"Humor is your defense mechanism. A wall you use to deflect anything that might cause you pain or force you to grapple with who you really are."

His smile faded, but he managed to keep it in place. "Yeah, and who's that?"

"A deeply insecure person. Someone who's afraid to reveal their wounds."

"I'm not insecure."

Caprice snorted. "Oh my god, yes, you are! *So* insecure."

"And you, Caprice," Julianna said, turning her way, "wear the mask of vanity. You're empty inside. A shell. You crave validation from others in order to escape your low sense of self-worth."

Her mouth hung open. It looked like she'd been slapped. I wanted to push back from the table, slip from the room, and lock my stateroom door until we returned to Puerto Rico.

"No, I don't," Caprice replied.

"Pause a moment and reflect on what you just said," Julianna said. "Is that *really* the truth?"

Caprice's eyelashes fluttered, and then her face crumpled, and her gaze fell to the table. "You're right. I want people to like me. I'm sorry, Mother."

I bit my lip. *Mother? What the fuck?*

"Don't be ashamed, child," Julianna said. "We all wear masks. It's how we cope with life. But they—" she eyed Chaz again "—are not to be worn here. They are not what Xclivity represents. This is a safe space. Here, you will open yourselves to others and finally be seen." Her gaze fell to the bracelet in Chaz's hand. "Will you allow yourself to be seen, Chaz?"

My skin crawled. I wanted to pull out my phone and text Nina under the table, tell her to put a rush on the Xclivity research, and to send a boat to rescue me while she was at it. But I couldn't. I didn't have my phone. I'd left it in my room—I didn't have anywhere to put it because of this goddamn dress.

Chaz rubbed the back of his neck and sighed. "Oh man, I don't know ..."

Caprice elbowed him. "Just put it on, you idiot!"

"Fine, okay. Lay off." He rolled his eyes and clicked it into place.

"There's a bracelet for every guest. Each in your favorite color and customized to fit," Julianna said, passing the case to Alex, who selected a purple band and contemplated it for a moment before regarding Liam with his lips pressed into a tight line. *Click.*

Julianna set the case in front of me next. Two bracelets glimmered up from the soft velvet, one silver and one terracotta orange. It was clear which one was mine. I took the silver band and twirled it between my fingers, noting the hue exactly matched the color of my dress. My initials were engraved on the back in sans-serif font—the *wrong* initials: V.M. Via Miller. I fought the urge not to roll my eyes. The last thing in the world I wanted to do right now was wear this thing.

Julianna sensed my reluctance and edged closer. "I know you and your sister have walked a difficult path, Via. You both have scar tissue to repair. It's why you're here. The universe has brought you to us to heal. That's what your bracelet represents. Healing." She set her hand on my shoulder. *Put it on.*

I didn't move. The room fell silent. The bracelet felt heavy, like a shackle. I still didn't understand why it was so important I wear the damn thing. I didn't want to; my instincts were shrieking for me to put it back in the box and slam the lid. This was all so fucking weird.

My face flushed with heat. Quinn was staring at me, her eyes pleading.

You do owe it to her to try, Therapist Olivia said.

I pressed the ends together, the clasp clicking shut in the shape of a miniature infinity symbol. *Cute.*

Julianna gave my shoulder a squeeze. "Well done, Via."

"It's Olivia, actually."

"Pardon?"

"I go by Olivia, not Via."

She studied me for a long moment, her lips puckering like she'd stuffed her mouth full of sour candy. "Certainly." She took the case and continued around the table and set it in front of Darren. "We call this voyage the Transcension because it's an opportunity for us to do just that—to rise above our painful pasts, to bring our wounds into the light and declare that they no longer control or define us."

Darren retrieved the final bracelet and studied it as Julianna hovered above him, her face taking on the understanding look of a middle-school counselor. *I've been where you are, son. I know how you feel.* "I sense your uncertainty," she said. "You're trying to discover who you are apart from your parents, aren't you? You've been searching." A muscle near his temple twitched. He didn't glance up. "You *will* find yourself on this trip, Darren, I promise. But first you must commit."

Click.

Tim clapped Darren on the back. Kerry gave him a single nod, the severe angles of her face smoothing ever so slightly. The woman never smiled. I was starting to wonder if she was carved from granite.

"That's what The Work is all about," Julianna continued, trailing around the table. "Striving to attain a state of positive harmonic frequency. During our time together, it's Xclivity's job—*my* job—to help each and every one of you discover who you really are. And I promise you, there is nothing more profound than that knowledge. But it will only happen if you are willing to engage with the process, to truly do The Work."

I cringed, dreading whatever multi-level-marketing invitation would surely fall out of her mouth next—some sugar-lipped, timeshare-style pitch. *For the low, low price of ten thousand dollars, you too can be this whole and complete!*

Julianna's gaze swung my way. "Olivia, tonight we begin The Work with you."

What? No, let's not.

Footsteps rose behind me, and I twisted to see Marco setting a trunk the size of a large cooler on the floor.

"What's that?" I asked, feeling unsteady as I pushed to my feet.

She only gestured in response, sweeping her arm toward the trunk with the movement of a game show hostess about to pull back the grand prize curtain. Behind her, across the room, I spotted Carmela staring at the trunk, looking haunted, her lips pinched, her face knotted.

"Please," Julianna said, "I'd like you to open it."

A nervous laugh bubbled up my throat. "And what happens if I don't?"

Julianna edged in front of me and took my hands. My palms were sweating. "No one will force you to do anything you don't want to do on this trip. You can choose to keep it closed. That's what most people do when facing their fears. They keep them locked away. They never realize how strong they truly are. But you, Olivia, are strong. I can sense that."

It all felt too intimate, the way she held my hands, her fingers threading with mine in tender compassion, her dark eyes soulful and searching. I felt naked beneath her glare, like she'd stripped me from my dress to get a better look at the pale, frightened creature beneath. It made me want to jerk free and bolt from the room, but something about her words and the authenticity with which she spoke kept me standing there, nailed to the floor thinking, *You know what? You're right, I* am *that strong.*

I moved past her and squatted in front of the trunk. My fingers shifted unsteadily toward the latch and hovered there, unable to draw any closer.

"You can do this, Olivia!" Quinn encouraged from the table.

I flipped the latch.

The lid sprang open and the sensation of falling overtook me—the feeling that the floor had unstitched itself beneath my feet. Waves of vertigo crashed against my skull and threatened to sever my shaky grip on reality.

A shriek rose up my throat. I stumbled back.

"Holy shit!" someone said.

Inside the trunk, a mass of scaled bodies coiled and writhed with oily motion. Forked tongues flicked from between lipless mouths. Black marble eyes swayed and rotated my way. The sound of hissing filled my ears in a long, sinister rush that nearly loosened my bladder. I didn't know how many snakes there were. Dozens? A hundred? It didn't matter; even one was too many. I'd been terrified of snakes for as long as I could remember.

"Olivia, it's okay, they're harmless," Julianna said. "Breathe." She sounded impossibly far away, like she was speaking through miles of static. Her hand slipped over mine and pressed it to my stomach. "*Breathe.* Welcome the fear and *breathe.* Imagine the worst thing that could happen and remain in that moment until the fear subsides."

I didn't have to imagine. The last time I'd been this close to a snake, the worst thing *had* happened.

"Good," Julianna said. "*Good.* Come." She edged forward and tugged me with her, a step closer toward the boiling mass of scales. "If we let them, our fears bind us. They stunt our growth and keep us trapped." Her hand slid from mine, and I watched in horror as it coasted over the snakes, hovering there for a second before, with an unsettling ease, she took a lime-green serpent and let it coil over her forearm. She then raised it and offered it to me. "Face your fear, Olivia. Take the snake. It won't hurt you."

The snake lifted its head and wavered expectantly in front of me, its tongue flicking in and out, tasting the air with little darting movements. Eyes ringed in yellow pigment locked with mine, the pupils black, the gaze alien and cold. Beads of sweat erupted across the back of my neck.

"Take the snake, Olivia," Julianna repeated. "You are stronger than your fear."

As if drawn higher by some invisible magnet, my hand rose, my fingers trembling.

"This is how you move forward," Julianna said.

Breathe, I told myself as the snake slithered from her arm toward mine. *Just breathe.* The sensation of cool, dry leather brushed my fingertips.

"This is how you overcome."

And I ran.

CHAPTER NINE

A rattlesnake bit me when I was six years old. It was one of those light-bulb-flash memories you never forget, no matter how hard you try. You know the kind—those awful, childhood recollections that leave sear marks scorched across the meat of your brain. Close your eyes, picture it, and you're right back there in that moment, clear as day.

I'd woken with the sun and slipped from the tent to pee. On my way back to the campsite, I slowed to marvel at my surroundings—the red-washed cliffs and pastel-pink buttes, the vistas of wrinkled rock towering all around me, jutting toward a creamsicle sky. I've always loved mornings. Even as a little girl, I'd loved that first beautiful blush of dawn when everything was still and quiet, and you felt like God painted something for only you to see. That was how I felt in that moment, like I was standing in the middle of a miracle.

The fangs sank into my ankle without warning.

I heard no brittle keratin vibration. No dry *chicka chicka chicka* rattle shooing me away. Just a lazy step and a quick in-and-out strike that left me on the ground wailing. What followed came in a blur of color and sound. Vague sensations and images that, like a slide projector, were delivered one sticky frame at a time, *flash-click, flash.*

Flash-click. A bearded man racing toward me, the smell of tobacco wafting off his checkered shirt as he picked me up and roared for help.

Flash-click. The man running, my head thumping on his shoulder with every step.

Flash-click. Pressure around my ankle, the skin swelling like a vise, my leg going numb.

Flash-click. Pain firebombing its way through my blood.

Flash-click. The taste of venom pooling metallic at the back of my throat, my eyes flooding with tears.

Flash-click. An endless stretch of agony waiting for the chopper before hearing the rhythmic *thwap, thwap, thwap* of rotor blades chewing air.

Flash-click. My father's face above me in the hospital, his cheeks shining with tears.

Flash-click. Men in green scrubs peering down at me from behind their surgical masks, their heads outlined in a waxy-butter light.

I almost lost my leg that day; I nearly died.

But nobody here knew that story. Nobody except Quinn.

"Olivia, wait!" Quinn screeched. "Come back!"

I burst through the dining room doors and barreled outside

with the feeling of that long-ago rattlesnake venom smoking through my veins. My ankle throbbed with phantom pain. I ran faster, my heels clacking against the deck until the ringing *snap!* of my high heel breaking sent me tumbling into a row of sun chairs so hard I felt the impact in my teeth. And then I sat there, staring up at the navy-tinged sky, fighting back tears, telling myself things like, *Don't cry, Olivia. Don't do it.* And, *You're stronger than this. You really are.*

I wasn't. The tears came anyway. I pinched the bridge of my nose and focused on slowing my racing heart. The boat hummed with gentle vibration. Stars glittered overhead with ancient fire. I shivered in my barely-there dress, feeling vulnerable and exposed, which I now understood to be the point of the trip. I would be forced to expose my darkest secrets and most intimate fears to a complete group of strangers, because that's what The Work was all about, right? Overcoming your fears? Putting them on parade for others like I'd done a moment ago, so they could watch you unravel in real time?

"Why did I come?" I whispered. "*Why?*"

"Olivia?"

A figure drifted my way, floating between panels of light—my sister the ghost, dressed in red.

"Why did you run off?"

I pawed the moisture from my eyes, untangled one of my legs from the sun chairs, and pulled myself to my feet. "Why do you *think* I ran off?"

"I'm sorry. I know Julianna can be a little intense at times."

"What else did you tell her about me, Quinn?"

A look rippled over her face, a brief curl of the lips followed by a narrowing of the eyes—*a sneer?*—there one second and gone the next. She reclined against the railing. "My first Xclivity event was overwhelming, too. I didn't know anyone. I remember standing in the corner drinking my wine, thinking, who are these people and why are they all so weird? Why did I come here? I felt so out of place. I just wanted to go home."

I wrinkled my nose and took a step toward her. "You're actually going to make this about you? What the fuck was that? The bitch had a box full of *snakes!*"

"Let me explain, will you?" Quinn snapped.

I rolled my eyes and waved a hand. "Fine. Explain."

"At my first meeting, they were talking about the same things. Facing your fears and living an integrated life. Achieving your potential. Doing The Work. All of that. When they asked me to tell my story, I tried to leave, but I couldn't. Not because I wanted to stay, but because I was a coward. After spending so many years by myself, I didn't have the courage to face another night alone."

The comment slid between my ribs like a cold metal blade.

"So, after a while, I opened up and told them everything. Just blurted it out to a room full of strangers, guts and all. Can you believe that? I didn't look up the entire time. Not once. Not until the very end. When I did, I thought they'd all laugh at me. But they didn't. Not a single person. They just listened. Like, really listened, you know? I could tell they cared. Especially Bryce." She wiped her eyes and laughed. "I was still so lost when I met him, Olivia. Barely hanging on by a thread."

I wanted to scream at her, *What does any of this have to do with the goddamn snakes?* But I couldn't hold on to my rage with her looking so broken and frail. "Quinn ..." I trailed off, not really knowing what to say next, just feeling like I had to say something to keep her talking because I was finally getting some answers about her life and what she'd been up to the last few years.

She shook her head. "I was in pieces back then. Bryce didn't have to stand by me. None of them did. They could have abandoned me like ... like so many others have." Her eyes tilted toward mine and then fell. The phantom blade slid through tendon and hit bone. I hadn't been the one to abandon her—she'd abandoned me—but that's not how Quinn saw it. In her eyes, I'd been the one who'd given up on our relationship. The one who'd walked away. "But they didn't," she continued. "They accepted me, warts and all. They saw me." She swept a hand from her chest to her waist. "*This* me. The person still trapped inside. The person I could become."

"That's great," I replied. "I'm happy for you. Seriously. But don't you think it's time you and I talked about *us?*"

She continued without pause, like she hadn't heard me. "The reason I'm telling you all of this is that it took a family for me to heal. And that's exactly what Xclivity is, Olivia—a family."

I'm your family. I wanted to say. *You wouldn't let me in!*

"It took a while, but they brought me back to life. They helped me remember who I was. And they can do the same for you and me."

A flash of anger rippled through me. We didn't need Xclivity or any of its mind games to work things out. We just needed to talk. "You know this is a cult, right?"

Quinn's eyes narrowed, all the warmth draining from her face. "Why would you say that?"

"Seriously? All the self-improvement talk? All the crazy-ass terms? Doing The Work. I mean, come on. There are better ways to help people deal with trauma than surprising them with a chest full of triggers." I clenched my jaw. *Go easy,* I told myself. *Take it slow.* "Look, can we just clear the air here? We need to talk about what happened."

"Olivia, stop."

But I couldn't. I had to expel the poison. I'd carried it for too long. I had to get it out. "No. If we're ever going to move forward, you need to hear my side of the—"

Her fingers jetted out, and she sunk her nails into my wrist with painful force. I snapped my hand back, but she wouldn't let go, her fingernails digging deeper, her face twisting into a snarl, teeth bared. She looked like an animal.

"Let go, Quinn!" I hissed. And then softer: "Please, you're hurting me."

She blinked and looked at her hand like it didn't belong to her, like someone else was applying pressure to her fingernails, ordering them to sink in.

"Quinn ..."

Her hand unfurled, leaving four angry crescent moons behind, pressed into the delicate skin beneath my palm. One was already plumping with blood.

"I'm sorry." She took a step back, the moon draping her in a gory light. "I—I don't know why I did that. There's a process. A way for us to work through things without—" she waved at my hand "—without something like this happening."

I brought my wrist to my lips and sucked. The bright taste of pennies filled my mouth. "We can't ignore things anymore. That's what we've done for years now, and it hasn't gotten us anywhere. We have to talk."

"And we will. We *will*. I promise. But not here. Not like this." Quinn's voice faltered, cracked. "Xclivity has a certain way of doing things. Methods that provide the right structure for difficult discussions like these. Trust me, I know from experience." Her jaw bunched, and she popped off a nervous laugh. A tear cut down her cheek and clung to her chin like a jewel. "I brought you with me because I want us to be close again. I truly do. But you have to give this process a chance, okay?" She sucked a slice of lip between her teeth as she waited for me to respond. There was something tender in the look; I had the distinct impression she'd crack and fall to pieces if I said the wrong thing.

"Okay," I finally conceded. *If it will get you to talk.*

A smile swam across her face, and she rushed forward and pulled me into a hug, squeezing so tight, I thought she might snap a rib. Then she stepped back and took my hand. "Look, tonight hasn't gotten off to the best start. Come on, what do you say we go have some fun?"

I tensed. I couldn't stomach the thought of seeing the others so soon after the production I'd made in the dining room. I faked a yawn. "Actually, I think I'm going to head to bed. It's been a long day."

"Really? It's still early, and it's been so long since we've spent any real time together." Her voice trembled, and I felt the conversation turning south again. I didn't want another meltdown. And the truth was, I *did* want to get to know my sister. The *real* her. Whoever she was beneath all of this. Even if I didn't want to admit it, I knew Quinn was the only family I had left.

I hesitated, then sighed. "Sure. Okay. Let's go."

"Yeah?"

I nodded. "Yes, on one condition."

"What's that?"

"No more snakes."

CHAPTER TEN

Quinn led me back through the dining room, toward the bow, where I could see everyone sitting around a glass-walled fire pit spitting blue tongues of flame.

Everyone except Julianna.

They looked up as we approached. Quinn settled next to Bryce as Caprice patted an empty cushion beside her. She handed me a glass of water as I sat. I took a long sip, feeling awkward, like a kid waking from a particularly nasty night terror only to realize it was all a dream. *No monster, see? Nothing there.*

"Thanks," I said to her. "Sorry for my reaction earlier."

"Don't be. All those snakes? I would have done the same in your situation. That was awful."

"Are these events—" I waved a hand vaguely at the ship "—always so intense?"

"Sometimes. If it makes you feel any better, I wasn't ready for the whole, *you're an empty shell thing*, either."

"I'm sorry. That had to hurt."

"It wasn't awesome." She swept a hand through her hair and

bit her lip. "But honestly, it's what I needed to hear. Julianna is good like that. She'll really help you grow if you give her a chance."

"Yeah, she's ... something." I paused, tried to change the subject. "This ship is incredible, isn't it?"

Caprice pulled a tube of lip gloss from her clutch and reapplied it, smacked her lips. "It slays. Not that anyone would know. There's no Wi-Fi. I haven't been able to post on my socials all day. A ship like this has to have Starlink, right?" She snapped the clutch shut and turned my way. "Hey, are you getting a signal? Let me see your phone."

"I left it in the room."

She sighed and flung herself back into the cushions. "I haven't gone this long without posting in forever. It's absolutely killing me."

A ball of anxiety throbbed to life behind my ribs. I regretted not stopping by my room to grab my phone on the way out here. I suddenly needed to confirm if what she was saying was true—that there wasn't a cell signal.

"My followers probably think I'm dead or—oh, shit, Chaz, you idiot!" Caprice's gaze shot toward the bow where Chaz stood perched on the railing, rocking back and forth with his arms spread wide, a drink in one hand, his face angled toward the stars.

"I'm the king of the world!"

Caprice rushed for him, and I followed. The two of us closed on him fast, but Marco reached him first. He pulled Chaz from the railing and held him suspended by the collar like a puppet before setting him down.

"What the hell, man?" Chaz slurred, shaking free, his highball glass falling from his hand. It clinked off the railing and plunged over the side into the ocean.

Marco cracked his knuckles and said nothing.

Caprice smacked Chaz on the chest. "You're going to get yourself killed, you know that?"

He snorted. "What? I was only having a little fun."

"She's right," Marco said. "You wouldn't last five minutes in your state. Fall off the bow, and the ship would pull you under. I've seen my fair share of men get chopped up in the propellers." Something about the way Marco's eyes came alive on *chopped up* rattled me. Not just that, but it was a weird thing to say. How many men had he seen get chopped up? How many had he chopped up himself? I had no idea, but every time I was near this guy he set off alarm bells.

"Whatever, bro, that's cap," Chaz said, brushing past him, heading toward the couches. We followed, and when we were out of Marco's earshot, Caprice turned to me and mimed a shiver.

"That man gives me the creeps."

"I know, right?"

"I overheard Bryce say he was ex-military," Caprice continued. "I wonder what he's doing here?"

"I don't know. Maybe Julianna thinks we'll be attacked by pirates or something."

"Yeah maybe, but still …"

"Olivia, Caprice, come sit down," Quinn called from the couch. "We're about to get started."

About to start ... *what?* Another snake session? Bobbing for apples in barrels full of scorpions, maybe? I suddenly wished I'd carried through with my threat of going to sleep. I *was* tired. I'd woken at four-thirty this morning to catch my flight, and my eyelids were growing heavier with each passing second. *Tell her you're exhausted,* Therapist Olivia offered. *Smile and say goodnight.*

But I did neither of those things. My legs carried me back to the couch where two servers swirled among the furniture, passing out mugs of what looked like tea. When I moved to take a sip of mine, Quinn set her hand on my wrist. "Hold on, we need to wait for—oh, here she comes."

Julianna breezed past me and settled into a chair across the fire. The others fell silent, and I groaned inwardly, preparing myself for another psychobabble speech.

"Cheers, everyone!" she said, hoisting her cup before draining it with one long drink.

Quinn downed hers then glanced my way.

"Well?"

"What is this?" I asked, eyeing the brown liquid skeptically. Or was it black? I couldn't tell in the low light.

"Just something that'll help you relax," Quinn said. "Drink it. It's harmless."

Darren took a sip. "Interesting." He took another. The others were doing the same, Caprice swallowing hers with a laugh, Tim smacking and wiping his lips. Chaz tossed his back like a beer and unleashed a shotgun belch. And then they were all waiting, staring at me.

Again.

"I'm okay. Really. I have a headache."

The cup trembled in my hands. I didn't want to drink it. I wanted to set it down. I moved to and stopped when Quinn whispered, "Please, Olivia. Don't embarrass me."

"It's really not that bad," Darren said with a nod.

My muscles clenched. I could feel Quinn's gaze washing over me once more with its pleading heat. *Goddammit.* Whatever this was, it couldn't be worse than snakes—or could it? I didn't know. But if Darren was willing to do it, and the others were, then what danger was I really in? The thought didn't help much as I brought the mug to my lips and took a drink. The liquid was surprisingly cool as it passed over my tongue, the flavor not altogether unpleasant, herbal and earthy with notes of black licorice, like a shot of Jägermeister without the alcohol.

"Not bad, right?" Quinn asked, studying me with a wry smile playing over her lips.

"No," I replied, staring into the cup. "Seriously though, what is it?"

But she'd turned away, already deep in conversation with Bryce, so I sank back into the cushions and gazed at the stars. They swirled together overhead like a Van Gogh painting and draped the yacht in a soft, blue light. Time skipped. My skin tingled. I rubbed my eyelids with the pads of my fingers. A rolling sensation filled my arms, like my heart was the moon and my blood the tide. A muffled panic fizzed through my chest, followed by a distant thought. *Shit, I'm high.* Part of me, a large part, wanted to sneak away and slip back to my room—sleep this off. Another part argued to stay here and enjoy the sensation. Besides experimenting with an edible several years back, I hadn't been high in a long time. And I had to admit it wasn't the worst feeling in the world. My muscles felt like butter.

Caprice's voice floated toward me like a balloon. "Alex, if you were a Muppet, who would you be?"

I searched for him and spotted his glasses glowing in two blue circles to my left, illuminated by the flames. "Oh, that's a good question. I have no idea. I'd have to think about it."

Liam scoffed. "You'd *obviously* be Fozzie."

"The bear?" Alex asked. "Isn't he a comedian? I'm terrified of public speaking."

"Well, yeah, but he's sensitive like you, love." He took Alex's hand and brought it to his lips with a kiss. "It's my favorite thing about you."

I stared at Liam. I was having a hard time getting a read on their relationship. The guy was an emotional roller coaster—sweet one moment, sour the next. It's probably why Alex stuck with him. He saw what Liam *could be* and not what he actually was. An asshole.

"He's also insecure," Alex said with a smirk before nudging Darren. "What about you? Who's your Muppet doppelgänger?"

"Man, I'm with you. I have no idea. Let me think about it." Darren ground his palms into his eyes and blinked overly hard before popping his jaw. He was definitely feeling the same way I was.

"That's easy. Oscar the Grouch," Kerry sniped out of nowhere. "His room is always trashed, and he never moves out."

Darren's face fell. "Ouch, tell me how you really feel."

"I am, Darren. You're almost thirty. The fact that you still live at home is ridiculous."

"Not the time, Kerry," Tim said in a lowered voice. "We've discussed this. He'll move out when he's ready."

"It's never the time. And you babying him isn't doing him any favours."

Darren winced, clearly stung, and a flash of annoyance ran through me. What a bitch this woman was to put her son on blast like this to a bunch of strangers.

Chaz snorted a laugh, and Kerry appraised him. "You think that's funny?"

Chaz shook his head and held up a hand, struggling to maintain his composure. "No, I was just …" He snorted again. "I was just thinking Caprice's Muppet would be Miss Piggy."

Caprice elbowed him so hard, he nearly toppled off the couch. "OMG, you're such a dick!"

"Enough, children," Bryce said with a slight edge to his voice, "or I'll send you to your rooms."

Julianna leaned forward. Shadows pooled in the hollows of her eyes, giving her a skeletal appearance. "New game. Ask and answer. Let's get to know each other a little better. I'll ask someone a question, and they'll answer. Then they get to ask someone a question. There's only one rule. You have to tell the truth."

My stomach dropped. Even among friends, I'd never done

well with games like these. My mind turned to a blank slate every time someone put me on the spot. I'd sit there, trying to think of an answer, before inevitably spouting something awkward that made everyone cringe. And that was with people who knew me. Playing ask and answer with this uneasy group of strangers would be the equivalent of water torture. The anxiety sparked again, cutting through the high, clear and bright.

Julianna surveyed the circle, her hair shimmering with firelight.

Don't pick me, I thought. *Please, don't pick me.* In my current state there was no way I'd be able to lie. Just getting a sentence out legibly would be difficult. If she asked me a question, I was pretty sure I'd start to cry.

"Liam," she said, "I'll start with you. Tell us about your most relaxing experience."

I breathed a sigh of relief.

Liam massaged the corners of his mouth. "Yeah ... I don't think anyone would want to hear about that."

"Now you have to tell," Alex said. "Spill it."

"If you insist." Liam leaned back and kicked his feet up on a footrest. "When I was in my twenties, I went to Thailand, to Phuket, with my company at the time. A bunch of us boys wound up on the beach with a couple locals. Well, long story short, after a few too many cocktails, the clothes came off, and we had a—"

Alex flashed a hand up. "Okay, stop. You were right. I don't want to know. Next question."

"It was a long time ago," Liam said. "A little harmless fun."

"*Next* question," Alex repeated.

"Fine," Liam huffed. "Hm, let me think. Which one of you poor saps should I embarrass? Which one ... which one?" He scanned the group, his eyes finally landing on Bryce, his lips splitting wide with a grin. "Okay, Mr. Hedge Fund Manager, what's your net worth?"

"Oh, now things are getting interesting," Caprice chimed.

A muscle in Bryce's jaw twitched. "Not nearly as much as you might think."

"That's not an answer!" Chaz spouted. "How much?"

"Fifteen million." Bryce looked mortified, like fifteen million was fifteen dollars in his world, but what did I know about what a successful hedge fund manager made? It sounded like a lot to me.

Tim whistled. "That's nothing to spit at."

"It was a hell of a lot more. The market got away from me last year. I took some bad positions." He took a drink of water, his eyes never leaving Liam's as he placed his glass back in the sweat ring on the side table. "Do you want to ask anything else?" A challenge hung in the question. A threat—*do it and see what happens.*

Liam's grin faded. He shook his head. Bryce stared at him for a second longer and then turned to Darren. "Darren, is there anyone here you're attracted to?"

My throat knotted. Christ, what were we—twelve?

Darren rubbed his pants. "Seriously?"

Quinn smiled and straightened. "Answer the question."

"Fine ... yes."

Alex popped an eyebrow. "And who might that be?" But I already knew the answer because Darren was looking directly at me.

"I knew it!" Caprice said.

I felt a spatter of butterflies explode behind my ribs. Was I attracted to him? I wasn't sure, but for some reason, the idea wasn't entirely off-putting, like it was with most men. Maybe there was hope for me yet. Maybe there was hope for this trip.

He mouthed a *sorry* and turned his attention to my sister. "Quinn, what's your biggest regret? If you could change anything about your life, what would it be?"

A whirlpool of emotion swam over her face. Rage? Anger? Despair? I didn't know. But I *was* certain that the question was one she didn't want him to ask. Her eyelids flipped shut, and I could almost hear the gears in her mind churning toward an answer. When she opened her eyes again, they were aimed directly at me. "I would change my relationship with my sister."

"What, specifically, would you change?" Julianna asked.

"All of it," she replied. "Everything."

CHAPTER ELEVEN

Growing up, my sister felt cold to me, like an actress playing a part on the stage of her life. I often imagined a little woman helming the controls in her head, a miniature playwright in a director's chair calling out the next scene with a megaphone. Laugh, but never too hard. Cry when appropriate, carefully and on command. Make sure to say the right things.

As a child, I was lonely. I didn't have a lot of friends. But I had a sister I liked to annoy. I'd slip into Quinn's room and hide in her closet. When the doors slid open, I'd explode out with my hands raised and issue a howling *boo!* I wasn't exactly sure why I did it. Maybe to tease some genuine emotion from her: a shriek or a laugh or some other reaction I could categorize as human. *There you are. I see you.*

But there were other times when I snuck into her room to watch her and try to understand what made her tick. Something about the way Quinn moved through life so detached and distant bothered me. I wanted to understand it, to understand *her*. I never did. I caught glimpses, though.

One memory in particular still haunts me.

I'd fallen asleep in Quinn's closet and woken to her sitting near her sunlit window, staring at a butterfly that had fluttered inside and landed on her hand. Back then, I loved butterflies. They reminded me of angels. I'd spend hours in our backyard garden watching them, marveling at the grace of their wings and how those subtle, fragile movements made them seem like a floating miracle, so weightless and free. I wanted to move through life like that. I wanted to be that free.

Sometimes I'd turn and find my father staring at me from the porch with tears in his eyes. *Your mother lives in them, you know that?* he would say. *Butterflies were her favorite thing.* That's what I was thinking that day as I peered through the slats in Quinn's closet. I'd never seen a butterfly so beautiful. A swallowtail in full golden bloom dusted in iridescent blue. *It's her.* I thought. *It's really Mom.* Quinn stared at it for the longest time, her forehead puckered in concentration, her lips in a slight part, and I remember thinking, *Quinn sees Mom, too.*

And then she snatched it and plucked off its wings.

I shrieked and burst from her closet in tears. *Why did you do that! What's wrong with you? It was her!*

Mom's dead, she said, staring at me for the longest time, looking at me like I was an insect, like she wanted to rip off my wings. When I could no longer stand it, I fled her room, thinking *I hate her, I hate her, and she hates me, too!* It wasn't until much later that I realized Quinn's feelings for me ran far deeper than that; in a way, she'd been at war with herself from the moment I was born.

———

I woke in my cabin to splinters of light leaking past the edges of the curtains, turning the backs of my eyelids a rusty, DayGlo orange. I flipped them open with a groan then reached for my phone on the nightstand, thumbed the screen, and squinted at it.

No bars. Unreal. Caprice was right. How a ship like this, with all its polish and shine, didn't have any Wi-Fi was beyond me. I'd tried to find a connection last night after returning to my room, only to hit a spinning circle of death, which eventually resolved into a page reading DNS_ERROR_NO INTERNET.

Something was different about the screen this morning, though. A flutter of hope unspooled through me when I spotted the red notification icon pinned to my messaging app. New texts! They must have come through during the night, likely when we'd sailed through a stray cell pocket. I scanned them greedily: a reminder from my dentist's office confirming my appointment for a crown next week, a text from a friend asking how I was doing, and then this from Nina:

I did some digging. Xclivity offers self-improvement courses and professional-growth seminars. Coaching and mentorship. That kind of thing. Technically, they're legit, but the corporate structure is uber complex. I can't make sense of it. There are quite a few holding companies with no assets or operations. It's probably nothing to worry about—a lot of businesses do this for tax reasons. Just forget about it and enjoy yourself. Doctor's orders. I'll handle things on this end until you get back. Talk soon.

Nina's words rattled through my head. *Probably nothing.* Damn near every case I'd ever investigated had started out with those two words. But those *probably nothings* were different than *this probably nothing*. This *probably nothing* involved a trunk full of snakes and drinks laced with, what? Barbiturates? Psilocybin? Some substance that made you tell the truth? I still had no clue. And, worse, this *probably nothing* involved Quinn. I thought again about her full-on freak out when I brought up talking about our relationship. The way she went feral and lunged for my wrist. The way she sunk her claws into my skin. *There's a process ...*

The scab on my wrist pulsed painfully in response, a parting gift in the shape of Quinn's fingernail. Strangely, it didn't bother me nearly as much as the rash that had blotched to life beneath the Xclivity bracelet. I have a mild allergy to certain metals, which is why I rarely wear watches, but when I do, they're easy enough to remove ... unlike this thing. I couldn't get it off no matter how hard I pulled or how much I fiddled with the latch, the infinity symbol mocking me, no longer looking cute. I'd even tried to break it a few times, but it wouldn't give. *I'm here forever, bitch.*

My head fell back to the pillow, and I closed my eyes. I didn't want to get up, didn't want to face whatever the day had in store. I was a creature of habit. Give me a pot of coffee and a to-do list over a lazy weekend any day. With no objectives to complete or goals to accomplish, no cases to research, I was useless.

After dozing a few more minutes, and with a heavy dose of reluctance, I pulled myself out of bed and padded across the floor to the glass slider. There, I flung the curtain aside to paradise. A curving slice of emerald sea lapped against a sugar-sand beach. Farther back stood a verdant jungle with trees so thick and green they seemed like something from a movie. A few fluffy white clouds drifted above the island, the sun still working its way into place somewhere to the east, bathing everything in a flood of golden light.

The air felt luxurious against my skin as I opened the door and stepped outside, the temperature perfect. Somewhere in the mid-seventies if I were to guess. A beautiful day for some zip-lining? A nature walk through the jungle while reciting personal affirmations? Another forced confrontation with a box full of snakes? I still didn't understand what had happened yesterday, and I needed to talk to someone I trusted to gain some perspective. I had to talk to Nina.

I raised my phone and swept it in a long arc across the horizon, hoping to catch a signal. No bars. Nothing. *Of course.* With a long stretch, I trundled back inside toward the full-length mirror on the wall and studied my reflection. My hair lay in a sleep-tangled mat on top of my head, and the skin beneath my eyes was smeared with dark circles, my cheeks splotched red. I looked vaguely humanoid, like a creature from deep space here to study the population, to try to blend in. *Because that's what you need to do,* I told myself. *Blend in and get through the rest of this trip in one piece.*

But first I needed a shower.

I headed for the bathroom, stopping when I heard a knock at the door. I didn't want anyone to see me in this state, a walking disaster wearing a mustard-colored T-shirt and a pair of worn sweats. And, shit, what if it was Darren?

Go away, I thought. *Just go.*

The knock came again, louder this time and with more insistence, a muffled female voice cutting through the door. "Room service."

Thank God. "Coming." I eased over and swung the door wide to find Carmela standing behind a cart covered in silver dishes.

"Good morning, Miss Miller," she chirped. "I have your breakfast."

"I didn't order anything."

"Ms. Nadar insists all our guests start the day with a well-balanced meal. You have a savasana session on the beach at ten. You'll need the energy."

I stepped aside and tucked a wayward chunk of hair behind my ear. "Okay, sure. Come on in."

She wheeled the cart past me and removed a silver plate cover, revealing a fillet of raw fish served on a bed of green paper moated with rice.

"What is that?" I asked.

"Tuna sashimi paired with nori and rice."

"Nori?"

"Dried seaweed. It's full of vitamins and minerals. Try it. It's not as bad as it looks."

My stomach knotted, and I shook my head. It looked pretty bad. "No, thank you. I'm not much of a breakfast person." *And that isn't breakfast.*

Carmela continued busying herself at the cart, humming as she retrieved a carafe from within and filled a glass with a lumpy green substance. I took a tentative sniff when she passed it to me.

The smell of celery and cruciferous vegetables filled my sinuses, cabbage and arugula, and possibly beets. I shuddered and handed it back.

"Are you sure you don't want to try it?"

"I'm good."

She set the glass back on the tray and then paused for a second, looking at me like she wanted to say something.

"Everything all right?" I asked.

"Yes, I um ... well, I wanted to thank you."

"For what?"

"For last night at dinner, with Mr. Conrad."

"Oh." It came rushing back: Liam lashing out at her after she spilled his wine, calling her a bitch, dabbing at his stupid shirt with his bow tie waggling away beneath his chin. A laugh bubbled up my throat when I remembered him flapping his arms in panic, looking like a stork stuck in the mud.

Carmela's cheeks darkened.

"Sorry," I said, taking notice. "I'm not laughing at you. I'm laughing at *him*." I mimed wiping my shirt, making a few squawking sounds as I did. "Don't let him get to you. The guy's an idiot."

Carmela smiled. "It's not always easy."

"Seriously, you can't let people like that dictate how you feel. How often do the guests on these Xclivity trips treat you like that, anyway?"

"More often than I would like."

"I hope they pay you well."

She rubbed her wrist, her eyes ticking sideways. I knew

whatever she said next would be a lie, but she just stood there, looking at the floor like she was lost, not saying a word. I crossed my arms. "Carmela, tell me they pay you well. Wait—they pay you, right?"

Over the years, Nina and I had researched a series of suspicious deaths that occurred on cruise ships—all women, every case poorly investigated and hastily classified as suicides or accidents. We learned a lot about how cruise companies exploited their staff, working them seventy to eighty hours per week without any days off, paying them wages that were more competitive than what they could make in their home countries but were still too low to survive on. In some cases, they didn't pay at all.

"They do," Carmela finally replied, looking up. "I'm ... I'm lucky to have this job." There it was again, that fake, customer-service smile curling over her face like molded plastic with just enough teeth shining through to let me know I'd hit a wall. She turned to leave, but I moved with her and blocked the doorway.

"Hang on a moment. Please. I run a true-crime podcast, and I can't help but feel like something with Xclivity, with this entire trip, is ... off."

Her smile broadened. "There's nothing wrong. Xclivity is a wonderful company to work for." The statement tumbled out in a way that sounded both rehearsed and unbelievable—a mouthful of cardboard.

"I've helped a lot of troubled people, Carmela. I can help you, too, if you'll let me." I took her hand and gave it what I hoped was an assuring squeeze.

She gnawed on a sliver of cheek in consideration, blinked. The corners of her lips twitched. Her mouth opened and snapped shut. She closed her eyes and shook her head as though in silent argument with herself before reaching into the breakfast cart for a napkin. She scribbled something on it, glanced behind me toward the hall, then pressed the napkin into my hand, along with a key card. "Not here. Find me when you get back. I'm not working dinner tonight. The staff quarters are downstairs at the back of the boat, past the gym. I'm in room 116. We can talk there." She started for the door, pausing halfway. "Stay portside. You'll avoid the security cameras that way." Then she was gone, breezing back into the hall.

I opened the note and read it. Read it again.

My brain sizzled. Time ceased to move.

After a while, I stood and flushed the napkin. I no longer needed it; the words were seared in my brain in electric blue ink. It was a warning—one that chilled me to the bone.

You aren't safe. Do whatever they say.

CHAPTER TWELVE

The speedboat skipped over the water toward the beach. The ocean misted around us, slapping against the gunwale, sending jets of brine arcing outward in gushing rainbows.

I'd exiled myself to a back-corner seat, trying to hide my panic from the others as they'd arrived in groups of twos and threes. Caprice and Chaz. Bryce and Quinn. Tim, Kerry, and Darren. Liam and Alex. I hadn't said a word to any of them. I hadn't even waved. All I could think about was Carmela's note and the flurry of questions it had unleashed.

Why wasn't I safe?

What, exactly, did that mean?

How deep was Quinn's involvement?

Goosebumps rippled over my arms, despite the sun's warmth. The island excursion hadn't even begun, and already I wished it were over. I wanted to talk to Carmela, needed to know what she'd meant. It was the only thing on my mind.

The boat's motor guttered out, and we floated into a slip where two Xclivity staff awaited our arrival. They moved with practiced ease, winding the boat's docking lines around a pair of cleats before helping the passengers off. "Please mind the gap," the captain said as I stepped onto the dock. He gave me a nod and a smile, and I briefly wondered if he was also the yacht captain. I had yet to see whoever was steering the ship.

"You okay?"

I jolted. Alex stood directly behind me with his arms cocked off his hips, his curls frizzed into an unruly tangle on top of his head. In his glasses and pineapple-patterned Hawaiian shirt, he looked like a tour guide ready to lead a tropical field trip—one I didn't want to attend.

"I'm good," I said. "Thanks."

"That shit with the snakes last night was the weirdest thing I've ever seen. Super strange. Freaky, really. I'm terrified of what they'll do to me tonight at the Purification Dinner."

The hair on the nape of my neck rose. "The Purification Dinner? What's that?"

Alex shrugged. "No clue. Liam mentioned it yesterday. I didn't press him for details."

Jesus. I couldn't handle another freaky-ass meal. Just the thought of it made me weak-kneed. I was already running the excuses through my head. Maybe I'd find a way to get sick. "Yeah well, if they do anything, I'm guessing it can't be worse than a box full of snakes."

He pondered that for a moment. "Maybe."

I didn't ask him what his Trunk O' Trauma would contain, and he didn't volunteer any information. We just walked in silence, trailing down the beach after the others with the sand crunching beneath our feet until I asked, "Hey, have you gotten a Wi-Fi signal yet?"

Alex scratched his head. "On the yacht? No. I asked Chaz about it this morning though, and he said they're working on it. Technical difficulties, I guess. And we are at sea, so it's all satellite, which can be spotty at times."

"Figures." A few feet ahead, a hermit crab scuttled sideways into the surf. I watched it go, one of the pincers flashing open before disappearing beneath a white rope of foam.

"So, you pumped for some meditation?" he asked.

I glanced at him. "I thought it was yoga?"

"Oh, maybe. Liam said something about a meditation session, but I don't think he knows, either." I frowned at the mention of his name, and Alex took note. "He's … not as bad as he seems, you know. He's just a peacock. He likes putting on a show. Which he kind of has to do being in tech and all. It's hard to stand out. You have to be assertive. But what he did to that waitress last night—and how he talked to you—that was fucked up. I'm sorry."

"You don't have to apologize for him."

"I guess not, it's, well—I wish people could see the Liam I see. He's so sweet at home. Nothing like that."

I'd seen a few glimpses of Liam's sweet side, but it was still difficult for me to envision him and Alex curled on a couch in front of a movie, feeding each other spoonfuls of Ben and Jerry's.

"How long have you two been together?" I asked.

Alex scrunched his face. "Three years this week. I've actually planned a little surprise for him. I *have* to tell someone, even though I totally shouldn't. Can you keep a secret?"

I nodded.

"I'm going to propose!"

He beamed. I gave him a half-smile and tried to look happy. "That's wonderful, Alex." It wasn't. Liam would use Alex up, drain him. It made me sad. Alex seemed like a genuinely good person. I didn't want it to happen.

"Thanks," Alex said. "I'm going to do it tomorrow evening on the upper deck, right before sunset. I packed some chocolate and champagne to celebrate. A few of the staff are going to prepare everything ahead of time."

"That sounds perfect. You'll have to let me know how it goes."

"Oh, you'll know. I'll either be sobbing uncontrollably or walking on air." He fluttered his fingers as if to accentuate the mental image. "But enough about me. I still can't believe you're actually here. You have no idea how much of a stan I am. I'm dying to hear more about your podcast. Do you mind if I ask you a few questions?"

"Not at all," I said. "But I think they'll have to wait. Look." The group had stopped ahead of us, everyone standing near what appeared to be a circle made from volcanic rock. My eyes lingered on Darren stretching near his parents, wearing a tank top and a pair of camouflage shorts. He turned my way, and the corners of his lips kicked up into dimples.

"Olivia!" Quinn's voice pierced the air, high and bright

shard of glass punching straight through my eardrums. "Hurry up! We're about to get started!"

"Here we go," I said, rolling my eyes at Alex before making my way over to her. She waited for me with her arms crossed, looking fresh-faced, her lips lightly glossed and her skin glowing. I didn't know how it was possible she was this chipper. I felt like shit after whatever weird drink she'd forced on me last night. I hadn't slept well at all.

She placed her hands on my shoulders and guided me back a step. "Stand here. You're one of the points, see?" Three polished white rocks lay before me, one at my feet and two more connecting me to Bryce and Quinn in the shape of a triangle. An expensive-looking turquoise bowl patterned with leaves sat at its center.

To my left, Darren settled into a matching triangle with his parents while, to my right, Caprice and Chaz stood face to face. Across the circle, Liam and Alex did the same, each group separated by the same white rocks with a bowl similar to ours placed between them.

"Good morning."

I swung around to see Julianna strolling toward the head of the circle, wearing a beige linen tunic and a pair of flowing white pants. Her hair fell from beneath a sage-colored bandanna, cascading over her shoulders. Marco took up position to her right, his bald head gleaming, his face already dappled in sweat. As was mine. It was at least ten degrees warmer this far from the water.

"Welcome to Utopia, Xclivity's private island." Julianna spread her arms. Her tunic sleeves looked like angel wings. "Nature is where we go to heal, to commune with Mother Earth and to receive her blessings. Nature has a way of replenishing our vitality and filling us with a newborn sense of purpose."

Chaz snorted. "Yeah, oh-*kay.*"

Marco regarded him instantly, his slate eyes flashing. An electric ball of dread sparked to life in the pit of my stomach. The question hit again: Why was he here? What was about to happen? Everything about this moment suddenly felt wrong.

Julianna continued: "Xclivity was founded with the singular vision that we are not only an extension of the earth but of each other. Energy is timeless. Everything we touch, see, taste, smell, or hear is simply an expression of energy in different forms. We can harvest that energy. We can channel and direct it in wonderful ways if we know how. And once we do, our impact on this world will be boundless."

She paused, nodding at Marco, who bent and retrieved several bundles of dried leaves. He set one in each of the bowls as Julianna continued to speak. "But before we can make any impact whatsoever, we must discover our true purpose in life, the reason we are here. So many people exist in a state without purpose. They try to fill the void in their souls with meaningless things. Without direction, we become cattle, ingesting what's placed before us without thought or question. We binge on television like junk food. We numb our pain with alcohol, drugs, and sex. We spend our money on clothing and cars, on houses and electronics and jewelry, thinking these things will make us happy. Convinced that material possessions can provide the answers our souls long for when all they really do is blind us."

Marco pulled a gunmetal-black Zippo from his pocket and began lighting the bundles. Flavorful smoke filled the air—a pleasant, earthy aroma I immediately recognized as sage. I hadn't smelled it since college.

"To find our true calling, we must stop looking outward for something to fill us and begin looking inward instead. You need to examine yourself and ask the questions that matter. Your soul is crying out for something. What is it? Take a moment to listen."

My soul cried out for me to get some water. God, it was hot.

Julianna continued. "The truth is that most of us are broken. We are damaged by this world. We carry the shame of our past and believe we are unfixable, that we can never change. This is a lie. We can change, but we can't do it on our own. It takes a community. It takes a family. And that's exactly what Xclivity is. A family. *Your* family."

"That's beautiful," Quinn said.

"Yes, absolutely," Kerry added.

Shoot me, I thought.

Julianna nodded at each of us in turn. "If you'll let me, I'd like to take you on a journey of yourself. I want you to connect with your spirituality in a way most never do."

"Please," Caprice said.

Julianna's face went as smooth as a glass pond. "Close your eyes and inhale deeply. Clear your mind. Focus on the air as it fills your lungs, on the sensation of your feet connecting to the earth.

Feel the sun warming your skin. Let go of your thoughts, of all your stress and every distraction."

I scanned the circle, watched as Caprice took a deep, blissful breath—her eyes closed, her forehead Botox-smooth. Behind her, Darren winked at me and turned a few circles over his temple with his index finger in a *this is nuts* gesture. A laugh bubbled up my throat.

"Olivia," Quinn reprimanded. "*Please.*"

"Fine," I hissed back. I snapped my eyes shut. The sun baked against my neck as Julianna spent another five minutes droning on and on. When I opened my eyes again, Bryce was staring at me.

"How do you feel?"

"Amazing," I lied.

"Good. This is only the beginning."

"Now," Julianna said, "take each other's hands and raise them over your head."

Bryce stretched his right hand toward mine, and I reluctantly grasped it, then took Quinn's. We raised them. This was getting ridiculous.

Julianna tilted her chin toward the sky and inhaled, the picture of peace—lips soft, eyes closed, hands wide. "Open yourself to those around you. Let their energy course through you and release yours to them." She exhaled, long and slow. "Allow yourself to be one with the moment."

My shoulders burned. Sweat pooled at the small of my back. A mosquito buzzed near my ear. I tried to slip my hand from Bryce's to swat at it—but he tightened his grip in response.

"Focus," he said.

Another mosquito landed on my neck.

"*Feel* the connection," Quinn whispered.

A hot sting pierced my skin. "Let go!" I yanked my hand from Quinn's and stumbled backward into Caprice. Our heads cracked together as we went down in a tangle of arms and legs.

"Get off me!" she shrieked. "Get *off!*"

I rolled away from her, onto my side, and probed the spot where my skull collided with hers. "I'm sorry … it's the mosquitoes."

Caprice prodded her head with two fingers and then pulled them back like she expected to see blood. "Shit. I think you gave me a concussion."

"You're fine," Chaz assured her, though I could already see a welt taking shape, rising beneath her hairline like a miniature loaf of bread.

Bryce gazed down at me with pity. "There aren't any mosquitoes, Olivia."

"Yes, there definitely are, *Bryce*. Why would I make that up?"

"It's okay, Olivia," Julianna said, kneeling at my side. "It's not uncommon for someone to panic. Contemplative meditation can be intimidating at first. Especially when doing it together. Most people have forgotten how to trust others. To serve others. Which is why I think our next activity will be perfect for you."

"What's that?"

Julianna smiled and nodded toward the jungle. "The trust walk."

CHAPTER THIRTEEN

I've always had an eye for detail. I see the little things others miss—the extra breath someone takes before telling a lie, that slight hitch of the chest that means they're thinking about what to say next. Even as a kid, I'd noticed things: a dragonfly without its wing. A pet missing an owner. How my father spent his nights staring at his phone, lost in pictures of my mother. That's where he'd really lived—in his memories of her. I'd often catch him gazing at me, the corners of his lips curling down, weighted with grief. *You remind me of her, Via. She would have loved you so much.* Her memory pulled at him like a riptide; she clung to him and wouldn't let go. Even then, as young as I was, I knew there was something wrong with my father.

I just couldn't fathom its depth.

Seeing all those details made me a badass in my career. I reached for that superpower whenever I could. But right now, walking blindfolded through the jungle with Quinn, I couldn't see shit.

I stopped and brought my fingertips to the scarf. "This is crazy. I'm taking it off."

Quinn gently swatted my hand away. "No, you aren't, you'll ruin the exercise. Come on, Via, you promised you'd try."

"Oh my god, how many times do I have to tell you I go by Olivia now?" I massaged the clump of pissed-off tendons at the back of my neck. I knew they'd unleash a massive headache if I didn't drink some water soon—which, by the way, was where? I'd had yet to spot any bottled water, which made no sense for a tropical beach excursion. "Quinn?"

She didn't respond, and I stopped.

"You still there?" Dead air hung at the end of my question; a floating bobber of silence punctuated by the intermittent throb of cicadas. "Quinn, if you don't answer me, I'm going to take off—"

"Why does it bother you so much? Me calling you Via?"

Images flash-banged to life at the question in a flaring *whoosh!* The garage cracking open to a cloud of exhaust. A figure slumped at the wheel, hazy through the fumes. I knew who it was before they cleared. He'd already told me in the form of a note stuffed into my lunch box. *I love you, Via. None of this is your fault, Don't ever forget that.*

A fist formed in my throat, and I struggled to speak. "Because it reminds me of ... him."

"Oh ..." Quinn mumbled, her tone softer now, tender. She didn't need me to say anything else. She knew exactly who I was talking about. Quinn had loved our father. That was one thing we'd shared.

"Let's just get this over with," I said. "How much farther?"

"Not far. A few minutes. You ready to try again?"

"I guess," I groaned. A few minutes might have well been a lifetime. So far, I'd stubbed my toe twice—once so hard, I felt the toenail crack. It pulsed with every step, a tiny throbbing heartbeat, begging for me to rip the blindfold off and head back to the beach. But that was against the rules: No peeking during the trust walk. And no touching, only words. All of us had been paired off and sent into the jungle on our own separate paths. With no way to see each other, and no one to hear besides Quinn, it felt like I was walking on an alien planet.

Do whatever they say. Carmela's warning clanged in my head, and a chill ran through me despite the heat.

"Why are you being such a baby about this?" Quinn asked.

"Easy for you to say. You're not the one blindfolded."

"If you can't trust me to guide you through a simple exercise like this, how are we supposed to work through our issues and repair our relationship?"

My heart sank. She was right. She hadn't done anything wrong. And I *did* want to repair our relationship if only for our father. He'd always wanted us to be closer. *I know she can be difficult sometimes, Via, but it's only because she's not as strong as you. No matter how she acts, or what she says, she needs you. You have to look out for her. Promise me you will.* And I'd promised.

"Okay, fair enough," I said. "What next?"

"Keep going. The trail curves ahead, but not for a little bit. Until then, just take slow, easy steps, and I'll keep you on the path." The path that wasn't a path so much as it was a splinter of spongy earth, rising and falling beneath my feet like a buried roller coaster track, waiting to sprain my ankle. We walked in silence for a few minutes, me with my hands out in a zombie shuffle and Quinn trailing so quietly behind, I briefly wondered if maybe she'd thrown in the towel until she finally said, "Stop. There's a ledge in front of you, about half a foot high. Lift your leg slowly and step up."

"Like this?"

"No, your left leg. Yep, like that. Now your right. There you go! See? You can do this. Great job, Olivia!"

The compliment unleashed a wave of warmth: an absurd reaction to completing this simple task. But I didn't care. I couldn't remember the last time Quinn had praised me for anything, or at least with any amount of genuine sincerity. She was happy, happy for *me*. And something about that felt good, felt *right*.

Maybe there's hope for you two yet, Therapist Olivia added.

"Okay," Quinn said. "We're close now. A little farther, and then it'll be my turn."

We were supposed to exchange the blindfold at the end of the trail. I'd become Quinn's eyes for the return trip—the two of us one happy, trust-building team just like Julianna wanted. I walked with more purpose as Quinn called out directions, my toes no longer bashing into every blunt object along the path. *How 'bout that for The Work, Julianna?*

"Hold on," Quinn said. "There's a puddle here. Take a small step left and then a big step forward but be careful, there's a branch hanging over the trail. I don't want you to get hurt."

I visualized it—a gnarled arm stretching for my face—and then ducked underneath the limb without so much as a scratch.

"Perfect! You're doing *so* good! Okay, you'll go right here—"

I went right.

"No! In a few feet!"

A starburst of pain exploded in my shin as it collided with a stone. My fingers clawed empty air. Gravity took hold and sent me pitching forward, my brain conjuring images of me plunging headfirst toward a cliff base littered in sharp jumbles of rock, a bone-shattering pile of granite that would leave me with a nice collection of new knees and elbows upon impact.

Or, more likely, dead.

Oh, fuck.

I slammed into what felt like a bed of moss, and then spun lower through a wall of branches, thorns raking my shirt, flashes of pain erupting behind the blindfold in coronas of red and white light. My existence became one of violent sensation—*air-earth-air-earth-air*—before I thudded onto flat ground.

Somewhere above me, Quinn screamed.

My diaphragm spasmed. I fought for oxygen. The foul reek of sulfur filled my throat—a smell like a vat of eggs left to rot in the sun.

"Olivia! Are you okay? Please say you're okay!"

I tore the blindfold from my eyes and opened my mouth to respond but only managed to sputter and cough.

"Don't move!" Quinn screeched. "I'm going to get help! I'll be right back!"

No, don't leave, I thought feebly. *Stay here.*

"Quinn!" I squeaked. My voice came out shaky and far too low for her to hear. Not that it mattered—she was already gone.

I popped my jaw and took in my surroundings. I was lying on my back in a ring of muck bordering a swamp, the world coming back to me in a series of green and brown splotches: trees and mud and murky water. A thick canopy of fronds hung overhead, seams of midday light angling past the leaves and over the valley I'd carved through the vegetation during my descent downhill. A pair of shrubs dangled broken limbs.

My pulse quickened. Were *my* limbs broken? My arms?

I wiggled my fingers, and relief poured through me when I saw they weren't. They were heavily scratched, though, from my elbows to my wrists. The marks looked like little red river squiggles on a map. Painful, yes, but I'd survive, which was all that mattered. I palmed my chest and patted my ribs. No serious pain there, no fractured ribs, thank God.

Then I turned my attention to my legs.

Which were *sinking*.

I went cold. The mud was cresting my leggings like cake batter, swallowing my calves an inch at a time. My shoes were already buried in the slop and sinking deeper.

With a cry, I heaved on my left leg, and it came free with a wet *thwap*, but my right foot wouldn't give no matter how hard I ordered it to move. A fresh wave of panic ripped through me, and I plunged my arms into the mud, searching for something to take hold of, frantic to find something I could use to pull myself back onto solid ground. My fingertips skimmed a branch or a tree root, slimy but solid.

A lifeline.

I twisted my body and took hold of it, then pulled myself toward firmer ground with steady movements until the branch burped to the surface.

Not a branch. Not a root.

It was bone and tendon. Earth-stained fingers. A flash of something silver around the wrist. *An entire arm.*

I let go of it with a shriek, my fingers sawing through the dense clay, my arms pulling with every bit of strength I could muster. My stuck leg resisted like it was encased in wet cement. I grabbed a vine hanging from a branch and jerked harder, and my foot slowly came loose before it slipped free entirely. Then I was on solid ground, gasping for air once more.

The cloying stench of decomposing organic matter filled my nose.

Bile coated my tongue.

My vision burned black at the edges.

The weight of what just happened hit me like a wall of bricks.

You should be dead. Someone else died here.

I raised my head and took in my surroundings. The jungle pressed in all around me, thick with vegetation. I had no clue where to turn, no idea where to go. And there was no way I'd be climbing back up the hill I'd tumbled down. In my condition, it might as well be a cliff.

A splash broke through the thought, and I glanced behind me in time to see a long, reptilian tail glide into the water across the swamp. Greenish-yellow eyes burning lantern bright, heading my way. A crocodile.

Oh, hell no.

My throat constricted, and I sprang to my feet and barreled into the jungle.

CHAPTER FOURTEEN

The day I nearly died seven years ago began as it always did—with a run.

I loved running.

Sean Grieves took that from me.

After my father killed himself, I became a changeling fond of shadows and closets, taken in by my grandmother, who watched me cry for a year. Not a day passed without me blaming myself for what my dad had done. Despite what he'd told me, it was the only thing that made sense to my seven-year-old brain. I hadn't loved him enough. I hadn't behaved like I should have. If I'd only been nicer, kinder, friendlier, stronger, a better daughter, he wouldn't have abandoned me. He wouldn't have gone.

My grandmother tugged me from therapist to therapist in hopes they'd fix me—an assembly line of doughy-faced women who smiled at me with the proper amount of professional pity as they watched me play with dolls. *How are you feeling today, Olivia?* they'd ask. *Would you like to tell me what's wrong?*

I didn't want to talk about my father, *couldn't* talk about him. Not then, anyway, and most certainly not with *them*. When my grandmother finally realized therapy was a dead end, she tried a different tactic. She dragged me to a soccer field and informed me I was on the team. She'd paid the registration fee. I could scream all I wanted to, but I would play. That was that. So, I did. I played for a couple of years, and although soccer didn't stick—I didn't have the natural skill for the sport—running did.

It became something of a church for me, a way to process my feelings and escape the weight of my crushing grief.

Anytime the world grew too heavy for me to handle, I ran.

Anytime I thought of my father, I ran.

Anytime my heart felt like it would burst and shatter from all the pain, I ran.

I ran, I ran, I ran.

In high school, I joined the cross-country team and took second place in state.

By the time college rolled around, running was all that mattered. I treasured the mornings, ached for that first burst of fresh air and the fire that filled my legs when my body was in motion. I loved that moment when my body clicked on, and my brain shut off, and the only thing I had to focus on was taking my next breath, my next step.

I lived for the weekends, because the weekends meant getting out of town and into nature, away from the city with its constant noise and noxious traffic. All week I ached for the crunch of pine needles beneath my feet instead of the city's unforgiving pavement. I scoured the countryside for the perfect trail. I craved isolation and those few precious hours when I could be alone.

I'll never forget the day that all changed. A Saturday in September with a weather forecast promising rain. *No problem, I'd told myself, the clouds won't blow in for hours. Plenty of time for a run.* Something about that day felt like heaven, no cars in the parking lot, just me and the trail and my feet hammering out the miles, setting a record pace.

I never saw him coming. He exploded from the trees in the form of a rushing shadow. A camouflaged blur with eyes narrowed to slits. Then came the impact. The violence of it. The taste of dirt in my mouth, and the sudden bright gush of blood on my tongue. One minute I was running, and the next I was fighting for air. It happened that fast.

I loved running. In those days, it was all I had.

Sean Grieves took that from me. After that, when I ran, all I felt was fear.

Fear like I felt now, tearing through the jungle with leaves the size of dinner plates smacking my cheeks, vines tearing at my ankles. I could barely see, the canopy so dense overhead it nearly blotted out the sun. My heart machine-gunned in my chest. A switchboard of pain receptors scorched my side, breath shooting from my mouth in hot, ragged gasps.

Run, Olivia.

Run. Run. Run.

A figure flew from the brush.

Strong hands seized my arms in a vise-like grip and jerked me to a stop.

Sean. It was *him*.

Suddenly, I was back on the highway, leaping from the trunk with his hands clawing at my neck and his breath hot in my ear.

I screamed and raked my fingernails across his cheek and sent him sprawling back.

"Shit!" the figure howled. "Olivia, stop! It's me!"

The illusion shattered. Bryce stood in front of me, looking horrified, wincing as he pressed his fingers to the two red tracks I'd gouged into his cheek. "What's wrong with you?"

"I ... I'm sorry," I stammered. "I thought you were ..."

"Who? Who *exactly* did you think I was?"

"I don't know—someone dangerous! You came out of nowhere and attacked me!" My brain was on the verge of short-circuiting.

"*What?* I didn't attack you. I was trying to help you." He touched his cheek again and hissed.

"I'm lost in the jungle on some weird-ass island, and I don't know who ..." I swallowed hard. "I don't know ..."

The trees blurred. Tears dripped off my cheeks. My knees hinged, and I swayed left.

"Jesus, Olivia, are you okay?" Bryce's voice sounded muffled, like his mouth was full of cotton. He stepped closer and looped an arm beneath my shoulders, then ushered me toward a log where I sat. He offered me his water bottle, and I took several needy gulps. The water felt like a miracle.

"I'm sorry. I didn't mean to scare you," he said.

Scare me. The words reminded me of what I'd just seen. I stood and seized his wrist, started pulling him back through the jungle.

"Wait," he said. "You're bleeding!"

"I don't care. You need to see this."

"See what?"

I knew he wouldn't believe me, so I didn't answer and instead retraced my steps, following the path I'd cut through the brush. Bryce muttered something about me going in the wrong direction, saying that I needed to rest. But I ignored him and continued until the flat pool of murky water appeared through the trees, the surface sheened in bacteria.

"What are we doing here?"

"Shh," I said, scouring the swamp for the crocodile. When I didn't see it, I ducked out of the trees and pointed at the noxious ring of mud I'd just escaped. "There. Look."

He crossed his arms. "I don't see anything."

I gestured again. "Right there, next to ..." but the arm was already gone, reclaimed by the surface, the mud now a silty-smooth plane. The only evidence of my frantic escape was marked by the trail of grime running from the outer edge of the swamp into the grass. "It was there. I swear it was there."

Bryce scratched the back of his neck. "What was there? What are you talking about?"

I dragged him closer, still refusing to believe my eyes.

"There was a fucking *arm* buried in the mud!"

A trio of wrinkles formed over the bridge of his nose. He started to speak and stopped. Started again. "Are you sure it was human? I'm betting it was an animal."

"It wasn't an animal. I know what I saw."

His eyes narrowed. "You just fell down a thirty-foot ravine! You probably have a concussion."

"Do you know how many autopsy photos I look at, Bryce?" I was shouting now, my voice cracking. "It was a human arm! And there was a crocodile, too!"

"No crocodiles live this far north."

"An alligator, then."

"Nope," Bryce insisted in a frustratingly calm voice. "None on this island, anyway." He raised his hand and rubbed his brow. The chrome glint of his watch flashed, and my brain sizzled with the image of the silver band wrapped around the decaying wrist of the arm I'd pulled from the mud. *Oh, God.* I suddenly knew what it was.

An Xclivity bracelet.

CHAPTER FIFTEEN

Back in my stateroom, I stepped out of the shower and stared at my reflection in the mirror. It felt like I was looking at a stranger. My hair hung in a limp frame of my face and my eyes were cupped in dark circles. A yellow and blue patchwork bruise bloomed over my hip, leeching a painful rainbow of color. Another one ran down my thigh, the shade of a plum. My arms were bandaged and cross-hatched in scabs. I looked and felt like shit, but nothing was broken—and I'd *definitely* been through worse.

Barely.

This trip no longer simply felt *off*. It felt dangerous. Every fiber of my being screamed for me to get the fuck off this boat. To run. But there was no way off, no way to run. Not in the middle of the Caribbean. Sure, I could attempt to hijack a lifeboat, but I had no idea where they were or how to captain one if I did. And even if I could, I wasn't going to leave Quinn behind. Not yet. I couldn't abandon her without knowing if she was truly in trouble, or if she was part of the problem.

Had she meant for me to wind up in that swamp? Had she sent me down that hill on purpose? I didn't think so—she'd teared up the moment I'd emerged from the tree line spattered in mud, sobbing and apologizing like crazy on the boat ride back to the yacht. Her concern seemed genuine enough, sure, but what the hell was Julianna doing sending us into the jungle blindfolded in the first place? And why on that path, where something like that could happen?

I replayed the fall: the crack of my shin against stone and the uneasy totter that followed, that awful moment before gravity took hold and sent me tumbling down, down, down ...

Rocks battering my spine, branches punching my ribs.

That awful dead-air rush before I smacked onto wet earth. The rotten stink that followed. Quinn's scream raining down from somewhere above me. Tearing off the blindfold to the sensation of sucking, of my legs being pulled under.

Digging through the mud for the stick that wasn't a stick, but an arm.

Because there *had* been an arm.

And an Xclivity bracelet.

I hadn't mentioned the bracelet to Bryce. Over and over again, he'd tried to convince me that what I'd seen was simply a PTSD-triggered stretch of my imagination. "It happens," he said. "Head injuries are strange things."

Sure, whatever you say, Bryce.

His insistence put me on edge. And how had he found me so fast, with me plowing full throttle through the jungle after my fall? The foliage was beyond thick, nearly impossible to see through. How had he been right there? It didn't sit right with me, didn't make sense.

Nothing on this trip did.

I tugged on a worn pair of jeans and a T-shirt, and then absent-mindedly reached for my concealed carry holster—which wasn't there. Because why would I possibly need my nine-millimeter here of all places, on vacation? One of the first things I'd done after recovering from my assault was to purchase a Springfield Hellcat and learn to shoot. I carried the gun everywhere I went. After Sean, I felt naked leaving home without it. And right now, I felt naked as hell.

With my paranoia pinging, I grabbed my phone and scrolled to the camera, then turned a slow circle. I watched the screen for the flickers of infrared light otherwise invisible to the human eye that signaled the presence of hidden cameras—something I'd picked up from an interview on my podcast with a security expert. I'd found them once before in a vacation rental and promptly left, but thankfully didn't see any here.

Exhausted, I settled into the club chair near the balcony and massaged my temples. Outside, the ocean rolled past in a hypnotic, slow-motion slosh. The island was gone, the yacht once again cutting through the water toward God knew where.

God, I wanted off this yacht.

For a moment, I considered crawling into bed and passing out. I wanted to. I was beyond exhausted. But despite how bad I felt—and I truly felt like shit—there would be no early bedtime for me. I still needed to talk to Carmela. She was the only one on this ship who could tell me what was going on.

At six-thirty, I pulled myself from the chair and limped into the hall. The Purification Dinner (whatever the hell that was) was in full swing, voices and laughter filtering down from the dining room along with the cheery clink of silverware and glass. Even with my injuries, Quinn had insisted I attend, telling me how integral the dinner was, backing off only when I showed her the quilt of bruises lying beneath my shirt.

Sorry, I don't think I can handle it. I need to rest.

Quinn said she understood, but I knew she was disappointed. What a shame to miss whatever fun activity Julianna had planned for the evening. I envisioned Julianna passing out boxes of the finest velvet packed with black widows, smiling and fluttering her hands in a jangle of bracelets, gesturing for everyone to open them. *Go on, face your fear—see what's inside.*

With a quick glance behind me to make sure no one was watching, I headed for the back of the boat toward Carmela's room. I eased down the hall and into the lobby, abruptly changing course when movement near the bar sent me scurrying behind a column.

"You're supposed to be working dinner tonight." Marco's voice. *Shit.*

"That's not what the schedule says." I didn't recognize the other person talking—a woman, another member of the crew. "I just checked it."

"I don't give a fuck what it says. You're needed upstairs. You go where I say to go."

"Yes, sir," she replied, with a sudden flutter in her voice.

The woman's footsteps pattered my way, followed by Marco's. My stomach dropped. He couldn't find me here—not like this.

Silently, I edged left around the column as they passed to the right, certain Marco would spot me and ... do what? Drag me outside and throw me overboard? Toss me over his shoulder and haul me upstairs to eat dinner with the rest of the gang? Of the two, the second option seemed worse.

I waited until I could no longer hear them, then slipped through the lobby and down another corridor, careful to keep portside as Carmela instructed. My nerves cooled to a dull simmer when I passed an empty gym and spotted a sign reading, *Crew Quarters,* with an arrow pointing down a flight of stairs. I took them, and the boat transformed from polished steel and lustrous wood to grease-splotched walls and rubber tile floors. The smell of bleach hung in the air, mixing with pungent undertones of diesel.

I passed several doors and found room 116 tucked away next to what appeared to be an engine compartment. The hidden machinery vibrated the floor as I pulled out the key Carmela gave me and held it against the lock. The door clicked open to a room that wasn't a room so much as a closet, sporting a twin-sized bed the size of a cot. There were no windows, just four stark white walls and a ceiling bearing a single fluorescent tube. Carmela sat at a small desk crammed in one corner, her gaze darting past me toward the hall when I entered.

"Did anyone see you?"

"No." I shut the door and was immediately overwhelmed by a wave of claustrophobia. The space felt like a slightly larger version of a car trunk. "Tell me what you meant this morning. Why am I in danger?"

Carmela shrunk back in the chair without a word.

Too strong, Olivia. "Sorry," I said, taking a seat on the corner of her bed. "Today wasn't great. I'm a little rattled. Let's start again, okay? Why am I in danger?"

Carmela clasped her hands. "How do I know I can trust you?"

"You don't. You have no reason to. But I can tell you're scared. And I know what it's like to be afraid. I was abducted when I was younger and nearly murdered. It's why I do what I do now. Why I try to help people. But I can't be caught down here with you. It wouldn't be good for either of us. We have to be quick."

She surveyed me with an intensity that made my skin itch, then sighed. "What I have to tell you, I've never told anyone. What I said earlier was true. You are in danger, but this will make it worse. If you want to leave now, I'll understand."

A chill cut down my spine. The way Carmela was looking at me right now—with her forehead trimmed in sweat and her face two shades paler than when I walked in a moment ago—made me want to bolt and never look back. I nearly did. But I managed to steel myself. I had to know what was going on. There wasn't another choice. "Go ahead. Tell me."

She grabbed a framed picture from the desk—a photo of a much younger Carmela with long, straight hair and a face that looked untouched by time. She wore a cornflower-blue dress, her arms looped around the shoulders of a boy I guessed to be about two years old and a girl that appeared slightly older—maybe four.

"Yours?" I asked, nodding at the photo.

"Yes, Diego and Elena." She cradled the frame and gazed at

it with a tender smile, the whites of her eyes turning pink. "My children are why I wanted to talk to you." She set the photo back on the desk with a sigh and rubbed her hands. When she finally spoke, her voice slid out in a whisper. "My name's not Carmela. It's Margaret. Margaret Vallejos."

I leaned forward. "Spell it for me."

Carmela ... *Margaret Vallejos* ... paused for a second before spelling her last name, one letter at a time. I recited it in my head several times over, so I could text it to Nina later—*if* my phone picked up another signal.

"I've been on *The Athena* for six years now," Margaret said, "but I've been with Xclivity for much longer." She exhaled and surveyed her feet. "I can't leave. They won't let me."

CHAPTER SIXTEEN

The room lurched, and I fought for balance. "Who won't let you leave? Xclivity?"

"Yes, although that wasn't always their name. In a different life, I was a Sacramento prosecutor. I'd built a case against a local company—Consumer Advocates, Incorporated. It was one of those multi-level marketing companies that charged its members to sell their products. Consumer Advocates told new recruits all they had to do to get rich was bring in more people beneath them and they'd get a cut of their sales."

"And what did Consumer Advocates actually sell to the public?"

"Discount packages on groceries and bulk goods. Stereos and televisions. Appliances. That kind of thing. My client—a woman named Diane Sumner—wanted to sue them. But all she had to offer were accusations and conspiracy theories. She said Consumer Advocates made leaving the organization incredibly difficult. She told me they were bankrupting their members. That they'd bankrupted her."

"Had they?"

"I don't know. Maybe. She didn't have any evidence to

support her claims beyond a few bank statements, and..." Margaret trailed off and looked at the floor. "Sorry, this is difficult for me to talk about."

Alarm bells clanged in my head. I wanted to tell her to spit it out, to remind her we needed to hurry, but I knew if I pushed her too hard too fast, she'd shut down. Trauma couldn't be rushed. It was a truth I knew all too well. "It's okay. Take your time."

She sucked in a long, labored breath and blew it out. "After the meeting, after I told Diane there was nothing we could do, she walked straight out the door and into traffic. A city bus ran her over a block from my office. She died instantly."

I inhaled sharply. "Jesus."

"She had three kids. Two were the same age as mine."

"I'm sorry."

"So was I. I couldn't help but feel responsible. So, I kept looking into Consumer Advocates. Their members were difficult to pin down. I met with a few of them, the ones who would talk to me, anyway. Most wouldn't; the second I mentioned the company, they clammed up. I wasn't getting anywhere. But just when I was about to let the entire thing drop, I got a phone call from a man who said he had something for me. I met him in a public park, and he gave me a folder and left without a word."

"Did you get a good look at him? Did he give you his name?" My mind was already in sleuth mode, searching for the little details she'd missed, scratching for information I could siphon to Nina when I got a chance. I already knew we'd be targeting Xclivity next.

"Not really. And no. He was wearing a ball cap and glasses.

He seemed paranoid, looking over his shoulder every few seconds. Definitely scared."

"What was in the folder?"

"A few financial statements and some bank transactions. Accounting records. The company was a shell—a typical pyramid scheme, but worse."

"How so?"

She reclined in the chair and stared at her hands. "They preyed on the lower middle class, on those with just enough money to steal but not enough to do anything about it. Single mothers like Diane. The elderly and the disabled. Vulnerable segments of the population that society likes to ignore. They charged these people exorbitant amounts to join the company and then piled on annual membership fees. We're talking thousands and thousands of dollars here."

My eyebrow arched. "So, these people joined Consumer Advocates for what—the right to sell discounts on TVs?" It sounded like a creepy version of Costco.

"That was only the hook. What they really offered was community. A place to belong. They promised to help people take control of their lives. A path to financial independence. Their members were zealots. They sold a lot of packages to people, not that it mattered. The majority of those fees and commissions flowed straight to the top. Diane was right. The more I looked into them, the more I discovered how many people's lives they were ruining."

I thought of Quinn. Our paths had diverged radically in the

years following our father's death. She blew through her share of our inheritance with alarming speed. She'd been desperate for cash after that. Nearly homeless at times. What price had she paid to ascend Xclivity's ranks? And what terrible things had they done to her after she did? A hard shiver raked my arms. I wasn't sure I wanted to know.

Margaret continued: "The more I investigated, the more illegal activity I uncovered. Money laundering and tax evasion. Fraud. Even weapons trafficking. But that wasn't the worst part."

"No? What was?"

"Consumer Advocates went after anyone who tried to blow the whistle on them. They were aggressive. Threats of violence. Financial ruin. Worse. Several members disappeared." Margaret shook her head. "I put together a case—the best of my career. It would have been national news."

"What happened?"

Her knee bounced in place. "I worked late the night before I was going to file the suit. My car was the last one in the parking garage. One minute I was unlocking the door, the next I was in a van with a bag over my head. I thought they were going to kill me." She looked away. "Sometimes I wish they had."

I went stiff. "Why would you say that?"

"Because, when they took off the bag, I realized they'd driven me home. They knew where I *lived*. They parked across the street so I could ..." Her voice cracked. She closed her eyes and pinched the bridge of her nose, took a long, jittery breath. "So I could watch."

"Do you need a break? You don't have to continue if it's—"

Margaret's hand whipped up, her eyes flashing to mine. "Yes, I do. I've been silent for too long." She straightened and her expression hardened. "The curtains were open. My husband was asleep on the couch, but there was another man there, standing beside him. He had a gun. He ..." Her voice hitched. "It was Marco. He ... he shot Vince twice. Once in the chest, another time in the head."

Ice water poured through my veins. I set my elbows on my knees and leaned forward. "You're telling me this organization murdered your husband?"

"I screamed," Margaret continued without answering me, tears rolling down her cheeks. She didn't bother to wipe them away. "Another man marched in front of the window with ... with my kids."

"No," I whispered.

"Elena had just turned four, so she knew enough to be scared. She was crying. I could tell she was terrified, but Diego ... he was only two." Her voice cracked. "The man—he brought the gun to my baby's head. My little boy. I was certain he was going to shoot him."

The lump in my throat grew. I could barely speak. "They didn't?"

"No. But they said they would if I didn't behave. They were forced to rebrand because of me. Because I'd tipped off a few of my contacts in the police department, who were running a parallel investigation. Unfortunately, it never went anywhere before Consumer Advocates dissolved." She dabbed her eyes and released a sad laugh. "It's hard to prosecute a business that no longer exists.

The police dropped the case. I thought they might actually let me go after that. I was so stupid."

"So, what happened next?"

"I met Julianna. She told me the only way I'd ever see my kids again, the only way they'd live, was if I worked for Xclivity."

A sinking sensation overtook me. I knew where this was going. "They turned you into a slave, didn't they?"

"Yes. I spent a month establishing Xclivity's organizational structure, drawing up the formation documents, making sure everything was bulletproof from both a business and a tax perspective. I set up their bank accounts and advised them on the best ways to move money without drawing attention. Instead of another multilevel marketing structure with a big downline, I had them focus on expensive, executive development programs and leadership courses. Self-improvement seminars catering to entrepreneurs, but only people they could isolate and break down psychologically first. It took a few years for Xclivity to really take off, but once it did, it was wildly successful." Her face creased. "All because of me."

I knew telling me this story pained her, each word like spitting out a shard of glass. Normally, I'd pause an interview when someone reached this point and offer them coffee or water, or a few minutes to regain their composure, but we didn't have a few minutes. I needed to wrap this up and get back to my room as soon as possible. The smell of diesel—and the details of this story—were making me sick.

"None of this is your fault, Margaret."

"Isn't it, though?"

I paused, then said, "What happened to your children? Where are they now?"

Her chin quivered and the lines on her forehead deepened to knife cuts. Her eyes tilted toward the ceiling, her lips pressing together as she bit off a sob. "They gave them to the members."

"What do you mean, 'gave them'?" I couldn't make sense of the statement, her words not slotting into place fast enough.

"Xclivity *raised* them. Every year, they forced me to watch videos of *my* children with ... with *their* families. Holidays and birthdays. Sporting events. School concerts. Dances. Their entire childhood. My son's graduation. My daughter's *wedding*. All these clips of my babies growing up without me. They were collateral. Xclivity did it to keep me in line. To make sure I remembered what would happen if I ever tried to escape." She dabbed her eyes, sniffed. "The worst part is that my kids looked happy." Another sob crawled up her throat. "They didn't ... they didn't need me anymore. They don't know I exist."

My mind ground to a halt. This was so calculating and cold, it stole my breath. I reached over and set my hand on hers. She said nothing, just continued to cry before pulling back to wipe her nose.

"So, you haven't seen your children in person since they took them?" I asked.

"No, not until yesterday."

"I—wait, what? Your kids are ... *here?*"

Margaret passed me the photo frame, her tears jeweling on the glass. I took it and gazed at the two long-ago children it contained, at the girl with her mother's nose, and the boy with brown hair and round, dark eyes that looked ... *familiar.*

Why do they look so familiar?

"My son is. You've already met him," Margaret said. "They changed his name to Darren."

CHAPTER SEVENTEEN

Sick.

It was how I felt now. That word kept leaping to mind as I stumbled from Margaret's room—*sick, sick, sick*. Her pleas looped through my head: *You have to get my son off the yacht. You have to save him, Olivia. You have to save yourself.*

And Quinn. I had to save my sister.

Or was that even possible? Was she trapped or was Quinn just another one of Margaret's captors?

One way or another, I had to find out.

I hadn't been in any true danger since the incident with Sean. Sure, the podcast came with its fair share of crazy, but nothing anywhere close to this. I felt it throbbing all around me, the ship oozing with threat. I needed to get off this boat, had to get *away*.

My head spun, and I took a moment to collect myself near the end of the corridor. Margaret had tried to give me a note as I'd left her room—a letter she'd written to Darren.

Take this. Give it to him when the time is right.

No, I'd told her. *It's too dangerous.*

And it was. A letter like that would land both of us in hot

water if it was discovered. If I gave it to Darren, odds were he'd turn it over to his parents or to someone else in Xclivity. He needed the proper context before reading something like that. He needed to hear Margaret's story from her own lips. *You can give it to him yourself,* I'd told her as she slipped it back into her desk, looking dejected. *I'll get you out of this.*

You won't be able to, Margaret had replied. *They don't tell me what happens to the guests on the third night. All I know is they disappear when we reach Elysium. When I wake on the fourth day, they're gone.*

The arm from the swamp flashed to mind.

The bracelet.

Acid boiled at the base of my throat, and I struggled not to vomit. It was all so fucked up, but I believed Margaret. No way was she lying. *No way.* I knew a liar when I saw one. But how could I possibly convince Darren, a guy I'd only recently met, of *any* of this? How could I tell him his parents weren't his parents at all, but rather his abductors? That everything about his life was a lie? That his real mother was right here on this ship? Even with Margaret's letter it would be impossible.

And what about Quinn? How strong was Xclivity's hold on her? What about Alex and Chaz? I couldn't keep them in the dark, even though they likely wouldn't believe a word I said.

Questions rolled in, one on top of another.

How powerful was Xclivity, *really*?

How were they making people disappear?

What else were they involved in?

My scalp prickled with fear. With no Internet and no way to reach Nina, taking action felt hopeless. I didn't know what to do next, didn't know how to proceed. But after what I'd just heard, I'd be up all night, trying to piece together a plan.

I froze when I neared my room.

My door hung open a few inches, even though I'd closed and locked it behind me. I stood there, staring at it for a full minute, trying to decide whether to go inside or run. But what choice did I have? It didn't matter where I went at this point; this boat had turned into a floating prison.

With my nerves sparking, I took hold of the doorknob and pushed.

Bryce stood in a fitted charcoal suit near the balcony, waiting for me, his hands clasped behind his back. He turned when I entered, his antifreeze-colored eyes sweeping over me in a way that made *me* feel like the intruder. "Hello, Olivia, how are you feeling?"

"What are you doing here?" I asked.

He brushed a piece of non-existent lint from his chest, and then blinked toward a tray with a silver-domed dish resting on the ottoman at the end of my bed. "I brought you some dinner. I figured you'd be hungry."

"Thank you," I offered, grudgingly. *Get the fuck out of my room.*

"I also brought a present." He produced an orange plastic bottle from his pocket and gave it a single shake. Pills rattled within. Painkillers, maybe? Worse? His eyes narrowed. "Where were you just now?"

"I needed to stretch my legs a bit. They were sore."

"These will help," he said, handing me the bottle and the water.

"Thanks." I took them and set both aside. As bruised and exhausted as I was, there would be no drugs for me tonight—and no way in hell was I going to take any pills from Bryce.

He frowned, and the scab I'd left on his cheek curled down in a way that made his otherwise handsome face sinister. "You really need to rest. And these will help you get some sleep."

"I'll take them before I go to bed."

"How about now?"

"Seriously?"

He nodded, his eyes boring into me, shining like sheets of ice.

Screw it. I was too exhausted to play his game, so I'd play one of my own. I wanted him gone. I snatched the bottle and shook two oval-shaped tablets onto my palm. They looked like the Tic Tacs I used to camouflage the alcohol on my breath as a teenager. The same white shell, but certainly with no minty-fresh flavor hiding underneath. I popped them into my mouth and feigned a dry swallow. Then I gave him a little-kid *ahh* and stuck out my tongue. "There you go."

"Good." He moved closer and put his hand on my shoulder. I stiffened. "I really am sorry about what happened today. Tomorrow will be better, I promise." He grinned. "No more trust walks."

I gave him a strained laugh. *Go.*

"Goodnight," he said, before trailing into the hall and closing the door. The second it clicked shut, I shot into the bathroom, turned the lock, and spit the pills into the toilet, then rinsed out my mouth. Terror poured through every part of me, every inch. I could smell it seeping from my pores as I slid to the floor and shook, my heart pumping in my chest, my hands shaking. I had to figure out a way to get Darren and Quinn off this yacht. *And Chaz and Alex, too.*

But how? How, how, how?

I groaned and rubbed my temples. It all suddenly felt impossible.

Get it together, I thought. *You can't fall apart yet. Not yet.*

I stood and drifted over to the dish Bryce left behind and pulled off the lid. A pepper-encrusted steak swam in a pond of Kool-Aid-pink juice. A healthy serving of au Gratin potatoes was piled next to the meat, the plate rimmed in asparagus. My stomach growled. I hadn't eaten anything since breakfast, but I wasn't about to tear into a meal hand delivered by Bryce, the pill man.

Exhausted, I flung myself onto the covers. A pair of mints rested on the pillow. I unwrapped one and popped it into my mouth.

Fuck Xclivity.

Once I found a way off this boat, I'd sic Nina on them. I'd focus the podcast on ripping Xclivity apart, member by member. I'd put them on blast to everyone who'd listen. I'd turn all of my listeners against them. But first I needed to …

Needed to …

What?

I ground my knuckles into my eyes and shook my head. The room blurred, the walls winking in and out, like I'd stumbled in from a hard night on the town after ten too many shots. My gaze fell to the food I hadn't touched. I hadn't eaten anything but—

The mint. I eyed the empty wrapper, and I knew what Bryce had done.

Shit.

My chin hit my chest, and the world spun to black.

CHAPTER EIGHTEEN

I woke to total darkness, to a scream.

My clothes were sopped with sweat, my skin fever-flushed. I unglued my tongue from the roof of my mouth and drank in a shivery gulp of air. My legs ached, as did my arms. For a horrible, disorienting second, I couldn't remember where I was. And then it came back to me.

The ship. The yacht. Bryce and the mint.

Fuck.

I hoisted myself from the bed in a low-grade panic, only for my legs to turn to rubber the second my feet connected with the floor. I collapsed and lay there, thinking, *Get up, Olivia! You have to get up!* My head spun in protest. My tongue went numb. I wanted to pass out—but I couldn't.

There was no time to waste.

And I'd just heard *something*.

Slowly, I forced myself back to my feet and hit the bathroom light. The stateroom came to life in a soft glow, and I fumbled my way toward the door and cracked it open. Buttery trails of light dripped down the hallway and puddled on the carpet in a way that made my head spin. It felt like someone had filled my eyes with oil as I slept. I ran my tongue across the back of my teeth, across my gums, which tingled. My entire body did—more than tingled, in fact. Itched. It felt like a nest of termites were scuttling just beneath the surface of my skin, trying to break through.

I stepped into the hallway and listened.

But I heard nothing. No scream.

Maybe I'd imagined it?

I had, I decided, retreating back into my room about to close the door when a shriek split the air, followed by a single word. "Help!"

My blood turned to ice. Every hair on my body rose at once. I recognized the voice instantly. *Margaret.* My breath came shallow and fast, my heart beating like a hummingbird in my chest. Another cry carried down the hall, severed by the meaty *slap* of a palm striking a cheek.

Shut the door! Therapist Olivia screeched. *There's nothing you can do!*

It was true, especially in my condition. Every cell in my body screamed for me to do exactly that ... but I couldn't. Margaret was in trouble because of me. They'd somehow discovered I'd been to her room. It was the only thing that made sense, the truth of it humming in my bones. *They know, they know!*

Shut. The. Door.

My hand drifted toward the doorknob and stopped. After everything I'd been through, praying for someone to help me from that trunk seven years ago, feeling the same terror I now heard strangling Margaret's voice, was I going to sentence her to the fate

I'd barely escaped? Could I do that to her? And if so, would I be able to live with myself afterward?

Because if I shut this door, that's exactly what would happen. She would die.

And I knew I'd never forgive myself.

As quietly as I could, I slipped into the hall once again and snuck toward the commotion. The carpet bunched thick between my toes, my sight cutting in and out with every step. I struggled to focus, to remain on my feet. It felt like staggering through a dream. But I knew this was no dream. My heart was beating so hard, it felt like it was about to explode through my chest.

The lobby where Quinn and I had first entered the ship appeared in front of me. Only a few lights were on, the windows dark with night. I pressed against the wall and edged toward the corner, then peeked into the room. Two shapes were knotted together in conflict—a man and a woman. In the dim glow of the room, they looked like shadows dancing around a fire, intertwining and pulling apart in a violent frenzy.

One of the shadows broke loose and came into focus.

I gasped when I glimpsed Margaret's face. Blood streamed from her nose and splattered the cream-colored carpet—so much so, I wondered if it was broken. Her right eye was a swollen mound of flesh, her left eye peeled wide with fright. She cried out, and Marco clamped a hand over her mouth. "Shut up, you stupid bitch!" he growled. "You'll wake the entire ship!"

Waves of terror crashed over me as I watched him savagely yank her through the door and out onto the deck. I hung there paralyzed, staring at the blood spatters staining the carpet, thinking, *Go back to your room, go back!* Needles of fear pricked the base of my neck, the fine hair on my arms rising. How could I do anything against this man? He was so big, so violent. Pure muscle. He'd kill me in a heartbeat.

Just like he'll kill her.

Shaking, I scanned the room for a weapon—anything I could use. The chairs were askew, the tables covered in dirty plates, pieces of furniture knocked out of place. An empty beer bottle on a coaster caught my attention. It wasn't much.

But it was something.

Outside, the moon hung in a curving yellow sickle that drenched everything in bone-colored light. Ahead, farther down the deck, Margaret thrashed in Marco's grip, still fighting, rag-dolling her legs and arms as he dragged her toward the railing.

Fuck, fuck, fuck, fuck.

Gripping the glass bottle, I crept after them, keeping to the shadows, willing my feet not to make a sound. Fear churned oily in my gut, my legs filling with water as I drew near and crouched behind a chair. That's when Margaret bit Marco's hand.

And tried to run.

She made it a foot before he snatched her collar, ripped her back, and slammed his fist into her stomach, all in one violent motion. A volley of air exploded from her mouth, and she collapsed to her knees. Without waiting, he forced her back to her feet and thrust her head toward the railing, one hand around her neck, the other grasping her waist. My pulse went into overdrive—and I knew what he meant to do. Dear God, I knew.

He was going to throw her over. And it was all my fault.

You can't let this happen, Olivia.

My fingers tightened around the bottle. I'd only get one chance at this. One shot.

I stood.

Clack. Clack. Clack.

The sound came from my left, sending a fresh ripple of panic through my veins.

Clack. Cl-clack. Clack.

My breath hitched. I followed the noise toward a thin chain stirred by the breeze, rattling against a pipe. When I looked back, Margaret was staring directly at me from over Marco's shoulder, her jaw slick with blood. She couldn't speak the words, but I read her lips.

Help me.

I heard the footsteps rushing behind me too late.

An arm encircled my chest with lung-crushing force. A hand clamped a cloth over my nose and mouth. My eyes watered as the sharp scent of acetone filled my sinuses and rushed straight for my brain. I coughed and spit, thrashed and kicked. It didn't matter. The hand remained glued to my mouth, the fumes molten as the deck turned to a collection of smudged edges and blurred lines.

Oh, Jesus, no, please, no!

I fought to remain conscious, a series of images working through the haze in a gruesome, stop-motion flicker: Marco glancing back at me as he sunk his hands beneath Margaret's armpits. Marco heaving her higher, shoving her over the railing. Margaret toppling backward, seeming to hang there for a moment, caught in midair—her arms wheeling, legs kicking, her mouth stretching wide—before she vanished from sight.

Her scream was the last thing I heard.

CHAPTER NINETEEN

There's this recurring dream I have of my sister. Of Quinn standing at the kitchen counter with my father, perched over a mixing bowl, baking cookies on a chilly afternoon. Her cheeks are speckled with flour, both of them laughing. I hover there for a moment, watching the two of them, thinking, *They look so happy.* But when I enter, Quinn swivels my way, and her smile fades. Then she asks me a question—the *same* question—over and over again, on repeat, until I snap awake.

What are you doing here?

It was that question pouring through my head now, in a soft flurry of sound. "Olivia, what are you doing here?"

Pressure curled over my shoulder. A firm, too-tight pressure. The pressure of strong hands pulling me toward the railing, about to fling me overboard ...

"Olivia, c'mon, you have to wake up!"

I shrieked. Bright splinters of panic peeled my eyes wide. My arms rocketed out in front of me, fingers grasping clothing, fingernails scraping skin. A face blurred and took shape, delicate features framed by a wave of strawberry hair: Quinn.

"Shit," she cried. "Via! Let go!"

My fingers loosened, and I skittered away from her, over the floor, until my back pressed flat against the wall of my room. *Why am I back in my room?* The movement unleashed a tidal wave of pain, my brain pulsing against my skull, feeling like a soft-boiled egg as a wave of nausea slid through my gut.

"Hey, calm down." Quinn placed one hand on my arm and brought her other hand to my cheek. "Why are you on the floor? What happened?"

Something bad. Something awful. I fought for the memory. It hung somewhere in front of me—a wisp of smoke curling out of grasp, a nightmare there one moment and gone the next. Why couldn't I remember? I closed my eyes and rubbed them. My mouth felt dry, my throat parched. My joints ached from pressing against the cold, hard wood, my skull pounding and packed with sand.

"Come here," Quinn said, pulling me into a hug. Behind her, early morning sunlight streamed through the glass door. I squinted at it. *When did that happen? How much time has passed?*

The questions hurt my head. *Thinking* hurt my head. As if on cue, the room swayed and my stomach knotted. I pushed Quinn away and raced into the bathroom, barely reaching the toilet before my stomach turned itself inside out. Then I knelt there, curled forward, vomiting with my forehead resting on the porcelain. It wasn't until my fifth dry heave that I remembered.

The falling. Margaret.

No.

A sudden weight settled behind my ribs—a feeling so heavy, it felt like it would pull me to the floor.

She was gone.

Oh, God, not just that. She was gone because of me, and there was nothing I could do about it. Nothing but survive and prove it happened. *If* I could survive. And why wasn't I dead already? Why had they brought me back here, to my room? Probably because today was the third day, the day we'd reach Elysium, whatever the fuck that was, and they still needed me to—

A hand settled on my shoulder followed by a voice: "Olivia, you're scaring me. Please tell me what's going on."

I turned to find Quinn standing behind me with her head in a tilt, her eyes bathed in concern. Could I trust her? Could I *really*? I still didn't know. But what choice did I have? Just stay quiet and pretend everything was fine? Keep my mouth shut and hide in my room, hoping to escape whatever bad shit was coming my way? It wouldn't happen. We were all going to disappear tonight. I didn't have time to play it safe. I had to tell someone what I knew. And despite everything, Quinn was still my sister. In this moment, she was all I had. I made the decision.

"I ... saw Marco attack someone last night."

Her eyebrows ticked higher. "Who?"

"Carmela."

"The waitress?"

I stood and planted my hip against the sink, went woozy. "Yes. But her real name is Margaret."

"*What?* How would you know something like that?"

"She told me. I ... talked to her yesterday. I think it's why Marco assaulted her."

Quinn leaned against the shower and crossed her arms. "Where did this happen?"

"In the lobby. I heard her scream and snuck down the hall. It was bad, Quinn. She was really injured. I think he broke her nose."

"Can you show me?"

A bubble of panic rose up my throat, and I shook my head. I couldn't imagine bumping into Marco right now—or anyone for that matter. I needed a cold shower and a proper meal. I needed to think.

"Come on, we'll go together." She offered her hand. "You don't have to worry about seeing anyone. It's early. No one's up yet. If anything upsets you, we can come right back here, okay? I promise."

I didn't have it in me to argue, so I let her take my hand and pull me from the bathroom. Another wave of vertigo hit me as we walked down the hall, my forehead clammy with sweat. And not just from whatever shit Bryce had drugged me with.

From fear.

What if Marco saw me? What would he do? What would Bryce? And what about Quinn? An electric ball of dread buzzed at the base of my spine. Was trusting her with this a mistake? I suddenly didn't know.

We entered the lobby, and I stopped and gawked at the floor. There wasn't a drop of red *anywhere*. Nothing but tastefully patterned swirls of cream-colored carpet stretching out in front of me like nothing had happened. Like Margaret's nose hadn't been waterfalling blood last night ... which it most certainly had. *So* much blood.

What the fuck?

A glass clinked from across the room, and I nearly bolted. My gaze shot to a crew member busying himself cleaning a glass behind the bar—a man in a starched white shirt with a black bow tie who was looking our way. "Morning, would either of you like some coffee?"

I didn't answer. It was all I could do to remain in place with all the adrenaline coursing through my system.

"No thank you," Quinn said. "Olivia?"

I managed to shake my head, then took in the rest of the room—which had been cleaned and straightened. No dishes on the tables. Nothing out of place. And no blood.

Anywhere.

I sank to my knees and kneaded the carpet with my knuckles, feeling for moisture. Someone had to have cleaned the carpet. It was the only thing that made sense. But it was dry as bone.

Whatthefuckwhatthefuck?

I ground my palms into my eyes and fought back a sudden swell of emotion. Tears threatened to spill down my face. "It was here. I swear it was."

"What was?" Quinn asked.

I wiped my eyes and stood, glancing at the bartender, lowering my voice when he turned away. "Blood."

"Blood?" Her eyes narrowed and swept over the room, then came back to me. "Are you sure you saw this happen?"

Had I? Yes, the images were still too fresh, too vivid. Even with the drugs, I couldn't convince myself otherwise. I took her arm and pulled her toward the deck. Outside, the sky was hazy with clouds, the sun hanging behind them in an orange disc just above the ocean. The sight loosened something in my chest, and I bit back a fresh round of tears. Margaret was floating out there somewhere, alone and frightened.

No, I corrected. *Not frightened ... dead.* No one could tread water forever. And Margaret had been injured to begin with. She hadn't stood a chance.

"Olivia," Quinn pleaded, stepping closer, "please talk to me. Tell me what's wrong."

I took a breath and surveyed the deck, saw no one, listened for voices, the ocean the only sound. We were alone, but I still didn't want to utter the words here, so close to the windows and doors where they might be overheard. Without replying, I led her toward the back of the boat and the propellers. I didn't speak until we were standing behind a stack of chairs where no one could see us, and still I kept my voice low, just above a whisper. "After their fight, Marco pulled Margaret out here. And he ..." I hesitated, swallowed. I couldn't say the words.

"He what?"

"He ... threw her overboard."

Quinn tilted her head, her eyebrows slanting down. She opened her mouth and shut it, then let out a slow breath. Blinked and shook her head.

I stiffened. "I knew you wouldn't believe me."

Her face softened. "It's not that I don't believe you, I'm just trying to understand what you're telling me. Can you start again, slower, from the beginning?"

With a sigh, I said, "Something woke me last night. A scream. I snuck down the hall and that's when I saw Marco struggling with Margaret. She was trying to get away from him. I'm guessing he found out I spoke to her."

Quinn's brow creased. "What did you two talk about?"

"A lot of concerning shit." *Like we're all going to die tonight.* "Look, does it matter? I'm telling you it happened. Marco threw her over. And there's something else. Bryce, he …" I trailed off as Quinn's mouth settled into a hard line. Bringing him into this would be a mistake.

She inclined her head slightly. "What about Bryce?"

"Nothing. It's not important."

"No, tell me what you were about to say."

My face grew hot, and I swallowed. "I think—I think he drugged me."

"Bryce *drugged* you? What?"

"Last night, I was coming back from my conversation with Margaret, and I noticed the door to my stateroom was open. I almost didn't go in, but when I did, Bryce was inside waiting for me."

"Bryce was in your room?"

I nodded.

"Why?"

"He brought me some food, said he thought I might be hungry."

Quinn bit her lip, didn't say anything.

"He gave me a bunch of pills," I continued. "Said they were for the pain."

Her eyes widened. "And you *took* them?"

"No, of course not. But I did eat the mint on my pillow. I thought it was from room service, but I think he left it there for me. He put something in it."

The color drained from Quinn's face, like I'd pulled a lever and all of the blood in her head had flushed straight down into her legs. I'd hit a soft spot, something about Bryce she'd kept hidden. She didn't look surprised to hear this, which unleashed a question. If he'd done this to me, what had he done to her? I leaned in. "Quinn, are you in trouble?"

She blew out a long breath and closed her eyes, suddenly looked broken.

I set my hand on her back. "What you said earlier goes both ways. You can trust me. If anything's happened, I need to know."

She opened her eyes and glanced at the ocean. "Bryce has his moments but drugging you ... all this talk of killing someone. It's ... I just can't believe that." She hugged herself, looking fragile and lost. Since we'd boarded the ship, I hadn't recognized my sister, but I saw her now, and I didn't want to lose her. I had to find a way to prove I was telling her the truth.

"Here, I'll show you where it happened." I slipped an arm over her shoulders and guided her back down the deck toward the spot where I'd seen Margaret go over. I pointed at the lounge chair near the wall. "I was right there when—"

"Shh." Quinn's gaze flicked up and to the right in a barely-there motion, toward a black globe mounted to the bulkhead directly above us. My skin rippled. A security camera. *Shit.*

She turned away and gripped the railing, and I did the same. Something slick coated my fingertips when I touched the metal. Like a snake, cold fear slithered through me once more. I pulled my hand back to a dark slash of red staining the pads of my fingers. *Blood.*

Trembling, I showed Quinn—who set her hand on mine and gently pressed my palm back to the railing. When I looked up, her eyes were bulging, her nostrils flared. "Breakfast is soon," she said in a whisper so soft, it nearly washed away in the sound of the waves lapping against the yacht. "Bryce never skips it. I'm in room 310. Come by in thirty minutes." Then she was gone, striding away down the deck.

CHAPTER TWENTY

Where my quarters were elegant, Quinn's were palatial: a stateroom near the bow of the yacht with a curving wall of glass in the place of windows, offering a 180-degree view of the ocean. A sea of warm teak flooring ran beneath my feet and drew my attention to a chandelier hanging from the center of the ceiling, dripping with crystal. An incredible room, yes, but my eyes turned to Quinn the second she shut the door.

A thought had burrowed deep into the core of my brain on my way to her room, a parasite that would hatch a million squirming larvae if I didn't smash it first. I needed to make sure Quinn wasn't in on any of this, that she hadn't played a part.

I stepped close and forced her back a step. "Did you have anything to do with what happened to Margaret?" She opened her mouth to respond, but I stabbed her sternum with my finger before she could speak. I needed to provoke a reaction. If you surprised people and put them under enough stress, they'd usually slip and reveal something they'd otherwise keep concealed. "If you lie, I'll never forgive you, Quinn. Tell me the truth. Did you know?"

"No. And you're scaring me." Her hands didn't move as she said it; they remained plastered to her sides, her eyes unblinking as they locked with mine: no upward-flicking-sideways glance, no darting, nervous gaze.

I watched her for a second longer, then pulled my phone from my pocket and scanned the room for cameras before turning back.

"What are you doing?" she asked.

"Is this room safe? Are we being watched?"

She eyed me warily and shook her head. "*What?* No, Bryce would never allow cameras in here. Despite what you might think, he's a very private person."

I rubbed the bridge of my nose, exhaled, and then plopped down on the sepia-toned sectional sofa in the middle of the room. I was suddenly very, *very* tired. Quinn pulled a chair to the hot-tub-sized ottoman and settled across from me, looking frightened, rubbing her hands over her thighs as she glanced back at the door. "We have to be fast. Bryce won't be long."

I leaned in and set my elbows on my knees. My bruises from the swamp throbbed back to life beneath my shirt. "Talk, then. Tell me everything about Xclivity. No more bullshit. No more lies."

Quinn's gaze fell to her lap, and she wiggled her engagement ring, the diamond winking at me ludicrously from her finger. "I first learned about Xclivity at this recovery group thing I went to a couple years after ... you know, everything happened. There were a few members there. One of them—Kerry, actually—said I should think about attending an Xclivity conference with her. That it might help me heal." She chewed the inside of her cheek for a moment and blinked. "I don't know why, but I went. There were so many people. I'd never felt more overwhelmed in my life. I nearly left. I tried to, but Kerry spotted me panicking and calmed me down, then took me to our table. It got better from there. All I had to do was listen. Everyone was so warm. It felt like I was part of a family again."

My spine knotted on the word *family*.

"That's when I learned about The Work. It became, I don't know, addictive I guess."

I frowned. "Addictive?" It was a strange word to use.

"The Work is all about confession, about baring your soul to others. Letting go of all the toxicity in your life. You feel lighter afterward. It's why people share. And you wouldn't believe the things people shared, Olivia. Things *so* much worse than you and I ever went through. I wasn't even embarrassed when my turn came."

I imagined it—Quinn sitting cross legged in some elegant hotel conference room, sobbing out her story through a handful of tissues while those around her sipped organic juices and encouraged her with a slew of vague, new-age terms and positive affirmations. *Excellent, Quinn, let the toxins out. This is how you purify your soul.* The kind of people with glittering smiles who abducted and enslaved women like Margaret if they stepped out of line.

Quinn massaged her hand. "The first time I opened up was absolutely terrifying. But it helped me understand how much weight I'd been carrying. It felt like I was carving out all my scar tissue, just handing it over with every word. I truly think that's when I started to heal."

"But that didn't last, did it?" I didn't like to ask leading questions, but I needed to find out what Quinn knew and get the fuck out of here.

She twisted her mouth in consideration. "No, at some point, Xclivity became less about my personal development and more about recruiting new members. There was a big focus on fees, on keeping the classes full. I was good at it. *Really* good. That's when I leveled up."

I squinted at her. "What does that mean?"

"There are ways to accelerate your growth in Xclivity. Certain groups you can join, but you have to be nominated by a Steward. Nobody turns down a nomination. Ever. It's considered a huge honor. Bryce nominated me."

"He was your ... Steward?"

"Yes. When he picked me to join Imperium, I couldn't believe it. Of all the groups in Xclivity, Imperium is the most elite. I was flattered, but I had no idea what joining really meant. What it would cost me." Her eyes reddened. "There were these ceremonies where they made us ... do things." She sniffed, bowed her head. "Horrible things. To the Stewards. To each other. Sexual things. They even branded us." Her voice sounded fragile, like a glass about to topple and shatter.

"Why didn't you leave then?" I asked. "Why stay?"

Her face hardened. "I *couldn't* leave. I didn't realize it at the time, but they'd filmed the ceremonies, filmed everything we did.

Then they played the videos back to us and made sure we knew they'd release them if we left. They'd ruin us. Besides, even if I could leave, what else was I supposed to do? Go back to being a failure? Just give up after all I had invested in Xclivity? I gave them everything—my money, all my energy, the last five years of my *life*."

My heart lurched. Quinn wasn't thriving after all. It was a mirage. Xclivity had lured her in, groomed her, earned her trust, then spit her back into the world as their pretty little mouthpiece ready to rake in the funds. I felt for her, I did, but I was also furious that she hadn't come clean sooner. It would have helped if she'd told me all this before the trip when I could have actually done something about it. "If you knew how bad Xclivity was, then why did you drag me into this shit? Why pretend everything is so great until now? I mean, what the fuck, Quinn?"

Her eyes sparked. "I needed your help, okay!" She shook her head. "I wanted to tell you earlier, but they monitor everything. My email, my phone calls. Where I travel. I had to beg and beg to get you an invitation on this trip. They knew about your podcast, and they didn't want you here. They've been watching me more aggressively than ever as a result. So, I've had to play along until now. I didn't know what else to do." She sniffed, looked away. "You're all I have left."

Her words plowed into me, and I felt my anger ebb. I suddenly wondered how many others like her were trapped by Xclivity. How many women had this serpentine organization convinced there was no way out, and nowhere to turn—other than back to them?

I softened my voice. "Quinn, I'm sorry. This has all just been a lot to take in. It's not your fault. You were conditioned. Groups like this—they prey on people in vulnerable situations." *Like you,* I nearly added before biting it off.

Her tear-streaked eyes snapped to mine. "No, you're right. I shouldn't have involved you. It was selfish. And dangerous. Bryce will never let me go."

"There are people I know who can help with that kind of thing, but I need to be able to reach them. And we need to get off this ship." I felt the truth of the statement sitting on my tongue, the sudden weight behind the words. *The guests disappear.* "What's the deal with the Wi-Fi, anyway?" I continued. "Why can't I get a signal?"

Quinn swiped at a stray tear. She was fighting back more, struggling to remain in control. "Julianna thinks phones distract people from The Work. Communicating with anyone off-ship is prohibited."

I sat there, my mind reeling, trying to think of my next move. On a boat like this, there had to be a way to get a message out— some way to reach Nina. I just needed to find it.

"Is it really true?" Quinn asked. "What you said happened to Margaret?"

An image cut scalpel-sharp through my mind. Margaret splashing down alone, frightened and injured, with miles of empty ocean lying beneath her feet—treading water until her legs gave out. This, after decades of abuse, after Xclivity stole everything and everyone she'd ever loved. Anger bubbled in my chest. They'd do the same to Quinn if I let them. They'd do the same to me. "Yes. Xclivity abducted her children years ago. It's how they kept her in check. Darren is her son. Tim and Kerry raised him."

Quinn's lips went bloodless, her face paling further. "No …"

I studied her with my brow furrowed. "Yes, how do you not know any of this?"

Her shoulders slumped. I could tell my words stung. "Xclivity likes to keep things siloed. They honestly don't tell me much."

It made sense. Most criminal enterprises operated in the same manner. Information was power. People with information could sell you out. My heart fluttered. I needed to wrap this up. "Margaret also told me the guests are in trouble, that something is going to happen to us tonight. Something terrible. Do you have any idea what that is? You said you've been on these cruises before, right?"

"Bryce and I have been on a few cruises, but I've never tagged along for the Transcension."

The Transcension. This trip. God, I was so sick of these bullshit terms.

"Olivia," Quinn said, "if what you're telling me is true, we need to—"

A rattle came from across the room, a key card sliding into the lock. Quinn's lips moved in a whisper.

Hide.

CHAPTER TWENTY-ONE

I was already up and dashing across the room.

Where, where, where?

Past the bed. Around the corner. Into the bathroom. Sliding across the polished wood floor and nearly colliding with the freestanding tub, nowhere to hide but in a closet full of terry-cloth robes. I wriggled into it, pushing through a tangle of hangers before edging my way toward the back. I'd barely managed to close the door when I heard him.

"Where is she?" Bryce asked.

"Who?" Quinn answered, her tone high and light, like she had no clue what he was talking about.

Bryce didn't reply. The room fell into silence. The sway and creak of the boat and the soft clatter of the hangers beside me were the only sounds. The air felt charged; that static-filled beat between the lightning strike and the thunderclap.

"Don't play with me."

"What's wrong, baby? Why are you so stressed? Did something happen?"

Footsteps thudded and Quinn's voice went breathless. "Wait,

what are you doing?" The sharp *riiitch!* of fabric tearing cut through the air, followed by a chair crashing to the floor. "Stop it, Bryce!"

"Is Olivia in here? Where is she?" Bryce boomed in a way that made me flinch. The struggle grew louder, and a table crashed down with a *bang!* paired with the bright shatter of breaking glass. I heard more footsteps, someone running.

Quinn rounded into sight through the closet slats and flattened herself against the wall across from me, gasping for breath. The corners of her mouth were stretched wide, her nostrils flared with fear. "She's not here! Why are you doing this?" Her voice was no longer high and light.

Another pause. Another gaping silence. And then a hand flashed out—*Bryce's* hand—and his fist bunched into Quinn's now-torn shirt. "I'm done with your games." The way he said it, flat and even tempered, with no inflection at all, made me shiver. This was a man used to asking questions that got answered. His hand slid higher, toward her neck. "Now, I'm going to ask you one more time, and you should think very carefully before you respond." His fingers wrapped around her throat. "Where. Is. She?"

"In her room."

His grip tightened. "Wrong."

"Bryce, *please...*"

I stared at him with fury as his fingertips dimpled her skin, the pigment fading from peach to pink to white. My lungs burned in sympathy. Quinn swallowed, and I could see a vein pulsing beneath her jaw, leaping out in stark relief against her pallid complexion.

She tried to speak, but no words came out. The edges of her lips were turning blue. I was about to blow out of the closet, when Bryce's grip loosened and she took a gasping breath. "I ... I swear the last place I saw Olivia was in her room. She said she still wasn't feeling well."

"Liar." Bryce's hand contracted, and Quinn came back to life in a series of flailing movements, her fingernails clawing uselessly at his wrist.

"S-stop," she managed. "I ... can't ... breathe."

With a look of disgust he released her. She tipped her head back against the wall and sucked in several deep lungfuls of air. Her hand hung limp at her side, motionless, save for a slight tremor that ran down the length of her arm.

Bryce squared his shoulders. "You know I can tell when you're lying to me, right?"

"I'm not—" She coughed, shook her head. "I'm not lying."

He clucked his tongue with a disapproving *tsk, tsk, tsk.*

"Baby, I swear I'm not—"

He slapped her—a bracing strike that left a palm print welling on the bridge of her cheek. Heat bubbled across the back of my neck. She yelped and plastered her face against the wall. Her eyes welded shut, and she braced for another strike. I tensed, my muscles knotting, my fingers curling into fists.

A hanger rattled.

Bryce spun and his face furrowed. He cocked his head at the closet.

Took a step.

Another.

My throat constricted, a cloud of panic rising in my chest, my muscles going tense.

His hand was angling for the door when Quinn said, "Okay, okay, you're right. She came by earlier, but I don't know where she went afterward."

Bryce stopped, his eyes rolling toward the ceiling with a look of exasperation. I could see him fully now, his perfectly symmetrical features collapsing into a wince like he'd been slapped. Like Quinn had struck *him*. He ran a hand through his textured hair and turned back to her. "Why do you make me do this to you? *Why?*"

She slipped down the wall and cowered before him like a freshly scolded puppy. With a long, drawn-out sigh, he settled into a crouch in front of her, his voice going soft, threaded with notes of affection. "You know I don't like to punish you, baby. I picked you for a reason, remember? You're special."

I ground my teeth together so hard it felt like the enamel would crack.

He placed a knuckle beneath Quinn's chin and tilted her gaze toward his. "You understand how important tonight is to me, right?" He smiled, now the picture of warmth and love.

Quinn's face moved in a jerky, hitching movement I took for a nod.

"And you know what Julianna will do if it doesn't go as planned? Who she'll take it out on?"

Quinn gave another shaky nod. A single tear rolled from the corner of her eye and trailed down her cheek. "You."

"Yes. That's right. Me. And I can't have your sister interfering with anything else before then. She's already caused too many problems as it is. And it would be a problem if she doesn't show up to the Disclosure session in a few minutes like Julianna wants. Why do you think I'm looking for her?" He rocked back on his heels. "She needs to be there. I vouched for her because you promised she would behave if I let you bring her on this trip. You swore you would keep her in line." He appraised Quinn for a long moment, tilting his head to the side. "Will you keep her in line?"

"Yes."

"Then find her. And when you do, I don't care how sick she says she is. I don't care what bullshit excuse she gives you. You will drag her upstairs if you have to. You will make sure she comes, and then you are going to keep an eye on her. No more free rein of the ship, understand?"

Her head tilted up and down. "Okay."

He leaned in. "I need you to promise."

She shrank back. "I promise."

"Attagirl. Now get yourself cleaned up. You look like hell." Bryce stood and smoothed a set of nonexistent wrinkles from his sky-blue polo, then adjusted his collar in the mirror, staring at himself. "You know I love you, right? That I'd do anything for you?"

Quinn dropped her head and said nothing.

"Do you still love me?"

"Of course," she mumbled.

"See you in a bit."

It was a full ten seconds after the stateroom door clicked shut before Quinn said, "You can come out now. He's gone."

Quinn didn't move as I stepped out of the closet, her attention still centered on her knees, which she held accordioned against her chest. Tears streamed silently over her cheeks. It looked like she was trying to disappear.

"What an asshole. I can't believe he hit you," I said.

She let out a choking sob mixed with a laugh. "That was nothing."

"Seriously? Oh, Quinn." I knelt and pulled her close, and she went boneless, still crying—hadn't ever really stopped—just sobbing harder as she leaned into me. A fist formed in my throat. "I'm so sorry."

"Don't be," she managed. "It's not your fault. I got myself into this."

My eyes burned. I wanted to comfort her, but I couldn't. Bryce might come strolling back into the stateroom at any second, ready to take another swing. And there was something else—a ticking clock had started the moment I'd left Margaret's room. "Margaret said something bad happens on the third night. That's tonight, Quinn. We need to find a way off this ship."

"There isn't a way off."

"There has to be. Aren't yachts like these required to have—I don't know, rafts or something?"

She wiped her eyes and her lips trembled. "Yes, but there are too many security cameras. They'd catch us before we launched."

"We have to try," I muttered as another realization hit. "And we can't leave the others behind." In my panic, I hadn't considered them—Chaz and Alex and Darren. Especially Darren, who had no idea what Xclivity had done to the mother he never knew he had. The mother who'd sacrificed *everything* to keep him safe. The mother who'd died just last night.

"No, of course not," Quinn said. "Not that either of us would be able to convince them to come."

She was right. I imagined the conversation. *Hey guys, so Quinn and I are thinking of hijacking a lifeboat today because Xclivity is actually a cult that enslaves and murders its members. Oh, and rumor has it something awful is happening tonight—not exactly sure what—but we figured we wouldn't stick around to find out. You probably shouldn't either. Want to tag along?*

We'd sound crazy. It wouldn't work unless—

A thought ripped through my brain with the force of a nail gun. "Where do they keep the surveillance footage?"

She tilted her head. "The security room. Why?"

"Because that's how we prove what happened. That's how we get Chaz, Alex, and Darren to come with us. We show them what happened to Margaret. You said they record everything, right?"

"Yes."

"Can you get us inside?"

Quinn thought about it. "Maybe."

"Good enough for me. Let's go."

"We can't. We have the Disclosure session coming up."

"What is that, anyway?" I asked, annoyed.

"It's where we talk about everything that happened."

I hesitated. "Wait, you mean talk about what happened *with us?*"

She nodded.

"Oh my god. Who will be there?"

"Only the women. It's upstairs in the Sea Lounge."

A stone formed in the pit of my stomach. Even with the dire concern of getting off the ship taking up most of my mental capacity, the thought of discussing anything vulnerable in front of Julianna and Kerry, or even Caprice for that matter, made me sick. Quinn and I'd spent years avoiding our past, and I wasn't about to tear it open in front of a bunch of murderous strangers. "Quinn, no."

Her face fell. "We have to. We don't have a choice. You heard Bryce. If we don't show up, they'll—oh, shit." She looked up and her eyes locked with mine. "Actually, I think we should go. If we want to get into the security room, we're going to need a distraction."

CHAPTER TWENTY-TWO

Half an hour later, still shaken from Quinn's encounter with Bryce, I made my way to the Sea Lounge on the main deck. A tiled pool flanked by a row of miniature evergreen trees greeted me. Like every other room on the ship, designer sofas clung to the walls, looking as deep and comfortable as industrial-sized marshmallows. Beyond them, on the far end of the room, stood a glass door branching with rivulets of condensation.

I paused when I reached it to gather my strength. *This is just a distraction,* I told myself. *Just get through it.* Elysium was the real burning fuse. *The guests disappear on the third night.* But even knowing that, I didn't want to go into the sauna, didn't want to confront the hulking obstacle I knew lay inside. I'd had this conversation with Quinn a thousand times in my mind, but never in person, although I'd tried, over and over again. The last thing she'd said before I'd left her room looped through my mind: *Remember, for this to work, we need to make it look real.* With what we were about to discuss, I didn't know how it would be anything but.

I took a towel from a bamboo cubby, then pulled the sauna door open to a wet billow of steam. Shadows painted the walls.

Figures lounged in various states of repose, legs crossed, ankles locked, knees tucked to the side. Four sets of eyes swung my way. No one said a word. My heart fluttered as a volley of questions assaulted me. Had Quinn sold me out? Had she flipped back to Team Xclivity in the thirty minutes since I'd seen her, desperate to remain in Bryce's good graces? Would Marco be stopping by as a result, anxious to drag me from the sauna and feed me to the waves?

Focus, Therapist Olivia chimed. *You'll be fine. You can do this.*

"Welcome, Olivia. Please take a seat." Julianna's voice rolled toward me low and smoky through the fog. I forced a smile and settled next to Caprice. She appraised me with a Cheshire cat grin ringed in pink lipstick.

"Hey, you," she said in a voice dripping glitter. "How are you feeling? We missed you last night."

Worse, so much worse. "So much better," I replied. "Thank you."

"I'm glad you didn't seriously injure yourself." I squinted through the haze toward the voice and spotted Kerry staring at me in concern, her legs rippling with slender cuts of muscle.

"Me too," I said, suppressing the desire to rip her from the sauna, drag her by the hair to Darren's room, and force her to admit to him what she'd done. Or was she clueless like Quinn? Did she even know who Darren's biological mother really was? I had no idea, but I suspected the former. Something about Kerry's personality felt calculated to me. Cold.

Julianna lounged to Kerry's left, wearing a silver one-piece swimsuit and a matching pair of pendant earrings. Quinn sat to her right, her shoulders bunched, her foot bouncing, lips stapled into a straight line. She looked like a keg of dynamite ready to explode, and we hadn't even begun yet. *Great.*

"I'm glad to see you've recovered, Olivia. Welcome back." Julianna leaned toward a basket on the floor and retrieved a ladle full of water, which she drizzled over the heater stones. A fresh cloud of moisture filled the air, along with the fragrant scent of essential oils. "Let's begin, shall we?" She returned the ladle to the bucket. "Today is special. We must take what we are about to do very seriously. I cannot stress strongly enough that whatever is said here stays here. Is that understood? Nothing leaves this room."

Everyone nodded. Beads of sweat bubbled to life below my hairline. The heat was unbearable.

"The reason we hold the Disclosure session is because there are negative events in your past you have yet to deal with. And when someone doesn't address and work through their traumas, that trauma will control their present, which in turn, directs their future. In other words, the past is never just the past."

More nods. Already I couldn't handle this. I was in no mood for more of Julianna's brain food.

Julianna leaned forward. "We don't become the best version of ourselves by taking the path of least resistance."

"Nothing worth doing is easy," Kerry added unnecessarily. "Growth requires pain."

I shuddered. It sounded like the slogan from an office motivational poster, but in this context, it also sounded incredibly ominous.

"That's right," Julianna agreed. "Which is why today represents a big step in your personal development. I'm going to ask a series of questions, and I want each of you to really challenge yourself to be honest before you answer."

The room fell quiet. My temples throbbed. Quinn continued to bounce her foot.

Julianna spoke: "Take a moment and reflect on what you consider to be your deepest wound. It could be a negative belief about yourself, or something that happened to you. It could be something you did to someone else. Or something you failed to do." She paused and surveyed each of us. "What is your wound? What is that thing you never share with anyone?"

Silence again—the hiss of water hitting rocks.

Julianna laced her fingers together. "Does everyone have something in mind?"

Heads bobbed. Nausea crept back into my gut. I felt dizzy.

"Good, now hold that image in your mind, whatever it is, and keep it there. Focus on it. How does it make you feel?"

"Sad," Caprice said.

"Go deeper," Julianna replied.

"Hopeless."

"Better. Hopeless. Let that emotion pour through you, Caprice. Really soak in it. We all like to think we are stronger than we are, and we can simply bury our emotions and hide them from others, but we can't. Especially negative emotions. We have to experience them and work through them. We need to bring them into the light in order for our wounds to heal."

Caprice sniffed, then let out an exaggerated sob. Her pink lipstick glowed through the mist.

"Good," Julianna said. "*Feel* it. Let the emotion flow."

The sobs came faster, Caprice burying her face in her hands while Kerry cooed and rubbed her back. Julianna leaned in. "Now, Caprice, I'd like for you to share what's on your mind. Do you think you can do that?"

"Yes, but ..." She shook her head and held up a finger. "I ... I just need a minute first."

Julianna nodded. "Certainly. We'll come back to you. Who else would like to speak about their wound?"

Silence cloaked the room. No one said a word. The air seemed heavier than it had a moment ago; the water-saturated molecules bore down on my skin with an oppressive weight, the heat all-consuming. I felt like I might suffocate.

"Remember," Julianna said, "this is a safe place. You're with family here. All we want is for you to heal."

Family. I was so sick of everyone using that word. And Xclivity wasn't a family. It was a brood of snakes.

I looked at Quinn. Quinn looked at me. She swallowed: "I can go."

Julianna nodded. *The floor is yours.*

"I'm not sure where to start," Quinn said.

"How about from the beginning?"

Quinn ran her hands over her thighs, stared at them. "Okay, well, something about me that most people don't know is that I'm adopted."

Kerry inhaled sharply. I sighed. This had been the gulf dividing us ever since we were little—something my father never hid from either of us. We'd find out about it someday, so he made sure we both understood it didn't matter, that he loved us equally, that we were both his number-one girls. Somehow Quinn never got the memo.

"It was ... difficult for me," Quinn said. "I struggled when Olivia was born."

"Why do you think that is?" Julianna asked.

"Because my mother died giving birth to her."

I cringed at the way she said it—*my* mother instead of *our* mother, like I didn't count. A collective gasp ran through the sauna. It didn't matter how many times I'd heard about my birth growing up. It didn't matter that my father swore to me over and over again that he wouldn't trade me for the world. It didn't matter that my grandmother said those same things to me afterward with tears clouding her eyes. *You're all the best parts of her, Olivia, she still lives in you.* Anytime someone mentioned my mother's death, it brought me screaming right back to the fact that I'd killed her. I'd *killed* my mother and I'd never be able to change that.

"I'm so sorry, Quinn," Julianna said. "That must have been very difficult for you."

"It was," Quinn said. "We were so close. She was an amazing person. When she died, I felt so lost."

"How old were you?" Kerry asked.

"Seven."

"Oh my god, you were so young," Caprice said with a sniffle. "You poor thing. How did you survive?"

"Honestly? It was difficult. Our parents—my mother

specifically—struggled with fertility issues. Olivia's conception was considered something of a miracle. Being adopted already made me feel, I don't know, less-than. After Olivia was born, I knew I'd never be able to compete."

Less than? Really? Growing up, my father doted on Quinn the same way he doted on me. His affection was a recipe carefully measured out in cups: one for Quinn, and one for me, both of us seasoned with hugs and salted in kisses. But that wasn't how Quinn saw it. My birth was a hand grenade dropped into the middle of her perfect life; the bomb she never saw coming.

"Losing Mom tore Dad apart," Quinn continued. "And Olivia was this little piece of her she'd left behind. I caught him staring at her all the time. He never looked at me like he looked at her." She sniffed. "He never loved me as much."

"Jesus, Quinn, come on," I said, thinking, *You're pouring it on a little thick, aren't you?* "You know that isn't true."

"But it's how she feels, Olivia, and she's entitled to her feelings." Julianna crossed a leg and leaned closer. "Can I ask you a question?"

No, I thought. *Please don't.* "Yes."

"Is there *some* truth to what she's saying? Did you feel like your father treated you differently than Quinn? Perhaps with more privilege at times? Or with more care? And if so, was there a part of you that liked that?"

"What? No, absolutely not. That's ridiculous. Our father loved Quinn every bit as much as he loved me."

"You were too young to notice, Olivia," Quinn said. "You don't know what it was like before—"

"Mom died?" I interrupted. "Yeah, you've only told me a thousand times. I get it. I totally wrecked your life."

Julianna raised a hand. "Olivia, I'm going to have to ask you to lower the temperature. Please keep this conversation constructive."

You shouldn't be in this conversation to begin with! I wanted to shout. I mean, what the fuck were we doing in here with this woman, anyway? Despite what Quinn said earlier about staging a scene and storming out, this was all starting to feel a little too real.

I sank back and waved a hand to continue.

Quinn massaged her palm and exhaled. "It was more than how my father treated her. Olivia reveled in it. She enjoyed being the miracle child. She rubbed it in my face all the time."

I went rigid and let loose a shocked laugh. It was so far from the truth I didn't even know what to say.

"Mm," Julianna said thoughtfully, pressing a finger to her lips. "Can you validate Quinn's feelings, Olivia?"

"No," I replied. "Because that's a lie."

Julianna's eyes narrowed. "Is it? Remember that healing comes from honesty. It's okay to acknowledge that you've hurt someone. Don't let your pride get in the way of healing. No one here will judge you."

"Jesus. Okay, maybe I did at some point. I have no idea. It was a long time ago. I can't remember." I appraised Quinn. "There, better?"

"Well done," Julianna said in a patronizing tone as she added another ladle of water to the rocks, amplifying the suffocating humidity. "I appreciate your transparency."

171

I stared at her, baffled. Surely she didn't think I was being serious?

"It wasn't just that. Things came easier for Olivia, too," Quinn continued. "She was good in school and sports and pretty much everything she tried, unlike me. I struggled. I wasn't good at anything."

"That's how it was for me and Chaz, too," Caprice said. "Girl, I know how hard that can be."

Another lie, I thought, mentally checking off all the subjects in which Quinn had me beat: dance and fashion, art and music, the social scene and making friends. With her easy beauty and graceful approach, Quinn slipped between cliques like a chameleon while I had a difficult time finding my place with anyone.

"Anything you want to add there, Olivia?" Julianna asked.

"No," I spat. "Are we done?"

Quinn continued. "But that wasn't the worst part of my childhood. That wasn't my wound."

"No, what was?" Julianna prodded.

I knew where Quinn was going before she said a word. She was about to broach the one subject I'd told her was strictly off limits before agreeing to endure this charade. I locked eyes with her and gave her a firm shake of my head. I couldn't fake this. "Quinn," I hissed. "Don't." *Please. Not here. Not in front of all these people.*

She held my gaze and spoke. "My wound came when my father killed himself."

CHAPTER TWENTY-THREE

Losing my father plunged me into a depression so dark and deep, I sometimes fantasized about suicide myself. A mouthful of pills. A razor blade to the wrist. A bullet to the temple. It wouldn't take much. I ached to see him again. I wanted nothing more than to touch his face and hear his voice.

I loved my father. To me he was *everything*.

I never talked about his death with anyone. Discussing it felt like dragging sandpaper over a cut that never healed; it only left me in more pain.

And Quinn *knew* that.

"Losing him destroyed me," she said. "He was all I had left."

"That's not true," I replied. "You still had me."

"No, I didn't!" she snapped. "I didn't have anyone!"

I opened my mouth to reply and stopped. She had a point. When my father died, my grandmother initially took both of us in, but Quinn didn't last. My sister was fifteen the day my father closed the garage door and started his BMW. She wasn't the easiest child before his death but she turned reckless afterward. She dove headfirst into the wrong crowds at school and attempted to numb her pain with an ever-increasing diet of alcohol, drugs, and sex. When she landed her third citation for underage drinking in a month, paired with an arrest for public indecency—she'd been caught fucking a classmate in a department store dressing room—my grandmother abandoned her to the foster system.

Julianna gave Quinn's leg a squeeze. "Very good, Quinn. This is what The Work is all about. Press into this. Can you tell us why you felt so alone?"

I glared at Julianna. I wanted to strangle her.

"After our father died," Quinn said, "our grandmother took Olivia in, but she dumped me in a foster home."

"No," Caprice gasped.

"Yes." Quinn's shoulders rounded. "Olivia grew up with family, and I grew up with strangers I didn't know."

I remembered it well. Our relationship became one of twice-monthly visits. These sticky-skinned meetings were held in a local park where I'd witnessed Quinn's decay firsthand. It was like the very act of existing, of taking a breath, was devouring her whole. With every visit, she grew thinner, her eyes duller. Every time I saw her, I wondered how long it would be until she completely disintegrated.

"You didn't give Grandma much of a choice, Quinn," I finally said. "You were out of control."

Her eyes flashed at me through the fog. "That woman was *never* my grandma. She only loved you."

Something's wrong with your sister, my grandmother told me when I broke down and begged for Quinn to stay. *She's a bad egg. I'm doing this for you.* That meant it was my fault—another heaping platter of guilt I was forced to carry until I learned my grandmother had never wanted my parents to adopt Quinn in the first place. *She was never blood, Olivia. She was never family.*

"That's heartbreaking," Kerry said. "So, you didn't have anyone to support you through all of this?"

"No," Quinn replied. "No one. When Dad passed away, I lost myself. I no longer knew who I was. And when I fell apart, no one tried to stop me. No one cared."

"I cared, Quinn," I said softly.

Her forehead crumpled. "Did you? You weren't there for me when I needed your help."

My pity instantly swung to anger. "What was I supposed to do? I was just a kid!"

"I'm not talking about when we were kids, Olivia." Her gaze sharpened. "I'm talking about *after*."

The memory played on the screen of my mind like a projector: my nineteenth birthday—a rare, blue-sky winter day in January. I was still living with my grandmother at the time, going to Ohio State University, and she'd prepared a party for the ages. All of my friends were there, gathered in her living room, when I'd heard the knock.

Bang! Bang! Bang!

It came hard and sharp, overly insistent. *Another guest*, I thought, leaping to my feet.

When I opened the door, I barely recognized the creature standing on the other side. Thinning hair pulled back into a tight

175

ponytail. A mouth wreathed in scabs. Arms that fell from the sleeves of a too-large shirt, looking like hanger wires. Knuckles coated in grime. I nearly screamed when she flashed forward and seized me by the wrist. And then I was outside on the front porch, pulled into a hug.

Via, how are you? Can we go get some food?

Quinn? I'd muttered in shock. Two days after she'd turned eighteen, Quinn had left Ohio with her share of our father's inheritance and moved to Las Vegas. Besides the occasional postcard, I never heard from her. And when those stopped, I'd worried she was dead.

Embarrassed, I abandoned the party and took her to a TGI Fridays down the block. Quinn devoured her meal like a wolf. Her fingers crawled spider-like through her fries, her jaw snapping open and scissoring shut. She couldn't shovel the meal into her mouth fast enough. I just sat there, watching her, without touching my plate. When she finally spoke, it was to let me know she needed my help, that she'd run out of cash.

I just need a little bit, Olivia. A few thousand to get back on my feet.

And I told her no.

"Do you have *any* idea how difficult it was for me to come to you for money?" Quinn's voice ripped me from the memory. "How humiliating? You were all I had left. And you turned me down. How could you do that? How did you not see what kind of shape I was in? How desperate I was?"

Words leaped up my throat, and I locked them behind my

teeth. I wanted to remind her that I hadn't turned her down, that I'd offered to pay for a trip to rehab, that all she had to do was move back to Ohio and it was done. She'd called me a spoiled bitch and stormed out of the restaurant on the spot.

"You were a wreck, Quinn," I said. "You would have spent that money on drugs."

"How dare you judge me!" Quinn stared at me hollow-cheeked, looking ghoulish in the mist. "I had bills to pay. Debts to settle. I could barely afford to eat. Do you know how close I came to killing myself after you rejected me? I had to declare bankruptcy, Olivia. *Bankruptcy.* You have no clue what I had to do to survive after that. All I needed was a few grand. And you had more than enough!"

"Watch your tone," Julianna warned. "Both of you."

"Oh, fuck off, Julianna!" Sweat dripped into my eyes. This moment felt like a special kind of hell, and I'd had enough.

Her gaze went dark, poisonous. "You will *not* talk to me that way."

I stared at her, wanted to tell her I'd talk to her however I pleased, that I was sick of her shit, but something about the way she was looking at me, unblinking, eyes cold, gave me pause. I couldn't forget that, despite her flowery speeches and artificial encouragement, this woman was pure fucking evil. So, I said nothing and turned back to Quinn. "How would a few grand have been enough for you to turn things around after you blew through *ten million?* I don't even know how you spent that much as fast as you did."

Quinn blinked, her face shining like a wet moon through the steam, the whites of her eyes blazing like stars. Her lower lip trembled. "What do you mean, 'ten million'?"

"Don't play dumb," I said. "Your share of the inheritance. You got as much as I did and you wasted it all. Did you really think I was going to let you do the same thing with mine?"

Her face went slack, like she'd been slapped. "I got two-hundred thousand."

Caprice issued a sharp intake of breath. Kerry looked stricken.

My bullshit meter hit overload. What were we even doing? We needed to get to the security office and then get off this ship. Our lives were at stake, and here we were arguing over money—over lies *about* money. This was quickly going off the rails. "Stop lying, Quinn!" I said. "Just be honest for once in your fucking life!"

Julianna leaned in, her jaw hard, her mouth tight. "Enough! I will not allow this session to turn toxic!"

"I'm telling the truth," Quinn mumbled. "That's all I got."

I stared at her, at the truth splashed all over her face, at the absolute shock and the way she was gripping the wooden bench so hard her knuckles were white. "That's not possible," I said. I knew the details of my father's will. He'd never do that. He'd split his estate right down the middle—half for me and half for Quinn. My grandmother made sure of it. My grandmother who'd been the executor of his estate, and who'd absolutely despised my sister. Who'd kicked Quinn out of her house. Who'd told me point blank, Quinn wasn't family.

Oh, fuck.

My gaze fell to my hands—which were shaking, my fingers pruned.

"I *hate* you, Olivia. You destroyed my life."

I looked up. "Quinn, I didn't know."

But she was already gone, the door crashing open in a jet of superheated air.

CHAPTER TWENTY-FOUR

I found Quinn at the end of the corridor, near the central staircase. She stood on the bottom step, clutching the railing, facing away from me with her shoulders stooped, breathing hard. The image shot me back in time to the day of our father's funeral, Quinn perched over his casket, looking fragile and broken, like a leaf about to blow away. I stood there, wanting to take her pain for the briefest of moments, thinking, *Give it to me, Quinn, I can take it,* before remembering how lost I was in my own.

"Quinn," I said, setting my palm on her back. Her skin rippled beneath my touch. "Are you okay?"

She straightened and rotated my way. The whites of her eyes were tinged pink, her green irises almost luminescent in contrast. A muscle twitched near her mouth. "What do you think?"

"I didn't mean to—"

She raised a finger, waved it. "Just … don't. We don't have time. Come on."

She started up the stairs and I followed, feeling chastened, still spinning from her revelation in the sauna. All this time, and I'd never known what my grandmother had done to Quinn. How severe she'd been. How cold. But I couldn't lose myself in it right now. There were more important things to focus on.

Like securing evidence of Margaret's murder.

And getting off this ship. *The guests disappear.*

A few minutes later, we were making our way down a long corridor on the bridge deck. We passed no one, saw no one. The silence felt ominous. My hands began to sweat.

"Where is everyone?" I asked.

Quinn looked back at me without stopping. "The crew usually takes lunch around now on the lower deck."

"What about the men? Bryce and the rest of them?" Just his name on my tongue filled me with loathing.

"They're doing their Disclosure session upstairs in the garden. Bryce thinks the natural light helps people open up."

"There's a garden?"

"Yep. Right next to the saloon."

A saloon, too, because why not? I peered past Quinn toward a nondescript black door at the end of the hall stamped with a single, white-lettered word: *Security*. Quinn arrowed toward it, but I took her arm and brought her to a stop. "Wait, what if someone's inside?"

"There won't be."

"How do you know?"

"Like I said, they're at lunch. And Marco doesn't spend much time up here." She pulled a white card from a pouch zipped around her waist and tapped it against an electronic lock. Three squares blinked and turned green.

"You have a key to the security office?" I asked, surprised.

She pushed through the door. "Sort of. It's Bryce's master key. He keeps it in the room safe. He has no clue I know the combination." She fixed me with a look, one that said, *and if he finds out, I'm dead.* "Let's go."

I trailed after her into the office. Unlike the other rooms, it felt sterile. The walls were paneled in dark walnut with none of the decorations I'd grown accustomed to seeing throughout the ship. No modern art déco plastered on the walls, no velvet accents on the floor. Something like hospital light bled from the ceiling, falling over a rack of what appeared to be riot gear and cannisters of ... tear gas? I couldn't tell, but either way, it looked like Xclivity was well prepared to handle ... what? Pirates? A passenger uprising like ours? My pulse thumped hard in my neck. There was no question this room was very strictly off limits.

Quinn pulled a chair out and sat down in front of a laptop connected to two large monitors on the desk. She grabbed the mouse, and the cursor flicked past several icons on the desktop before settling on a blue video camera. *Click, click.* A checkerboard of images splashed over both screens. Quinn leaned back and looked up at me. "Okay, what time did this happen last night?"

I tried to remember. "Um, it was ... about one in the morning."

"Shit," Quinn muttered. "You don't remember, do you?"

"No. I didn't exactly think to look at the clock."

"Let's narrow it down to the camera, then."

I stared at the video feeds. There were so many, all over the yacht: a picture of a swimming pool I had yet to visit, a perfect blue square of aqua water stamped into the middle of the deck; the dining room, empty now, save for the tables; the lobby and the blind spot Margaret had identified; corridor after high-definition corridor, each one blazing crisp and clear.

Including Quinn's.

I recognized the painting on the wall near her room and the perfect shot of her door. My mouth went dry. With all of these cameras, how had Bryce not found me earlier? How had he not known I was in their room? Was the security system not linked to his cellphone? Or Marco's? Even with Julianna's Wi-Fi ban, I seriously doubted it. But what did I know? I had yet to see either guy use a phone, and I didn't have time to sit here wondering if they did.

I turned my attention to the shots of the decks. There were at least a dozen day-lit squares near the bottom of the screen, showing nothing but railing and frothing wake. "Do you know which one it is?" I asked. "You know the ship better than me."

"No. They all look the same." Her voice quivered. I could hear the panic rising.

Think, I told myself with my nerves close to frying. *Try to remember.*

I closed my eyes and forced myself to relive the moment from last night, scrubbing the memory for any detail that would help me identify the right camera. When nothing came, I replayed the morning with Quinn: Waking in a daze and flying down the hall to examine the carpet before racing outside onto the deck. Staring at the waves, the endless blue plane, all that water. Turning back toward the exterior of the yacht, then the railing ...

An image scratched my mind's eye.

"I've got it!" My eyelids flew open, and I scanned the security feeds again, reviewing them one by one until I spotted the orange life preserver lashed to the railing. I stabbed a finger. "There! That's the one!"

Quinn double-clicked the square, and the image widened. She pulled it onto the other screen and scrolled back through the feed. The time stamp skipped in the bottom corner, the sun setting in reverse. No movement. Nothing. "You sure it was this one?"

"I think so."

"You *think* so?"

"I'm sure. This is it."

She grimaced and went back to work. Moving slower, she scrolled farther back through the footage, both of us spotting the flicker of movement at the same time. And then they were there, Marco and Margaret standing frozen before us on the screen. Quinn hit play and my heart carved through my chest at the sight of Margaret's jaw covered in blood, her lips unstitching as Marco hoisted her higher.

Then she was gone.

Quinn's complexion bleached. "Oh my god. You were telling the truth." She pushed back from the desk. "This can't be happening."

I caught a slash of motion on the other display, a figure walking down the same hall Quinn and I had come down a moment earlier.

A *big* figure. Bald. Muscled. My knees nearly buckled.

"Quinn, look."

"Shit," Quinn, mumbled, staring at Marco. "No, no, no." Her hand flashed for her pouch and came back with a small thumb drive, which she clicked into the USB port on the laptop. A file folder opened. She rewound the feed containing Margaret, dragged the mouse over the footage from a small ribbon below, and copied it into the waiting folder. A status bar appeared—one moving way, *way* too slow.

A bolt of fear ripped down my spine. Marco was close.

Too close. We weren't going to make it.

Quinn must have had the same thought because she minimized the status bar and jumped to her feet. "Over here!" she hissed, rounding the desk and rushing toward a door on the far wall. We tumbled past it together, and a knot formed in my throat when I spotted the flash drive still blinking from the laptop.

CHAPTER TWENTY-FIVE

I stood shivering beneath the air conditioning spilling through a vent above us. Small lights flashed intermittently. I could feel more than hear the buzz of the computer equipment behind me. A server room, the space at least ten degrees colder than the rest of the ship. In my bathing suit, it felt absolutely arctic. Quinn hadn't been able to fully close the door before Marco entered the security office, leaving a sliver of space through which to see him as he lowered his tremendous bulk into the chair. He stared at the monitors intently, still unaware of the thumb drive flickering from the laptop on the desk, too busy looking for something else.

Looking for us.

The thought twisted through my stomach as he sat there, clicking away, reviewing the screens, his eyes bouncing left to right, his brow furrowed with concentration. Gooseflesh canvased my arms, my legs—and not just from the cold—but from what this man might do to us if he discovered us watching him. The violence he might unleash like he had on Margaret. The sheer physical threat he possessed. With our size difference, neither Quinn or I would stand a chance against him. So we stood there, not making a sound until, with a last click of the mouse, Marco finally pushed back from the desk and started to rise.

Leave, I whispered in my head. *Go.*

He didn't. He paused instead, his gaze tilting to the left—toward the cracked server room door. His eyebrows angled into a V, and I went stiff with panic. Quinn took a gulp of air. He stood, and the chair groaned in release. Footsteps thudded our way. The seam of light at our feet darkened in a slow eclipse, blocked by his wide frame. I braced, ready to spring forward the second the door opened. To do what, I wasn't sure—either run or attack—but I wouldn't go down easy.

My veins turned to ice. Time slowed.

Please, just go.

His eyes narrowed in contemplation. Then, with a grunt, he reached out and closed the server door.

Quinn and I remained in the dark, wordless, listening to Marco's footsteps fade down the hall until Quinn exhaled and said, "I thought I was going to have a heart attack."

"Me, too," I said, turning her way. "How did he not see us on the video feed? Wouldn't the cameras have recorded us coming up here?"

"Yes," Quinn said, considering it. "But he would have to pull up the right footage. And I doubt he was even looking for us to begin with."

"How do you know?"

"I don't. But like I said, he doesn't come up here that often. It's a ship, after all. There aren't that many places for people to go. The security system is kind of an afterthought." Quinn poked her head back into the office tentatively as she said it, then made her way to the desk and snatched the flash drive from the laptop. "Stash this in your room," she said, handing it to me, "and then come upstairs for lunch. It's outside on the sun deck. We can talk to the others afterward."

"Shouldn't we talk to them now? Or hide until we can?"

She considered it, frowned. "No. For now we pretend we don't know anything and play along. It would be more dangerous not to." She started for the door.

"Quinn, wait."

She hesitated, turned.

"I didn't know about the money. Grandma didn't tell me."

"That doesn't surprise me. That woman was the devil."

Was because our grandmother died years ago, taken by a heart attack on her daily walk to the park. It still hurt to know she'd passed away alone, that I hadn't been there to hold her hand. Despite how she'd treated Quinn growing up, she'd always been there for me, always loved me. And I never got to thank her for that.

"Seriously," I said, "I swear I didn't know."

Quinn closed her eyes and sighed, then opened them. "I believe you. And I'm sorry for what I said in there. I had to make it look real."

"So ... you don't actually hate me, then?" The question fell out of my mouth before I could stop it. I had to know.

"I—no," she stammered, then said, "I mean, yes, I did ... for a time, but I'm past all of that now." She pulled her bottom lip between her teeth and sawed at it gently in consideration—a tell I remembered from our childhood that meant she didn't want to say whatever would come next. "And, selfishly, I knew if I forgave you, I'd have no one to blame but myself. I needed someone to blame back then. You were right not to give me the money. I would have done exactly what you said. I know that now." Her lips quivered, and her gaze fell to her feet. "I had to hit rock bottom. Going broke is what it took."

I stepped closer—hesitantly, slowly—and when she didn't stop me, I pulled her into a hug. And then we stood there, neither of us saying a word as a single thought swept through my head like a cool bank of rain. Quinn was hugging me. My sister was *actually* hugging me. A lump formed in my throat and I let the tears come, didn't even try to hold them back. "I've missed you."

"Me, too," she replied. "So much."

I stepped back. "I promise I'm going to fix the money thing. I'm going to make this right."

She wiped her eyes. "I don't care about the money. It doesn't matter anymore. Not as long as I have you. But we can talk more about it later. We need to get out of here." She reached for the doorknob and stopped, her face ashen. "Olivia, we have to act normal. If they find out we know about this, *any* of it ..."

"I know," I said. She didn't need to finish the sentence. *They'd kill us.*

"Give me a few seconds before you follow," she said. "I don't want anyone to catch us up here together."

I nodded, and she slipped into the hall. And then I stood there for a full minute, watching the door, about to leave, when an idea sparked—an opportunity I couldn't pass by. I returned to the desk and clicked on the browser icon at the bottom of the screen. When the page loaded, I surfed to my email and began to type.

CHAPTER TWENTY-SIX

Despite the wall of tropical heat that hit me the second I stepped outside onto the sun deck, I felt cold. The clouds from earlier had burned away, leaving behind a navy sky a few shades lighter than that of the ocean, everything blue, blue, blue. There was so much water everywhere I looked, so much space. The swaying, empty vista left me feeling untethered, like gravity might somehow work in reverse out here and send me hurtling upward at any second.

A buffet table sat near the bar, looking picked over. I grabbed a plate and made a show of considering the options—sandwiches and potato salad, fruit and chips, slices of cold cut meat lying next to exotic cuts of cheese. I didn't care about any of it, but I also didn't want to turn around, didn't want to lay eyes on Bryce and his smug grin or Julianna's beatific, holistic expression. And I certainly didn't want to see Kerry and Tim, or anyone else for that matter. But I couldn't stand here studying lunch forever, either. So, with a great deal of reluctance, I filled my plate and forced my feet into motion.

There were two tables to choose from. Both were covered in thick white tablecloths, both set with glassware, glinting sharp with sunshine, sending bright shards of light slicing straight through my retinas. I wavered between them for an awkward moment, unsure of where to sit, until Darren patted a seat next to him. I smiled as he waved me over, my relief fading when I noticed Liam stationed directly across the table.

"How are you feeling?" he asked with his fingers steepled beneath his chin.

"Yeah," Darren added. "Mom said you had a bad fall?"

Mom. The word hit my ears like a razor blade. "It wasn't great, but I'm fine."

"How did it happen, anyway?" Darren asked.

I raised an eyebrow. "Well, funny story—I *was* walking through the jungle blindfolded …"

Alex set his glass down, nearly choking as he laughed, spraying the tablecloth with water. A few stray drops misted my arm.

"Jesus, Alex! Come on!" Liam exclaimed, jerking back in his chair and rattling the dishes.

"What?" Alex said, wiping his mouth. "It was funny."

Liam wiped his shirt furiously, like Alex had sprayed *him* with water instead of me. "You're such a slob sometimes, I swear."

Alex's smile wilted.

Caprice spoke. "Are you sure you're feeling okay, Olivia? You look pale." She was staring directly at me, her cheeks freshly powdered, her lips heavily glossed. By the looks of it, her Disclosure session had gone much better than mine.

"I'm fine," I replied. "I just need to eat something." And I did. Even though I wasn't hungry, I needed to keep up appearances, needed to make sure it looked like everything was *good, grand, wonderful, great!*

"How are things with—" she jerked her head over her shoulder "—your sister? Did you two work everything out?"

"Mm-hm." I took a bite of the sandwich, hoping stuffing my mouth with food would dissuade any follow-up questions. After all, it was rude to talk and chew at the same time. Caprice kept her gaze on me, though, waiting for me to finish. Thankfully, Chaz groaned before I did and made a show of planting his head on the table. He looked terrible, his forehead bubbling sweat.

I leaned toward Darren. "What's up with him?"

Darren extended his pinkie and thumb and mimed taking a drink. "No booze. They axed the alcohol last night at dinner."

"Seriously?" I muttered.

"You know I can hear you guys, right?" Chaz looked up wearily. "And yes, Julianna said we need to 'detoxify' or some shit." He raised both hands and wrapped the word in finger quotes. "Apparently, we need to be clearheaded today."

My nerves sparked, and Margaret's warning poured through my head for the umpteenth time: *The guests disappear on the third night.* It took every ounce of my willpower to remain seated, to not grab Chaz, Alex, and Darren and drag them from the table to my room to show them what Quinn and I had found.

"It's not going to kill you to spend a couple days sober, you baby," Caprice said.

Chaz groaned again and rubbed the sweat pooling near his temples. "Don't be so sure."

A wry grin crept over Alex's face. "I might have a little something-something stashed in my room, if it would help."

Chaz's face flushed with color, like the mere thought of a drink was enough to renew his vigor. "Really?"

"Yeah, I brought a bottle of Belvedere along. We can—"

Liam squeezed Alex's arm and gave him a single shake of his head. Alex blinked, suddenly looking abashed, then angry.

A clatter brought my attention to the other table. Tim had his head thrown back in laughter, Kerry shaking hers as Bryce looked on with a smirk, obviously pleased with whatever he'd said to elicit such a response. Quinn sat to his left with a hand plastered over her mouth, trying to contain herself. Then she lowered it and said something that sparked another round of laughter. *Hilarious.*

I stared at her: she seemed perfectly at ease, cracking up while wiping her eyes. Crying now, because whatever she'd said was so funny. Her face no longer carried the pallid complexion from earlier. How was she not freaking out like I was? How was she not as rattled and scared? Because I was scared shitless. Instead, she seemed rejuvenated, her skin vitamin infused and glowing, her fingers laced with Bryce's like he hadn't used that very hand to strike her this morning. I glanced at him, and he turned my way, his aviators ribboned with sunlight.

He was no longer smiling.

"Well, it looks like we chose the wrong table," Darren said.

I issued a flat laugh and twisted toward him, lowering my voice. "Listen, Darren, can we talk after lunch? I need to fill you in on something."

"Sure. What?"

"Oh, nothing important." *Just that we need to get the fuck off this boat as soon as possible.* My gaze flicked to Chaz as I said it, who was now eyeballing Alex with the manic intensity of a paper-bag alcoholic begging for change ... probably because he was an alcoholic.

"Seriously, though," he said to Alex. "Can I get that drink? I really need a drink."

"Chaz, stop it." Caprice's tone edged toward a warning. "You're embarrassing me. You promised you'd try on this trip. And this—" she waved a manicured hand at him, "—whatever it is you're doing here, isn't trying."

He glared at her. "You didn't tell me it was going to be a dry cruise. How do you expect me to work through our issues sober?"

"Our emotional entanglements," she corrected.

He threw his head back and rolled his eyes. "Whatever. I hate that term. That's all you talk about, anymore. Emotional entanglements. Freeing your soul. Experiencing paradigm shifts. Like I know what any of that means." He swung his gaze toward Alex, his eyes bloodshot. "So, how about it, brother? Shall we go have ourselves a little nip?"

"Sure," Alex said, casting a sour look at Liam, starting to rise. "Let's go."

Liam snatched his arm and jerked him back down, his face contorting into a snarl. "You're not going anywhere."

"Let go of me, Liam."

"No." He dug his fingers deeper into Alex's wrist.

"Let go!" Alex ripped his arm free and shot to his feet. His chair came down with a clatter. Heads rotated his way. Eyes went wide. Words spiked from Alex's mouth in a hot rush. "I have tolerated your bullshit for three years now, Liam! Three *long* years. And you know why I've done that? Because deep down, I've always believed that you are a good man. I've seen it. I know how kind you can be. How generous and gentle. But ever since you joined Xclivity, I don't even know who you are anymore. You treat me like—" his voice faltered, "—like I'm a burden. Like I'm nothing but baggage."

Liam's mouth fell open. "Alex, that's not true."

Alex stabbed a finger at him: "You aren't the man I fell in love with. We're done. All of this is *done*." He spun and took a few stiff steps, then paused and fished something from his pocket, which he hurled at Liam. My heart sank when I saw the small velvet box land on the table. "And to think I was going to surprise you with this tonight. Keep it as a memento! I'm going to go pack. As soon as we dock, I'm booking the first flight back to Chicago!"

With that, he twisted and strode into the ship.

CHAPTER TWENTY-SEVEN

"Alex," I said when I caught up to him. "Please, wait."

He didn't turn, didn't stop, just kept power-walking down the hall. I jogged a few steps and brushed his shoulder with my fingertips. "Alex—"

"What do you want?" he snapped, whirling toward me. He had his lips sucked between his teeth, his cheeks glowing red. His eyelids flicked shut for a long second, and he removed his glasses to wipe his eyes clear. "I'm sorry," he said, looking back at me. "You didn't deserve that."

"And Liam doesn't deserve you," I replied. "But we don't have time to focus on that right now. I need you to come with me."

A crease formed between his eyes. "What?"

The sound of the automatic door whooshing open behind us came before I could explain. Alex's face went feral, mean, then smoothed when he saw Darren round the corner instead of Liam.

"Hey?" Darren said. His voice rose on the last letter, a question hanging on the y: *is everything okay?*

"Is Liam still out there?" Alex asked, glancing behind him.

"Yeah." Darren gave him a slight grin. "He hasn't moved an inch. You really let him have it."

Alex's face crumpled. His lips trembled. I knew he was fighting back a fresh round of tears. It couldn't happen, though. Not here. A timer had started in my head the second I'd stepped out of the security office—a little hourglass dumping sand by the second. We needed to get off this boat before Xclivity murdered the rest of us.

The door whooshed again, and this time Quinn rounded the corner, tugging Chaz by the wrist. "Come on," she said, her eyes flashing a warning. "Let's go. They'll be in soon."

"Go where?" Darren asked.

"Remember when I said we needed to talk?" I asked.

He nodded.

"There's something we need to show you." I surveyed Alex and Chaz. "*All* of you."

I turned without another word, and we walked in silence, my neck prickling with panic, my legs itching to run. *Just stay calm*, I told myself. *Don't spook them.* When we reached my room, I opened the door to a smooth comforter and the pillows propped just so against the headboard. A towel sat on the foot of the bed, folded into the shape of a swan, a few mints resting near the beak. My blood turned to water at the sight, my chest tight with anxiety. Someone had been in here. Someone cleaned my room.

I headed for the closet, or more accurately for the safe *in* the closet, where I'd stored the USB drive before going upstairs for lunch.

"I'll get the TV set up," Quinn hollered from the room.

Without answering, I punched in the safe code, the last four digits of Nina's cell number. Difficult to guess, but easy to remember. The buttons blinked green. I pulled the miniature door open, and reached inside, my fingers searching for the rectangular memory stick ...

Which wasn't there.

Needles of fear swam down my back. My tongue went dry. It had to be there. I knew they could get into my room. But I thought *surely* a safe with a code ...

I searched the safe again. The memory stick was gone.

I cursed myself for my stupidity. *You idiot.*

"It's not here," I said, stumbling from the closet in a daze. "The flash drive is gone."

Quinn rotated my way, her face the shade of glue. "Please tell me you're joking."

My stomach clenched. *Oh, shit. Oh, fuck.* I walked to the bed and plopped down next to Chaz, who made room for me with a begrudging scoot to the side. The sickly sweet scent of alcohol leaching from his pores assaulted my nose. It made me want to puke. "Shit," I hissed. "Shit, shit, *shit.*"

"They took it," Quinn said watching me, looking stunned. "Which means "

"—they know," I finished.

"Took what?" Darren stood near the door with his hands jammed into his pockets, looking vaguely concerned.

I ran a hand over my face. "The video."

Quinn bolted upright. "We need to get off the boat."

"Whoa," Chaz said, coming to life beside me. "*Get off the boat? What are you talking about? Will someone please just tell me what the fuck is going on?*"

Quinn gave me a nod: *Tell them.*

I hesitated. How could I relay what I saw in a way that made sense? Without proof, it would sound like sheer lunacy. Still, what other choice did I have? Quinn would back me up, at least, but would that be enough? My head throbbed with the question, the morning's headache roaring back to life. "Okay, last night, I saw Marco throw someone overboard."

"What?" Chaz said, looking thunderstruck. "C'mon. That's ridiculous."

"You can't be serious," Alex added.

"We didn't expect you to believe us," I said. "Which is why we had proof. That's what we wanted to show you. We had a video."

"And now we don't," Quinn finished.

Here, Chaz actually scoffed and rolled his eyes at her. "*Rigggght*, did my sister put you up to this? She did, didn't she?"

I didn't answer.

"Who?" Darren blurted from my left; I'd forgotten he was even there.

I gave him a blank look. "Sorry?"

"You said Marco threw someone overboard last night. Who was it?"

"One of the crew." *Your mother.* "Her name was Carmela. Black hair"—*like yours*—"with dark eyes"—*also like yours*—"about yay high." I brought my hand to my collarbone. "We talked to her, remember? When we entered the dining room? She served you a glass of wine."

Darren rubbed the back of his head. "Yeah, I think I remember her."

Quinn edged next to me, the tendons in her neck popping like high-voltage transmission lines about to snap. "Look, it doesn't matter what she looked like. Olivia's telling the truth. I didn't believe her either until I saw it with my own eyes. A woman was murdered last night, and we need to get off this yacht before they do the same thing to us. And we need to do it *now*."

"Yeah? And how should we do that?" Chaz asked, back to looking bemused.

Quinn crossed her arms. "We steal a lifeboat."

Chaz laughed. "Oh my god. Pass me whatever you're drinking." He paused, then looked at Alex and arched an eyebrow. "Hey, can we still get that drink?"

"Focus!" I shouted.

"That does it," Chaz said, rising. "I'm done here. I'm gonna go pass out in my room. Wake me up when it's time for dinner."

He headed for the door. Quinn blocked his way. "You can't leave."

He tensed. "Seriously? You're really doing this? Get out of my way."

Chaz didn't seem like the violent type to me—he didn't have the look—but I joined Quinn, anyway, just in case. No one else would assault my sister today.

Quinn crossed her arms. "Chaz, you can't tell your sister about this. *Any* of it."

He snorted. "Are you kidding? Of course I'm going to tell her. Caprice is a little off-kilter sometimes, sure, but nothing like you two. You're both certifiable. Now move."

"No," we both said at the same time.

He frowned, no longer looking amused. Darren slid his fingers over my forearm. "Olivia, you have to let him go. You can't keep him here. You can't keep any of us here. And you shouldn't. If what you say actually happened, we need to talk to the others about it immediately. Come on, we'll go tell my parents together."

I shook my head furiously. "No, we can't do that. You don't understand. None of you can tell anyone about what you just heard. They're all in on this. Every one of them." I took hold of Darren's arm. "Your parents." I snapped my gaze toward Alex and Chaz. "Liam and Caprice. Julianna. Bryce. Something bad is going down tonight, I'm telling you. We need to go right now."

"Whatever you say," Chaz said, shouldering past me toward the door.

"Chaz, wait." More pleas bubbled up my throat as I followed him into the hall. "Please, don't—"

He stopped, and I smacked into his back. He didn't turn to face me, just stood there, staring down the corridor. I followed his gaze and my shoulders went rigid. Marco and Bryce were bulling their way toward us, both of them looking pissed. They stopped when the others spilled out behind me.

"Fellas?" Chaz said.

Marco's eyes narrowed. "You need to come with us. All of you." His voice was gruff—a concrete mixer churning gravel. It was an order. One I had no intention of following.

"Go with you *where?*" Chaz asked, cocking his head to the side.

Marco set his hands on his hips in answer, and the motion brought my attention to his waist, to the black flash of metal holstered there.

A gun. The man had an actual gun.

That's when I ran.

CHAPTER TWENTY-EIGHT

A shout rang out behind me: "Stop them!"

Them because Quinn was running with me—as were Darren and Alex, all of us racing away down the hall. But not Chaz. I peered over my shoulder and saw him still standing near the door to my room, rooted in place, looking stunned as Bryce plowed into him full speed. Marco surged past them as they fell, his mouth knotted in anger, his voice laced with rage.

"Get back here!"

I ran faster.

"This way!" Quinn yelled, bolting ahead of me toward the stairs.

I sprinted after her with Darren at my side, pumping his arms and flashing his teeth, and Alex behind us, huffing for air. We reached the staircase, and Quinn hit the first step and then leaped past the second to the third, taking them two at a time. Her legs were pistons, her elbows chugging up and down. It was all I could do to keep up.

"What ... the ... hell is happening?" Alex gasped as we crested the landing. "Why ... are they ... chasing us?"

"Because what I told you is true!" I fired back.

"Move!" Quinn shouted, angling for the door, the four of us swerving past a waiter carrying a tray cluttered in plates and cups. We burst outside onto the deck as a volley of glass erupted behind us. I stole a glance back and caught Marco tumbling through the door in a shower of broken dishes. His forehead was bleeding sweat, his entire face wrapped in a snarl. A liquid fear filled me, the knowledge that if this man caught us, we were dead.

I swung around in time to see the low length of pipe bolted to the deck head.

Alex didn't.

It caught him square in the nose. He flew backward and slammed to the deck, his glasses exploding off his face. I slid to a stop, about to rush back and help when I spotted Marco barreling toward us and froze. His feet slapped against the wood like canon-fire, his arms the size of my thighs.

Alex squinted up at me. "Go!"

I hung there, petrified.

"*Go!*" Alex repeated, then rolled over, and threw himself into Marco's legs.

He fell.

I ran.

Curving past tables and leaping over chairs. Sprinting with the wind shrieking in my ears. The yacht transforming into a smear of metal and plastic around me. Fire stitched through my ribs. My breath came in hot, painful snatches. Marco bellowed and roared behind me, sounding farther back now.

"Stop!"

I wanted to, *needed* to, but I ordered my legs to push faster instead, harder.

"There!" Quinn screeched, jabbing a finger at a series of bright white lifeboats with enclosed plastic shells. Each one hung suspended from the yacht by a pair of steel arms. "Get in! I'll get the pins! You two pull the wire release inside!"

Darren and I scrambled past her into the first boat we reached, her order flaring white-hot in my brain, the only thing that mattered in this moment. The only thing that would keep us alive. *Pull the wire!*

I looked for it, frantic, scanning the boat's interior. The metal *chink* of pins loosening came from outside, followed by the light patter of Quinn's shoes—and the thunder of Marco's.

"Got it!" Darren exclaimed, lunging for a wire hanging from the boat's ceiling.

"Wait for Quinn!" I shouted as he seized the braided steel, his arm coming down, about to pull. He stopped, and I rushed back to the door and beckoned her forward. "Get in!"

Quinn shot for the opening, and Marco sank his fingers into her hair and jerked her back. I gasped when I spotted the gun barrel resting against her temple.

"Get out," he growled.

"Okay," I said, raising my hands, about to step off the boat when Quinn's gaze sharpened. She gave me a barely-there shake of her head. And then, with one smooth movement, she lifted her feet, planted them on the boat's hull, and launched backward into Marco. He grunted with surprise as Quinn's shoulder collided with the gun and sent it skittering across the deck. They turned and scrambled for it, dropping to the wood in a mad hands and knees rush. Quinn reached it first, but Marco brought his hand down and tore it from her grip when she swung it his way.

Her eyes met mine and went wide. "Pull the wire!"

Darren pulled the wire.

The metal arms swung the boat outward, away from the yacht. Quinn leaped to her feet and ran toward me. "Hurry!" I said, leaning forward and extending my hand. "You can still—*Quinn!*"

The cry sounded like a stranger's scream instead of my own voice, a cold blade of horror knifing through me as Marco took his feet behind her, raised the gun—and fired. The last thing I saw was my sister crashing to the deck in a lifeless arc before she disappeared from view.

My heart pummeled my ribs. *He shot her! He shot my sister!*

The lifeboat hit the water with an abrupt splash and rocked in place. The hatch door banged against the hard plastic shell in time with the waves.

Thwack! Thwack! Thwack!

Tears smeared my vision, images of what I'd just seen ripping through my brain like bullets. Quinn leaping to her feet. Marco raising the gun. That single, flaring muzzle flash, aimed squarely at her back as the boat lowered.

Bang!

Ohmygodohmygodohmy—

"Hey!" Fingers cupped my face. Palms damp with sweat welded to my cheeks. Darren's sepia-toned features resolved—eyes bright with panic, lips pulled wide, a vein popping in his neck. "Snap out of it!"

I grabbed his wrists. "He shot her! Marco shot Quinn! We have to go back!"

"We can't!"

"We have to!" I cried. "We can't leave her!"

"She's dead, Olivia! And if we don't move right now, we will be too!"

Dead. The word hit me with the force of a shotgun blast. I moved, following him toward the bow and the console which sat nestled beneath the windshield in a bleary smudge of flashing lights and color. I scanned it in a daze, my brain cataloging what I saw: Steering wheel. Compass. Throttle. Switches and buttons.

Quinn is dead ... Marco shot her.

My eyes came to rest on an orange lever near the fuel gauge. Orange, the color of emergencies. *The boat release—a way to disengage from the yacht.* It had to be. There was nothing else. I wound my fingers over the lever and stared through the grime-encrusted glass. Outside, a chain was secured to the bow, attached to a metal ring.

Work, I prayed. *Please, work.*

I pulled.

Nothing happened.

I gawked at the lever, then at the chain. Nothing had changed. Darren shouldered past me and reset the lever, then smashed it down again to the same result: nothing. "What the hell?"

"We're stuck," I mumbled dumbly.

"This can't be the release," he replied. "There's got to be another."

But I knew there wasn't. In an emergency, people couldn't be trusted to think clearly, and a hunter-orange lever next to the throttle was about as obvious as it could get.

I retreated back to the bench and slumped down as a low rumble cut through the waves. The boat shuddered and heaved out of the water, ratcheting higher, rising back toward the yacht. We were no longer in control of the lifeboat.

We never were.

"Dammit!" Darren said, still working the lever—resetting it and slamming it down again and again as if it might lead to a different result at any moment. "Shit! Come on, you stupid thing! Work!"

The world blurred to a hazy sheen. The yacht was a cesspool I'd never escape no matter how hard I tried. Sure, we could leap into the ocean and let the tide carry us to our deaths, or tread water until we went hypothermic and drowned. Maybe, if we were lucky, we'd be killed by a shark or two before we got too cold. Or maybe they'd do to me and Darren what they'd done to Margaret—turn us into slaves and make us serve Xclivity members colorful drinks for the rest of our days.

A quick death seemed merciful by comparison.

The thought snuffed out as a shadow hurled past the lifeboat's windows, followed by a heavy splash. *Quinn?*

I rushed for the door and peered down through the opening.

"What was that?" Darren asked, pressing close.

"I think it was Quinn," I said, staring down at the still-rippling water. I couldn't see anything except the dark blue surface of the ocean lapping against the hull of *The Athena*.

Clonk, clonk, clonk. The gears churned and the steel arms rotated and swung the boat back into place alongside the yacht. Marco pushed through the doorway the second the boat came level with the deck, gun in hand, mouth in a grim line. "What the fuck were you two thinking? You're lucky I didn't shoot you, too."

I tried to conjure a response, but the words wouldn't come. All I could do was stare at the blood behind him, spattered all over the deck.

CHAPTER TWENTY-NINE

"Get out," Marco instructed, waving the gun at the door. I recognized the blocky, squared-off shape and compact barrel. A Glock 19, the same gun I often saw while training at the shooting range.

Darren stepped from the boat onto the deck first, and I followed with my head spinning. Bryce stood next to the door, waiting for us, a purple bruise blossoming beneath his ear. The sight made me feel slightly better. Chaz landed a blow, at least.

And then I remembered Quinn.

I swung toward Marco. "Where's my sister? What did you do to her?"

He crossed his arms and stared at me, his eyes as flat as two lead balls. When they angled left, toward the blood on the deck, and then the railing, a hot wave of grief flooded through me—and turned to rage.

I stepped toward him.

Hard metal pressed into my back.

"Don't even think about it," Bryce said. "Here's what's going to happen. We're all going to take a little walk, and you're both going to behave. No more running. No more games. Understand?"

I rotated toward him. "Bryce, what are you doing? We have to help Quinn. She might still be alive out there."

Something like pain rippled across the wet concrete of his face, a flicker of devastation before he clenched his jaw. "She's not." The concrete hardened. "She's dead thanks to you. You're the one who convinced her to run. She never would have done any of this on her own."

His words carved through me like a buzz saw. *Was it my fault?* I didn't know. He dipped his chin toward the pistol in his right hand. Another Glock. I wanted nothing more than to get my hands on it and open fire.

Marco shoved Darren. "Let's go."

We shuffled back into the yacht with its perfectly conditioned air and plush carpet; past a cinema I had yet to enjoy, spilling creamy light over a floor-to-ceiling screen; and into the glass-domed mezzanine overlooking the central staircase. A voice inside screamed for me to bolt, to tear down the stairs and make a break for it. Bryce hadn't restrained me, but I could feel him twitching with nervous energy, ready to pull the trigger. All he needed was an excuse, and I wanted to give it to him.

But where could I possibly go they wouldn't find me? And even if I *did* manage to evade these two assholes for a while, to somehow remain hidden, what would they do to Darren in the meantime?

What would they do to Alex and Chaz?

My vision swam with tears. I couldn't bear the thought of anyone else getting hurt on my account. Too many people had already. So, I followed their orders. I descended the stairs as ordered and zombied down a hall. The yacht felt cavernous and desolate—like we were strolling through a floating ghost.

"Take a right here," Marco said.

Darren stopped. "Why are you doing this?"

"Keep moving."

A scowl crept over Darren's face. "Wait until I tell my parents about this, you dick."

Marco grinned. "Yeah? You think I'll get in trouble?"

Darren opened his mouth to respond, but Marco took a step forward and slammed his fist into Darren's stomach before he could utter a word. Panic churned through my gut as he doubled over. I stepped between them and slung an arm around Darren's shoulders like it might protect him from any further abuse. He stood there for several seconds, fighting for air with a gob of spit swaying from his lower lip like egg white as I rubbed his back and said, "It's okay. I'm here."

Finally, after a series of shaky breaths, he straightened, wiped his mouth, and stared at Marco like he wanted to take a swing.

"Go for it," Marco said.

I placed my hand on Darren's arm and shook my head. "Don't. It's not worth it."

His eyes swiveled my way, the rage winking out when they met mine.

"That's what I thought," Marco said. "Now, move."

We trudged down a long hall and then descended another set of steps to the lower deck. The scent of solvent filled the air, of cleaning products and grease. Machinery vibrated the floor. The pulse of the engine thrummed somewhere behind the wall. Bryce ordered us to stop in front of a steel door with a heavy latch. Marco stepped past him and swung it open, then flipped a switch. A pair of LED tubes flickered to life above us, bathing shelves laden with bags of flour and sugar in a shower of antiseptic light.

Two figures were hunched in the corner with their heads reclined against the wall. One of them cupped a hand to his forehead and squinted at us. *Chaz.* The right side of his face was crusted in blood—a dark crimson waterfall that ran from beneath his forest of spiked hair all the way down to his chin. Alex sat next to him, his eyes ringed in black circles, both eyelids heavy and swollen along with the bridge of his nose. I winced. Just looking at him hurt.

"Get in," Bryce said, shoving me forward. Marco pushed Darren in next, and then we were both staring back at them as Marco slammed the door and killed the lights. I took a step back and nearly collapsed. It felt like standing in the middle of a cave.

"We need to find a way out of here," Darren said.

"There isn't one," Chaz replied.

"There has to be."

"There's not," Chaz said. "Believe me, we've already tried."

"He's right," Alex added. "This place is sealed tight. We're stuck."

"Shit," Darren muttered.

"Come over here," Alex said. "Follow my voice."

I snaked a hand out to orient myself, to feel for a shelf or a barrel to guide the way, and found Darren's arm instead. He laced his fingers with mine, and together we shuffled through the dark toward Alex. And then we sat. No one spoke. No one said a word. A fan kicked on overhead, clicking intermittently, the sound of metal scraping metal. The sound of madness. I didn't care.

All I could think about was my sister.

A sob bubbled behind my lips. I tried to bite it off and regain my composure, but it was no use. What was the point, anyway? Xclivity had us right where they wanted us. Scared and injured. Broken. Completely screwed. So, I didn't even try to hold the tears back. I sat there and let them come, ugly-crying in between gulping snatches of air.

I'm so sorry, Quinn ...

A hand squeezed my shoulder and brought me close. Fingers grazed my cheeks and thumbed my tears. "Hey, it's going to be okay," Darren said. "I promise."

"He's right," Alex added, setting a hand on my thigh. "We're in this together."

"I—he killed her," I managed to choke out. "He killed Quinn."

I felt Alex stiffen. "*What?* Who did?"

My voice faltered, and I had to pause for a second to collect myself. "Marco. She was trying to help Darren and me escape. She tried to save us, and Marco shot her. Then he ... he threw her overboard."

"Fuck ..." Chaz whispered. "Seriously?"

"Yes," Darren replied. "I saw it happen."

"Oh my god," Alex whispered, his voice pitching higher. "Holy shit. They're going to murder us, too." He rustled next to me and stood. Then he was slapping the walls and muttering to himself, throwing bags to the ground, the shelves clanging in the dark. "We have to get out of here. We *have* to! They'll kill us if we don't."

"We can't, genius. Remember?" Chaz said.

Alex didn't respond—I heard him fast-breathing, muttering, *shit! shit! shit!* as he continued to rattle around the room, banging away, until a sudden metallic crash silenced him. Then all I heard were his sobs.

"Are you okay?" Darren asked.

"I ... hit my head." His voice came out hollow, cracking as he made his way back toward us. "What are we going to do?"

"I knew I shouldn't have come on this trip," Chaz moaned. "Nothing good ever happens when I'm around my sister. I'm sure she had something to do with this. God, she sucks. We've never gotten along."

"Wait, you guys were having problems?" Darren asked. "Like what?"

Chaz laughed. "Isn't it obvious? We're like oil and water. Caprice drives me insane. She's never cared about anything or anyone but herself. I mean, why do you think she's an influencer? My parents have this dream we'll all be a happy little family someday if she and I can simply reconnect, but it's never going to happen. Especially after this. Besides, I'm pretty sure Alex is right that they're going to murder us."

Alex gulped and let out another sob.

"Not helpful," I snapped. "Saying shit like that won't get us anywhere."

Alex gave a tearful laugh. "It's okay. I shouldn't have come on this trip either. Literally just last night Liam told me I was holding him back. *Me*. Can you believe that? All I've ever done is support him. I dropped out of my MBA program at Northwestern so we could move to San Francisco. He said we needed to be where the tech companies were for his stupid app to succeed. So, I did it. I quit school because I believed in him. I even took out a loan to help him with the seed money. God, I'm such an idiot."

"No, you aren't," I said. "None of this is your fault."

"I don't know why I thought I could fix everything by proposing. I guess ..." He paused, sniffed. "I just couldn't let go of the idea of us, you know? I truly thought he was the one. I don't know what happened."

"Xclivity happened," Chaz said.

It was true. Chaz and Caprice's constant bickering, and the way Liam got a little too rough with Alex at times. Me and Quinn and our history of tragedy. All of us were tiptoeing through a relational minefield, trying not to step on a trigger. It couldn't be a coincidence. But what did it mean?

Only one person didn't fit.

I turned and peered through the black toward Darren. "What about you?"

"What about me?"

"You and your parents don't seem to hate each other, not like the rest of us."

"No," he agreed. "I guess not. Not in the same way, at least. To them, I'm more of a failure. A disappointment. Especially to my mother. I don't know if she's ever loved me, to be honest. I'm not sure if she even *likes* me."

"Why do you say that?" Alex asked.

"I don't know. All I've ever done is let her down. She wants me to take over Spark someday. But I'm not into the whole fitness thing like she and my dad are. It's not really my jam. I'd do anything besides selling supplements if I had the choice. Which I don't. They adopted me, raised me. They gave me a chance when I had nothing. I owe them everything."

A sour film coated my tongue. "Darren …"

He sighed. "It's why they brought me along. My parents think if I dive into Xclivity like they have, I'll come around. You know, if I just do enough yoga and meditate all the time, I'll become exactly who they want me to be."

At that moment, I wanted to tell him he'd never be who they wanted him to be because he didn't come from them. I wanted to tell him that Xclivity abducted him when he was too young to remember and murdered his real parents. But I couldn't. Not here. Not while sitting trapped in the middle of a storage closet with the panic level ratcheting higher by the second. What would telling him right now do except inflict more pain? More fear? So, instead I said, "Xclivity is into worse things than yoga and meditation. Way worse."

"I'm starting to believe that," Chaz said.

Alex groaned. "Seriously, what do you think they'll do to us?"

No one answered. No one said a word.

CHAPTER THIRTY

I dreamed of Quinn.

She floated beneath me in the water, her face cracking like porcelain, her skin peeling off in a sheath of delicate flakes. She held one hand outstretched toward mine, her voice drifting higher in an exhalation of bubbles. Questions that popped and fizzed in my ears.

Why did you give up on me?

Why did you turn me away?

I woke in tears to the clack of the door latch and a vein of light seeping across the floor. The others dozed beside me. I wondered how much time had passed. *Minutes? Hours?* In the dark, it was impossible to tell. Thirst raged at the back of my throat. I needed water in a serious way.

Light flared from the ceiling, and I snapped my eyelids shut to the afterimage of bleached muscle outlined in the door: a substantial torso and a thick neck, a head angled to the side in clinical observation. Marco maneuvered his bulk into the storage room as Bryce took position behind him, blocking the exit.

"Get up," Marco ordered.

"What time is it?" Darren asked.

"I said, get up."

We all struggled to our feet except for Chaz, who remained seated with his head reclined against the wall, pondering Marco with an impressive amount of disinterest.

"No."

"You sure that's the answer you want to give?"

"Fuck you."

Marco regarded him with a blank stare, then crouched and slammed his forearm into Chaz's trachea and held it there. Chaz came to life in a frenzied scrabble of motion. His hands clamped over Marco's wrist, and he attempted to dislodge the big man's weight. Marco leaned in harder in response. Chaz coughed and sputtered, his lips frosting blue, his cheeks bruising with color. A vein throbbed near his temple.

"Let him go!" I said. I wanted to drive my knee through Marco's teeth, steal his gun, and empty the clip in his chest. I wanted to gouge out his eyes and squash them beneath my feet for what he'd done to my sister. But I couldn't—not with Bryce eagle-eyeing me from the door, looking for an excuse to join the fun.

"You're going to kill him!" Alex added.

Darren edged closer. "Seriously, he can't breathe."

With a grunt, Marco rocked back on his heels, and Chaz rolled onto the floor and began hacking.

Marco stood and toed him with his shoe. "Still want to argue?"

"Asshole," Chaz said in a raw, cracking tone as he pushed to his feet.

"Call me whatever you want, but if you disobey me again, I'll break your arm. Now, let's go." He took Chaz by the shoulder and thrust him toward Bryce, who spun him around and bound his wrists behind his back with a thick plastic ring.

Bryce's eyes fell on me: "Your turn."

If there's one thing I've learned from my podcast, it's this: you never, ever let anyone bind you. You're dead the moment you do. Bound girls become dead girls, decorating the bottoms of ditches. You never comply. Make enough noise, put up enough of a fight, and someone will always call the cops. But that plan goes to shit when guns are involved and you're stranded in the ocean with no one to hear you scream. In that case, you comply.

I reluctantly shuffled over, my quads coming back online in a storm of pins and needles. Bryce pulled my hands behind my back and wound a zip tie around my wrists. He cinched it tight, and then did the same to Alex and Darren before waving all of us into the hall.

Alex frowned. "Where are we going?"

Bryce shoved him. "Walk."

We moved down the corridor and up the stairs, retracing our steps from earlier. We wound our way from the lower deck to the main deck, then from the main deck to the bridge. From there, we climbed higher still, taking the staircase to a level I had yet to visit. Marco paused in front of a frosted glass door and passed a key card over a scanner in the wall. It blinked green and the door slid open with a pneumatic *whoosh*.

Outside, a three-quarter moon hung suspended in a cloud

of stars. With no light pollution, they glittered savagely—a sea of diamonds scattered across a lush velvet sky. Normally, the sight would have stolen my breath, but tonight it only left me feeling cold. Out here, we were truly and utterly alone.

Behind us, the door latched with an ominous click.

A slight breeze scrubbed my arms.

The ocean lapped against the yacht in a gentle hiss.

A concentric glow rose from the floor of the deck, ribbons of light taking shape in the form of that lazy-eight curve I'd grown to hate—the infinity sign. My arms pimpled with gooseflesh as forms materialized behind it, long shadows unspooling down their faces in campfire fashion, dark pockets of black welling beneath their eyes. I counted five figures in total, all robed in white.

Julianna stood in the middle. Her raven hair fell to one side in an elegant braid, the strands threaded with jewels, her face relaxed, her hands clasped at her waist. To her right stood Kerry and Caprice with equally elaborate hairstyles—Caprice with her cheeks dusted in glitter, Kerry with eyes outlined in smoky eyeshadow. Tim and Liam were stationed to Julianna's left, their robes glimmering with silver brocade patterns. Infinity signs, of course, but there were also star shapes and other symbols I didn't recognize woven into the material.

No one moved. No one said a word.

A full body tremor ran through me. My knees filled with water. I didn't know what was about to happen, but I knew with certainty it wouldn't be good.

Finally, when the glow of the infinity symbol peaked, Julianna stepped forward and spread her arms, the sleeves of her robe swaying in the soft ocean breeze. "Hello, Olivia. Hello, Darren, Chaz, and Alex. I apologize for the way you've been treated the last few hours, but we had to take precautions for the safety of everyone aboard." Her face fell. "As you all know by now, we lost a very important member of our family today." She focused on me. "Olivia, I'm so sorry about what happened to Quinn. She was one of our rising stars. We had big plans for her. She will be missed."

No she wouldn't. I knew Quinn meant nothing to her. I heard it in her voice. She sounded no different now than she had while giving her yoga sermon on the beach. Calm, cool, and collected. Nothing but another fireside chat full of hot air.

"Just tell us what you're going to do to us," I spit, pissed, trying to cover my fear. "What is this?"

"*This*—" here Julianna pressed her palms together in reverence, and the others echoed the motion "—is the Transcension."

"Thanks," I said, "that really clears things up."

"Silence."

I followed the voice, and a flare of heat punched through my chest when I spotted Bryce. He'd donned a robe and joined the others, each line in his face looking like a knife cut, the slant of his eyebrows and his hard blue eyes weighted with rage. The way his teeth flashed behind his lips and his nostrils flared made him look like a bull ready to charge. I knew why: he blamed me for Quinn's death.

And I blamed *him*.

I stared at him with a fury of my own. I poured all of my hate into the gaze. For the first time in my life, I'd actually felt my sister surfacing, trying to connect. Not the synthetic, costumed version she'd displayed as a kid in order to gain my father's affection—the girl who smiled and laughed in all the right spots but never seemed at ease with the world or her place in it. Not the teenager my grandmother had abandoned and left fraying at the seams. And certainly not the secluded, bitter woman she'd turned into after, bent on self-destruction.

The *real* her.

The Quinn who'd made herself vulnerable, who'd turned to *me* to help her escape Xclivity and no one else. For a brief second, I'd seen a glimmer of what things could be like between us, the relationship we might have had. One freed from the weight of the past. A future spent supporting each other, of actually *being* there for one another through life's ups and downs despite all we'd lost. But no longer. Quinn was gone, all because Bryce and Xclivity had promised her a life full of pretty lies.

Alex strained against his zip ties, his face contorted in anguish. "Liam, why are you doing this? Tell them to let me go!"

Liam raised a single finger and placed it against his lips in response.

"Please, I know we've had our problems, but—"

Alex's head whipped back as Marco wrapped a strip of cloth over his mouth so tight, I expected it to saw through the corners of his lips. Marco glowered at the rest of us. "No one says another word."

No one did.

Julianna smoothed her robe. "We make this voyage only once every three years, when the moon's orbit synchronizes with the latitude and longitude of this very place. This alignment releases a tremendous amount of celestial energy, and that energy is focused here where you now stand. Welcome to Elysium, the purest energy vortex known to man."

Her words left me speechless. There was no question the woman had lost her mind.

Chaz rolled his eyes. "Awesome. Now let us go."

Marco backhanded him with a resounding smack.

Julianna continued. "Here, we can better connect with ourselves and with each other, as well as to a greater power. Some call that power God, some call it the universe. However you perceive it, there is a force at work here that is impossible to deny. You can feel it, yes?"

"Absolutely," Caprice chirped.

"It's incredible," Kerry said, tilting her head back so her face was bathed in starlight.

Bryce pulled the air in through his nose. "It's everywhere."

My legs were shaking. I swallowed an insane urge to laugh. *What the fuck?*

"It is," Julianna said, "and with this energy comes clarity. Here, one can slip free from the many entanglements preventing them from achieving their true purpose."

Liam nodded, the others murmuring sounds of assent. I suddenly felt dizzy with panic. This was all building toward something awful—I could feel it—and I wanted out before it started. My entire being was shrieking for me to get far, far away.

"Healthy relationships are essential to our wellbeing," Julianna said. "We need to surround ourselves with those who will lift us up and avoid those who tear us down. However, we often find ourselves in a position where—no matter how hard we try—we are unable to disconnect from unhealthy relationships. In those situations, we must extricate those people from our lives. We must *transcend* them."

She looked at Marco. "Please guide Alex into position."

My pulse thrashed in my ears. *Into position? What?*

Alex went rigid.

Marco took hold of his wrists and yanked him backward toward the edge of the deck.

My heart slammed against my ribs. *Oh, Jesus ... no.*

Julianna rotated toward Liam. "Liam Conrad, what I'm about to ask you to do," she appraised the rest of them, "what I'm going to ask of each of you to do, will be incredibly difficult. But I believe all of you possess the strength to rise to this moment. You wouldn't have been chosen if I didn't." She returned her attention to Liam, her face tranquil, her smile warm. "Liam Conrad, do you vow, from this point forward, to devote your mind, soul, and body to the tenets of Xclivity? Do you swear to strive for spiritual enlightenment at all times, and to uphold our shared vision of a better future?"

His head bobbed up and down, but his eyes were on Alex, his eyebrows knitting together in a way that made me think he was as confused as I was regarding what was about to happen.

"Yes."

"Will you dedicate your time, energy, resources, and focus to Xclivity and our cause above all else?"

Another nod. "I will."

Julianna continued: "Do you understand that with true commitment comes true sacrifice?"

"I do."

"Then take this moment to tell Alex how you truly feel. Hold nothing back."

Liam stepped past Julianna toward Alex. When he spoke, it was with the stiff cadence of an overly rehearsed speech. I could picture him practicing it in his stateroom mirror earlier, crooking his chin, trying to nail the inflection, the hand gestures. Give a little turn of the wrist here, pause for effect there. Make it dramatic. "Alex, for too long now, I've sacrificed my goals and dreams to make you happy. For too long, I've placed your needs above mine."

Alex's eyes narrowed.

"Lately, I feel like you're angry with me all the time. I can't do anything right. I travel for work too much. I spend too much money. I don't prioritize our relationship like I should. I treat you poorly in public, or get too angry, or seem too depressed." He paused and gave a weary shake of his head. "And I won't argue that some of those things may be true, but I have a *vision* for my life. A purpose. I want to leave my mark on the world before I'm gone, and I'll never be able to do that unless I have the freedom to explore my own path."

Liam looked back at Julianna, and she gave him a reassuring

smile. He squared his shoulders and continued, speaking with more confidence now.

"I didn't realize how much of my life revolved around making you happy until I joined Xclivity. From the day we met, I've done nothing but support you, and you've done nothing but smear my accomplishments and talk poorly about me behind my back."

A vein thumped along the side of Alex's neck. His face flushed and blazed red.

Liam crossed his arms. "I'm just tired, Alex—tired of *us*. I wanted things between us to work out, I really did, but after doing The Work, I realize it never will. I no longer want you in my life. You aren't healthy for me." Liam was saying this like Alex hadn't ended their relationship at lunch, acting like *he* was the one washing his hands of Alex.

Liam faced Julianna, and she gave him a glittering smile—the shape wide and warm. "Very good, Liam. True honesty is always difficult. That took a lot of strength."

"Thank you. I have to admit, I feel better now."

"That's wonderful. But you're not done yet."

Liam frowned. "What do you mean? Now what?"

Marco stepped behind Alex and swung open a gate in the railing, giving view to a dark panel of empty air.

Julianna's smile faded. "Now the two of you part ways."

CHAPTER THIRTY-ONE

Alex's eyebrows leaped toward his hairline. He took a step away from the yawning gap in the railing, only to be ripped back by Marco, who placed the barrel of the Glock against his temple.

Panic flooded my chest.

Alex's eyes filled with tears.

Liam stood there looking shocked, and a cold clarity filled me as I watched him, a realization that chilled me to the bone. I suddenly knew what the Transcension was. A test. No, more than a test—an exchange.

Murder someone, and you're in.

Murder someone, and they have collateral on you for life.

"Oh, darling," Julianna said approaching Alex. "The Transcension isn't something to fear. You needn't worry. Your journey doesn't end here." She ran her knuckles across Alex's cheek in a way that looked weirdly maternal. "This world isn't all there is. What waits for you beyond this plane is beautiful. Your energy will be everywhere. We are setting you *free*."

"Mmm!" Alex said through his gag, the tendons in his neck flaring. "Mm-mm-mm!"

Icy veins of terror slid down my back. I couldn't believe what I was hearing. It felt like I was watching an amateur stage play unfold in slow motion. I kept waiting for someone to call *scene* so we could all pack up and go home.

"Wait—" Liam stared at Julianna. "You want me to ... *kill* him?"

Julianna tilted her head like the question made no sense, like pushing Alex off the yacht in the middle of the ocean was the most reasonable request in the world. "That's such a crude word to use. There's no intention behind it. No deeper meaning. I don't want you just to kill him. What *I* want, Liam, is for you to liberate yourself from his toxicity. What *I* want is for you to grow into the strong, capable, and innovative leader you're meant to be. And, more importantly, I want *you* to take the next step in your growth with Xclivity. And this—" she gestured at Alex while offering Liam another beaming smile "—is the next step."

"I ... don't know ..."

Julianna's smile widened, giving her a manic look. The killer clown about to lunge with the knife. "Prove yourself to me, Liam, and you will be rewarded. We will fund your app. Nights like the one you talked about in Thailand will be commonplace. Sex. Money. Accomplishment. Your wildest dreams are all within reach. And know this. Alex won't be found. This will never be traced back to you. Elysium's currents are extraordinary. Anything that enters these waters simply vanishes."

Oh fuck. My mind splintered. My breath came in gulps and snatches. I had to get away, had to find a way out. But this situation wasn't the same as a trunk. There were no levers to pull, no magical buttons to push. I couldn't run, not out here in the open ocean. There *was* no way out.

Baby bird sounds crawled from Alex's mouth, indecipherable through the gag. He was openly crying now, weeping as Julianna fixed Liam with her tar-colored gaze. "You were instructed to invite the person in your life you felt was your shadow. The person who, for whatever reason, has prevented you from realizing your true potential."

She turned her attention to the others. "All of you were instructed to do this. And you have. Take a moment to look at them, to study them. To know who they are. We call this person your shadow because you carry them with you wherever you go. They weigh you down. They hold you back. They are always *there*, whispering that you aren't good enough or strong enough, that you aren't capable of achieving your dreams. And as long as you indulge them, as long as they remain in your life, you never will."

The statement hit me like a shotgun blast to the head.

I was a shadow. *Quinn's shadow.*

That was the real reason she'd invited me on this trip. I was an anchor preventing her from moving on with her life—the dark stain she couldn't scrub away, no matter how hard she tried.

But I wasn't her shadow anymore.

We *had* moved on, even if only for a few hours. *Both of us,* which meant Julianna's entire argument was bullshit, that she was bullshit.

"Your shadow is here for a reason," Julianna continued. "Have the last few days taught you nothing? These relationships are *not*

231

bonds to be salvaged. They are *not* redeemable. Their only purpose is to make you suffer." She paused, her face smoothing, going serene. "Which is why, to move forward, both with Xclivity and with yourself, you must scrub your shadow from your life. You must prove yourself worthy of happiness. And you must prove yourself worthy to *me*." She returned her attention to Liam. "So, Liam, I'll ask you one last time … are you worthy?"

Liam closed his eyes, then reopened them. He leaned toward Alex and whispered something into his ear. I didn't hear the words, but I saw their impact in the lines sprouting across Alex's face, and in the force of his tears. I heard them in the way he moaned through his gag, begging for his life. And I knew exactly what Liam was about to do.

Liam hung his head, raised his arm.

Oh, God.

And pushed.

Alex whipped backward, his eyes locking with mine for a millisecond before they disappeared. The splash that followed sounded like a boulder smashing through a sheet of ice. My heart stopped. I couldn't believe what I was seeing. He'd done it, Liam had actually done it. With his hands tied behind his back, Alex would drown. Alex, who'd planned a surprise engagement dinner for Liam, who'd *loved* Liam, who'd done everything for Liam, was *gone*.

"Oh, hell no!" Chaz shouted. "What the fuck, man!"

"This is insane!" Darren said. "We have to help him!"

"We have to go back!" I screamed. "We can't leave him behin—"

Fabric wound over my lips and cut me off. The taste of dirt and sweat filled my mouth as Bryce tied the gag. My stomach cramped. I fought against the sudden urge to vomit.

The Glock roared, and a blanket of silence fell over the group. Marco stepped forward with his gun held above his head, his eyes sliding from mine to Chaz's to Darren's and then back to mine. "All of you are going to shut the fuck up right now, or I'll kill you myself." He tilted his head toward Julianna. "Who's next?"

Julianna's gaze fell on Chaz.

His face went white. "No way," he said. "No fucking chance."

Marco placed the barrel of the Glock against his head. "Move or I shoot you."

Chaz moved.

"Caprice, step forward," Julianna ordered.

A vertical crease formed over the bridge of her nose. Her cheeks no longer blushed with color. She hugged herself and massaged the backs of her arms, her robe shimmering with the motion, rippling with moonlight. "I I can't do this. There's no way."

A crack slivered over Julianna's face—giving me a view of the dark chasm beneath, the madness waiting to swallow me whole. "You can and you will. You took an oath when you agreed to come on this trip. You knew a sacrifice would have to be made."

"Yeah," Caprice said, "but I didn't think it would be a *real* sacrifice! I didn't know you were being literal!"

A mad light danced in Julianna's eyes. She covered the distance between them in two steps and sunk her fingers into Caprice's hair, then jerked Caprice to within an inch of her face. Spit flew from Julianna's lips as she spoke: "Do you have any idea how many applicants I turned down for this trip? How many members of our family I rejected in *your* place, people who would kill for the opportunity to be here?"

Caprice shook her head. Acid boiled in my stomach. This was the real Julianna—the monster who'd forced Margaret to watch as her husband was murdered and her children were raised by strangers. I couldn't fully see it before, but I could see it now. And it filled me with terror.

Julianna wound her fingers deeper into Caprice's hair. "If you are to ascend in Xclivity, I need to know if you can be trusted. I need to know if you are worthy of the rewards. Are you worthy, Caprice? Do you belong?"

"Yes, Mother." Tears streamed down Caprice's face. She nodded and slithered out of Julianna's grip. Beads of sweat gathered near Chaz's temple as Caprice neared.

"Caprice," Chaz begged. "Please don't do this."

Don't do this, I echoed silently.

"Caprice, don't listen to this bitch! We're family! You're my sister!"

"Shut your mouth," Marco said, jabbing Chaz in the skull with the barrel of his Glock.

My eyes scoured the deck again for any possibility of escape, however thin—and saw nothing.

Caprice raised her hand, sobbing as she set it on Chaz's chest. "I'm so sorry, Chaz."

He went rigid, stiffening like her palm was a blowtorch.

Caprice looked back at Julianna. Julianna gave her a nod. "Do this, and the world will be yours."

This can't be happening, I told myself. *This isn't real.*

I screwed my eyes shut and imagined it—the slow, outward extension of Caprice's arm followed by Chaz tumbling for the water as gravity took hold. The awful splash that would follow.

The splash that never came.

I opened my eyes. Caprice's hand no longer rested on her brother's chest. It shivered at her side, instead, her fingers quivering. "I ... I can't do it."

"Oh, thank god," Chaz said, tilting his head toward the sky while blowing out a long sigh of relief. Tears snaked from the corners of his eyes.

Caprice brought her hands to her cheeks, crying and moaning more apologies. Julianna's face softened. She pulled Caprice into her arms and held her there, stroking her hair. "It's okay," Julianna said. "Not everyone has the strength."

"It's not right ..." Caprice let out another sob. "He's my *twin.*"

Julianna tucked a strand of hair behind Caprice's ear, thumbed her tears. "I know. I expected too much. You weren't ready for this."

Then, in a camera flash of motion, Julianna shoved Caprice past Chaz, off the yacht. Chaz's eyes bulged and followed her descent. He never had a chance to look back. Marco sent him after her, careening through the gap.

Splash! Splash!

I screamed into my gag. My eyes burned. I could hear them shrieking in the water, the sound about to make me retch.

Darren took a step toward his parents. "Are you guys going to do that to me? Have you lost your minds? Or are you going to let her kill all of us?" He paused. "Mom? Dad?"

"Bring him forward," Julianna ordered.

Marco snatched Darren's arm. Tim stepped in the way and took Marco by the shoulder. "Wait, hang on," he said, shooting an alarmed look at Kerry. "We can't do this. He's our son, for Chrissake!"

Kerry's gaze turned baleful. "No, he *isn't*. And you know that!"

Darren's eyes went wide with shock. He looked like he'd been punched in the face. "Mom ... why would you say that?"

"Take your hand off me," Marco growled at Tim.

Tim squared his shoulders and shook his head. "No—wait a goddamn minute. I'm not okay with this. Kerry, come on. This isn't us!"

Kerry straightened, her face firm. "It is. This is exactly why we're here."

He gawked at her, his brow collapsing. "No, it's asking too much."

"Marco, let Darren go," Julianna ordered, her voice icy. Her eyes were on Tim, her gaze hard. "We'll give Tim a few more minutes to decide if that's really the choice he wants to make. Escort Olivia into position."

Spots swarmed my vision. Fear spilled cold through my blood. I pressed against the wall of the yacht and shook my head. *No. Please, God, no.*

Marco released Darren and seized the collar of my shirt, then spun me around and dragged me backward.

Toward the railing.

Toward all that empty water.

Toward death.

My legs jutted and retracted, my feet trying to find purchase on the smooth boards of the deck that wouldn't come. Thoughts wheeled through my brain.

You aren't supposed to die.

Not here. Not like this.

Not after what you've already been through. What you've survived.

But I would, and I *knew* I would. Three people had already been murdered tonight. What was a fourth?

Marco forced me into position, my heels bracing empty air.

Julianna's voice slid toward me, flat and emotionless. "Olivia, you are an example of what happens when someone allows their shadow to remain in their life. Unfortunately, Quinn didn't learn that in time, and it cost her everything."

Her words filled me with a dull weight, and my throat knotted. She was right. I *was* Quinn's undoing. In Julianna's mind, I deserved this. And maybe I did.

The ocean slapped against the gunwale, black water and foam. The smell of salt hung in the air, the smell of death.

I could still hear Caprice and Chaz screaming in the distance.

I hung my head and braced myself, closed my eyes.

No way out. Not this time.

A shadow fell over my face.

I didn't need to look up to know it was Bryce. In his mind, I'd been the one to kill Quinn, who'd forced her to run. Not Marco. *Me.* So, who better than Bryce to take my life? Tears swam warm over my cheeks, a sudden, deep sadness welling within me.

I'm sorry, Quinn. I'm so sorry.

I refused to look up—I wouldn't give Bryce the satisfaction of watching me fall apart like this. He curled a finger beneath my chin and tilted my gaze higher.

I opened my eyes and my heart stuttered.

I couldn't breathe, couldn't speak.

Time slowed and came to a halt. It wasn't Bryce standing before me at all.

It was Quinn.

CHAPTER THIRTY-TWO

"Hello, Via," Quinn said.

I gawked at her, unable to believe what I was seeing.

Quinn was alive.

And not only was she alive, but she looked radiant with her hair styled into loose waves, her face shining and bright. Pendant diamond earrings hung from her ears, and her cheeks were freshly blushed. A silver necklace spilled over the neck of her robe, and her smile shimmered with lip gloss. Illuminated by the celestial light of the infinity sign, she looked like an angel—and maybe she was one—*because she died.*

Quinn plucked the gag from my mouth. Her eyes crinkled. "Did you like our little play?"

Play. I tried to process the word. My mind reeled as I struggled to keep up, struggled to understand what she was saying. And then her meaning hit me like a truck. She'd faked her death. Which meant—*holy fuck*—she'd faked *everything*. Her confession about Xclivity. The fight with Bryce. The scene in the sauna. The subterfuge to get the video. Our reconciliation.

All of it *faked.*

"You weren't supposed to see what happened to Carmela," Quinn continued. "After she got friendly with you, she just needed to disappear. Sure, I could have come clean when you wanted me to and sped all of this along, but that wouldn't have been *nearly* as fun as this. Seriously, you should see the look on your face right now." She rounded her lips into an O and popped her eyebrows in mock surprise. "It's fucking priceless!"

The others smirked behind her, all of them except for Tim, who looked like he was close to a heart attack.

"Wait—" I swallowed hard. "Is this a joke?" I knew how insane the question sounded, but I wanted to believe it so badly. I wanted Alex, Chaz, and Caprice to step through the door wrapped in towels, everyone chuckling and clapping at how they'd fooled me, telling me that I was on a hidden-camera game show, but the only one laughing was Quinn.

She blew out a breath that ruffled her hair. "No, this isn't a fucking joke. Although convincing everyone to play along took some work. They did wonderfully, though, don't you think?" Behind her, Bryce gave me a little turn of his wrist and took a mock bow. Marco grinned. I thought of the blood, of the *fake* blood, and whatever they'd thrown over the railing afterward in an imitation of Quinn's corpse. I thought of Bryce in his room, slapping Quinn, and Marco in the security office later, sitting at the desk with the flash drive winking up at him from the laptop—both of them knowing exactly where I was the entire time. Both of them fucking with me. I stood there reeling, my thoughts turning to a thick sludge, trying to understand why Quinn would do this. Which is what I finally said.

"*Why?*"

"Seriously?" Her expression flattened. "Why do you think? Why *would* I do this to you, Via?"

"Because of the money?" It was the only thing I could think of that made a sliver of sense.

Her nostrils flared with disgust. "No, not because of the money, although I knew about that, too."

"Why then?" I fired back. "What did I ever do to deserve this?"

Her features bunched, the corners of her lips going tight. "You were *born*."

I gaped at her.

"Mom and Dad weren't supposed to be able to have children. They weren't supposed to have *you*. *You* destroyed my entire life."

I strained against the zip ties. "That's ridiculous!"

"Is it? You took *everything* from me. My parents. My future. My whole fucking life!" Quinn clenched her teeth. "You don't know what I went through after Dad died. The things that happened to me in those foster homes, what the people there did to me. But you didn't have to worry about any of that, did you? No, for you, nothing changed. You just went off and lived your happy little life with Grandma."

My heart lurched. I wanted to tell her of course it changed, *everything* changed—I lost my father, too—but all I could do was stare as Quinn's eyes flickered back at me like guttered candles. "*That's* why I did this to you, Via. I wanted you to know what it feels like to think you have something real, only to have it all ripped away." Her face softened, and she shook her head, pulled in a breath. "None of this had to happen, though. Things would have been so much easier if you'd died years ago like you were supposed to."

Died years ago? What was she talking—

Time stuttered, and I felt the world shift. Sean ... she was talking about Sean.

My voice slid out in a whisper. "Oh my god ..."

The corners of Quinn's mouth tipped into a smile. "Now you're getting it."

"You knew him," I mumbled. "You knew Sean."

She knew, she knew, she knew ...

My *sister* tried to kill me.

"Of course, I did. I wasn't running with the best crowd back then. It wasn't hard to find someone as desperate as me. Sean was an idiot, though. He should have just shot you, but he couldn't get his hands on a gun. Criminal record and all that. Still, he convinced me it wouldn't be a problem. All he had to do was kill you and he'd get half of your inheritance. Simple as that."

"So, it *is* about the money," I said, still fighting for balance, struggling not to black out.

"Oh, it's about so much more than that, Via, but yes, I do want what's legally mine. What you and that bitch stole from me."

I heard her voice then, my grandmother's, whispering from somewhere near the back of my brain. *There's something wrong with Quinn.*

"I killed her, too, you know," Quinn said.

My eyes snapped up. "No, you didn't. She died of a heart attack."

Quinn's face darkened. "Because of me. After you refused to help me get back on my feet, I confronted her. Said I wanted what was mine. She told me I'd never see another cent. Said I was an embarrassment. A failure. Nothing like you. She even laughed at me, can you believe that? Actually snorted. But she didn't think it was so funny when I showed her the knife." Quinn made a gagging sound and placed a hand over her heart. "I only meant to scare her. But one look was all it took. *Bam*, heart attack. That was convenient."

"And then you came for me," I muttered.

"Yes, but you had to go and survive and start that stupid podcast of yours. Killing you became so much harder after that. Too many people watching. Too risky to try again so soon. Too suspicious. But it gave me enough time to get my shit together and do it right this time. To get you out here."

"They'll find you," I hissed. "My listeners will never let you get away with this."

"I doubt that. I'm your number-one fan, remember? I wasn't lying when I said I've listened to every episode. You didn't tell anyone where you were going, did you? Too embarrassed to admit you were off to see your train wreck of a sister."

I told Nina, I thought, holding on to that shred of hope like a lifeline.

Quinn shrugged. "Even if someone does start asking questions, I'm not worried. Xclivity has a way of making situations like these disappear."

"We are very talented in that regard," Julianna said.

I stared at her. "Why are you helping her? Why do you care?"

"You really haven't figured that out yet? With your background?" She gave me a pitiful shake of her head and clucked her tongue. "I care because Quinn is my daughter."

A weightlessness took over my body. A feeling like falling.

I studied her and saw it, Julianna's slender nose, and her upturned eyes, her prominent cheekbones and narrow chin. Her features were so similar to Quinn's, I didn't know how I'd missed it. Everything the *same, same, same.*

I struggled to remain upright, to breathe.

"Finding her wasn't easy," Julianna said. "The state took her from me when I was just a girl. I was proud back then. Foolish. I made mistakes, and I paid for them dearly. But nothing hurt as much as losing my daughter. That truly destroyed me. I spent years looking for her." Her eyes hardened to stone. "And when I found her, when I *finally* saw what she'd become, I knew she needed me in her life. She had to be reborn. It was the only way."

Reality wavered. I tried to speak. My voice lodged deep in my throat.

Julianna's glare deepened. "If I hadn't given her purpose, she'd be gone."

"And what's that?" My voice felt like sandpaper on my tongue, like someone else was speaking. "Murdering innocent people?"

She surveyed the boat and smiled. "Xclivity, of course. Restoring my daughter was *my* purpose. Giving her Xclivity is how I broke my pride. This family is hers now, and she has become its rightful Mother. I made her the Architect weeks ago. Nothing about this trip is my doing."

Quinn's in charge, I thought dimly. *She's been in charge this entire time.*

"This was what Quinn needed to move past her trauma," Julianna continued. "Removing you from her life is the only way she can fully heal."

Fresh tendrils of panic wound around my ribs, my heart dropping as I turned back to her. "Take the money, Quinn. I'll give it to you. To *all* of you. Just let me go!"

Quinn shook her head with a laugh. "Right, so you can play the victim *again* and spill everything on your podcast? Paint me as a lunatic to your listeners while you smear Xclivity to anyone who will listen? No, I don't think so. It will be easier for everyone—but me, mostly—if you simply disappear."

My fear transformed to rage. The only family I had left in this world, my *sister,* had never intended on giving our relationship a chance. She'd simply meant to turn me into her personal whipping post in order to exact her misplaced revenge. I flexed against the zip ties. I wanted to tear them off and wrap my fingers around her slender neck and squeeze until I'd crushed all of the delicate bones within. I wanted to claw her eyes out.

"Get it over with, then," I said. "What are you waiting for?"

"Nothing now."

I tipped my head toward the sky as she raised her hand.

Fuckyoufuckyoufuckyou!

Then snapped my head forward and drove it straight into her chest.

Lightbulbs flashed behind my eyes. My vision smoked. A hand reached for me through the haze—Marco, attempting to seize my arm—but I was already moving, pounding past Quinn as she toppled with a wail, racing across the deck. Hands reached for me, arms went wide. I bowled through them all, planted my foot on the bench near the railing ... and leaped over it with a cry.

The world went silent as I whipped through the air.

Snatches of color flashed around me.

White, black, silver, white, black, silver.

The wrong colors, all of them racing past. And then I saw it—the hue I was looking for. A square of *blue*. I twisted for it, flung my legs sideways, and arched my back.

But not far enough.

My wrist shattered the second it hit the deck, pain like fire tearing up my arm as the rest of my body smacked into the pool. So much pain—pain everywhere. All I knew. A ring of molten agony devouring my arm, blowtorch hot.

My eyes snapped open.

I hung suspended in liquid.

Bubbles poured from my throat in a chlorinated scream.

With it came a thought: *Move!*

My wrist ground like a loose bag of marbles as I pulled my thighs beneath my arms, followed by my knees and feet. And then my hands were in front of me, gloriously in front of me as I slammed my feet against the bottom of the pool and hurtled for the surface.

Air flooded my lungs, and the night came to life in a manic array of images and sounds. Quinn's wailing, anguished cries. Voices shouting, roaring from above. Figures racing to the edge of the deck and peering down. One of them pushed to the front, and I caught a glimpse of a face with a dimpled chin: Bryce, carrying a gun. A shout rang out as he raised it, a form slamming into him from behind.

Darren.

The gun flew from Bryce's hand and fell over the railing, hitting the deck a few feet from the pool. Darren arced over the railing next, and hammered into the water a second later, the crown of his skull missing the side by less than an inch.

More shouts, Quinn still screeching and sobbing, Julianna howling, "Get them! Shoot them already!"

Go! A voice cried in my head.

Splinters of fire tore up my arm as I pushed myself toward the stairs. My pulse hummed in my ears. Darren appeared in front of me, gasping, sputtering and coughing as he levered himself out of the water and his feet caught the deck.

"Shoot them, you idiot!" Julianna shrieked at Marco.

I followed, crouching to grab Bryce's gun with my good hand—and then we were running, bullets raining down from overhead. The doors exploded as we ducked inside the ship. Time ground to a halt. I hesitated, unsure where to turn, what to do.

What do we do? I thought. *Whatdowedowhatdowe—*

Darren's features slid through the panic, his eyes bulging, his hair matted to his forehead in brown streaks. He was shouting at me, yelling, "Olivia, come on! We have to hide!"

Hide. He was right—we did, and I suddenly knew *exactly* where to go.

CHAPTER THIRTY-THREE

We blew into the room as the first alarm sounded. Three ringing blasts followed by an announcement: "All staff return to your rooms and remain there until further notice. All staff remain in your rooms."

I pocketed Margaret's key and slid down the door to the floor, too stunned to move. The Glock slipped from my hand. A pulsing red light wept beneath the door as the mechanical voice continued to blare, repeating the message in different languages, Spanish and Italian and what sounded like Mandarin.

I wasn't sure, and I didn't care.

She played you. This entire time she was playing you.

Seven. Fucking. Years.

I closed my eyes. My pulse splashed across the backs of my eyelids, painting them in lucid red webs with every beat. My ruined wrist thumped beneath the Xclivity bracelet in an unending chorus of agony.

Bum, buh-bum, buh-bum.

I bit my cheek, still trying to comprehend my sister's treachery. All the years of therapy, of PTSD and trauma. All those nights waking up to the feeling of Sean's fingers squeezing the air from my throat. This trip—and my belief that my sister had changed, that our relationship actually stood a chance ...

All of it wasted, wasted, wasted.

I forced my eyes open. Margaret's uniforms hung in a neat row in the closet, and her toiletries still lined the sink of the small bathroom. Nothing had changed since she'd disappeared, which was good. The locked and empty room of a dead woman would be the last place they'd think to look for us. We'd been careful to avoid the cameras, to stick to the blind spot. They wouldn't find us in here. At least not right away.

Darren sat on the edge of the bed, rocking in place, his eyes two hollow pits of despair, his face scrubbed of color. Like me, he was in shock—only he didn't know it.

"All staff remain in your rooms."

I stood and stumbled to the desk and retrieved a pair of scissors, then made my way to the bed. "Let me see your hands."

Without looking up, he twisted to the side, and I snipped the zip tie.

I handed him the scissors. "My turn."

He took them, and his mouth fell open. "Holy shit, Olivia, your hand."

I forced myself to look. My wrist was plump with blood, my thumb curving inward at an awkward angle, the knuckle shifting laterally half an inch. My palm and forearm carried the angry purple-black of a storm cloud threatening rain. It made me swoon with vertigo, my stomach doing flip flops in a way that made me want to puke.

I glanced away. "Just cut it."

"Okay. Hold still," he said, positioning the scissors. The blades snipped, and a bolt of lightning flashed through my wrist, a hot, searing anguish that made me hiss. Tears threatened to spill from the corners of my eyes, but I couldn't cry, couldn't distract myself from what I really needed to do, which was to think.

What do we do now? How do we get away?

My brain felt like wet concrete. No answers came.

I plopped down on the bed next to Darren, exhausted. He stared into his lap and shook his head. "I've always known my mom didn't love me. But I didn't think …" He rubbed his eyes with his forefinger and thumb, let the words trail off, then started again. "My entire life I've tried to please her. To make her proud of me. But I've never been good enough for her. And I don't even know *why*."

"I do," I whispered.

He snapped his gaze my way, his eyes narrowing in a squint. "What?"

I steeled myself. I still didn't want to tell him about Margaret—not *here*, not like *this*—but I didn't know how much time we had left, and whatever happened to us, he deserved to know the truth, to know that he was loved. *Truly* loved. "Darren, the only reason you wound up with Tim and Kerry was because Xclivity forced them to raise you."

He recoiled. "*What?* Why would you say something like that?"

I stood and retrieved the photo sitting on the desk and handed it to him. "Because *she* told me."

He took the picture and studied it, his brow constricting. "Who are these people?"

"That's Carmela. But her real name is Margaret Vallejos. The girl in the picture is Elena. And the boy is Diego. Darren ... do you recognize him?"

He shook his head. "No."

A thought blazed, something I'd noticed about Darren on the first day of the trip, when he'd saved me from tumbling into the water. "Look at his hand," I said. "At the birthmark under his thumb."

Darren analyzed it for a long moment, then looked up, startled. "Why am I in this picture?"

"Because Margaret is your mother. Your *real* mother. And that girl is your sister."

He opened his mouth to speak, then shut it and turned his attention back to the photo. His eyes clouded, his lips pressing together. I knew the look. I'd seen it painted on Quinn's face dozens of times growing up. Those rare moments when her mask slipped, and I caught her staring at our family portrait in the hall, trying to puzzle out if she fit with us, if she belonged.

He ran his palm over his face and shook his head. "She can't be. My mother's ... dead. She died in Guatemala a few years after I was born."

"Tim and Kerry lied to you just like my sister lied to me."

"But why would they do that? What's the point?"

"To punish your mother. Xclivity is evil as shit. They recruit vulnerable people and take advantage of them. They brainwash them to do terrible things. Margaret found out about that and tried to stop them. Not Xclivity, but the group they were before this. She was an attorney, Darren. A state prosecutor. She was going to shut them down, so, they abducted her. They had to keep her quiet. You and your sister were their insurance policy." I returned to the desk and opened the drawer. Margaret's letter to Darren was sitting underneath a note pad, still tucked in the same envelope she'd tried to hand me. I retrieved it and passed it to him. "She wanted me to give you this."

He stared at it and swallowed hard, then took it. "This is all so insane."

"I know. An hour ago, I thought my sister was dead."

His eyes locked with mine. "That was beyond fucked up. I'm sorry."

"So am I."

He returned his attention to the envelope and took a breath. "I should probably read this now. I don't think we're getting off this ship."

Only if they throw us off. I couldn't stop the thought, couldn't change the channel in my head fast enough before the images flashed: Alex toppling backward off the yacht, Caprice and Chaz pinwheeling through space toward that flat sheet of dark water— all of them left behind to drown. And we'd be next if we didn't come up with a plan.

"We will," I said, crouching to grab the gun. "We won't give them a choice."

He eyed the Glock with suspicion. "Do you even know how to use that thing?"

"Yes, I—"

We heard the footsteps at the same time, muffled by the alarm. "Get in the bathroom!" I hissed. "Go!"

He moved as I aimed the gun, aligning the sights at the door. I exhaled in an attempt to slow my heart rate. Years of practice told me if I didn't, I'd miss. And I couldn't afford to miss.

The lock clicked.

The door swung wide.

Marco stood before me, his eyes glinting first with recognition and then with shock. I squeezed the trigger smooth and slow, like I'd been taught. The gun exploded and Marco flew backward, his hand crashing to his sternum. A deep choking sound rose up his throat, followed by a wet, strangled croak that let me know I'd hit him square. The choking sound grew wetter and then shifted higher into a laugh. The corners of his lips tilted into a grin, and he pulled his hand from his shirt. His impossibly clean, impossibly white shirt, not a drop of blood anywhere.

My head spun. I pulled the trigger two more times. *Bang! Bang!*

Marco didn't move, just stood there, grinning. *How?*

The answer hit fast and hard, and I knew: I cursed myself for not checking the magazine. The weapon in my hand was loaded with blanks, a prop used in Quinn's little stage play from earlier. *Fuck.*

"Wrong gun, bitch." His smile rounded into a scowl. "Play time's over." He stepped forward, pulled his Glock from the holster, and leveled it at my head.

A bright slash of metal arced toward his wrists.

The gun discharged as it fell from his hands.

My eardrums exploded with a high, piercing *rhee!*

The length of metal retraced its path and whipped straight into Marco's chin. His teeth clacked. Darren brought the rod back—a towel bar, I realized—then swung for the fences. Marco was ready. He stepped into the swing, and the bar caught him on the shoulder, Marco uncorking a vicious right hook at the same time.

But I was no longer watching.

I grabbed Marco's gun from the floor and replaced it with mine as Darren crashed into the wall and crumpled to his knees. Marco spun around and snatched the gun off the floor and leveled it at me.

He fired.

The room exploded, the sound concussive.

His brow bunched in confusion. It was my turn to smile. "Wrong gun, *bitch*."

He lunged.

I pulled the trigger.

We went down together, my wrist igniting with pain the second we hit the floor. Marco's face hung an inch from mine, saliva threading off his bottom lip, his blood seeping through his shirt, warm and sticky. He grunted and brought a hand to my neck, his fingers trembling as they gripped my throat.

But I knew he wouldn't squeeze.

He was already dead.

With a final breath, his eyes went dark and his head thudded onto my chest. I planted my legs against the wall and pushed out from beneath him, then rushed to Darren. He was lying on his back with his head cranked to the side, his eyes darting beneath his eyelids like little minnows. I ran my knuckles across his forehead and traced a finger over his ear. "Hey, you okay?"

He moaned and raised a hand, blinking several times before his eyelids peeled open. "Shit, that hurt."

"I bet. He got you pretty good."

He flashed me a painful grin. "Yeah, but at least I got him first."

"You saved my life."

"And you just returned the favor." With a grunt, he pulled himself off the floor and reclined against the wall, winced. "How'd he find us so fast?"

The question sparked a memory—Bryce locating me after I fled the swamp, just happening to be *right there*, waiting for me, ready to steer me back to the ship. And then Marco coming *here*, mere minutes after we'd rushed downstairs into the staff quarters, avoiding the security cameras the entire way.

How?

Darren rubbed his temple and groaned. His bracelet flashed ... and I knew. *The bracelet. Of course. It was so obvious.* I thought of the surveillance dead spot in the lobby. Even if the security cameras didn't catch you, the bracelets would. The bracelets turned us into a pair of walking GPS coordinates. The thought left me shaken, queasy: *This is how they knew you spoke with Margaret, Olivia. You're the reason she's dead.*

No. I couldn't go there. Not now.

Not if we were going to get out of this in one piece.

"This is how," I said, pointing at my bracelet. "They've been tracking us this entire time."

Darren groaned. "Shit. We're so screwed."

As if on cue, a squelch of static came from Marco's jacket, followed by a voice I recognized as Bryce's: "Marco ... Marco, come in. Have you located them yet?"

"Maybe not," I replied, still staring at the bracelet, noticing the crack from the fall for the first time. I looked up, a sliver of hope running through me. "I need you to break it."

Darren looked at me like I'd lost my mind, like I'd reached through his skull and pulled the fire alarm in his head. But I knew he could get it off. Even with the swelling. He'd just need to twist the bracelet hard enough and it would snap.

He shook his head. "But your wrist ... there has to be another way. We have a gun. Why don't we march up there and force them to dock the ship?"

The walkie-talkie squelched again. "Marco, are you there?"

"We can't," I said. "They'll know we're coming with these on. We wouldn't stand a chance. Which is why I need you to get this damn thing off me right now. I have a plan. It'll work."

He massaged the bridge of his nose, nodded. "Fine. Okay." He gently set his fingertips on the metal and began rocking the band back and forth with tender movements. The shattered bones of my wrist ground together like gravel. Waves of agony radiated up my arm. A thin line of sweat leaked from beneath my hairline.

"Stop," I wheezed. "*Stop*. You can't do it like that. You need to snap it. Twist it as fast and hard as you can."

He looked at me, his face flooding with concern. "Are you sure? I don't want to hurt you."

Was I? I'd run my entire life. Running was what I did best. From the memory of my mother. From what that did to my father. From Sean on the road that day, and after he'd died, from his ghost. And Quinn—I'd run from her for as long as I could remember. I was running from her now.

And I was *done* running.

"Yes," I hissed. "Do it."

He wiped his hands on his shirt and then took hold of the bracelet once more. His fingertips felt like soldering irons on my skin, my wrist throbbing like a bomb about to explode.

"Okay," he said. "Here we go."

I took a deep breath and ground my teeth together.

He twisted, and the bracelet snapped.

I screamed.

CHAPTER THIRTY-FOUR

They came with knives.

There were four of them: Bryce, Liam, Kerry, and Quinn. They stood outside the door to the crew galley on the lower deck, whispering to each other in their robes. The blades they gripped were wicked-looking things that curved like hawk beaks from their fists. Bryce held something else—a canister I recognized from the security room.

Tear gas.

Quinn edged toward the swinging door, crouched, and cracked it open. "Olivia, we know you're in there, and we know you have Marco's gun. We're not coming in, and I know you won't come out, so let's save everyone a lot of trouble and talk this out."

She leaned back and gave Bryce a grin. He returned it with one of his own, another shared ruse. Even now, after everything that had happened, they were still eager to make a game of slaughtering us—a fun little distraction to indulge in before returning to their lives of luxury.

"Darren, listen to Quinn, honey," Kerry chirped in a voice I guessed was her attempt to sound motherly, her tone high and light. "We really do just want to talk. We're not here to hurt you."

"Yeah, we're sorry for earlier," Liam added. "That was ... unfortunate."

Yes, I thought. *It would have been so much simpler if we'd jumped into the ocean.*

Bryce cleared his throat. "Listen, you've both proven yourselves to be resourceful individuals, and we're impressed. We've decided that Xclivity would be stronger with both of you as members. If you slide the gun out now, I will personally guarantee your safety. You will be one of us. You have my word that no harm will come to you."

I rolled my eyes. *This fucking guy.*

"Ready?" he mouthed to Quinn, then to Kerry and Liam. They tightened their grips on the knives and nodded. He moved to pull the pin from the canister as I stepped out of the utility closet behind them and cleared my throat. They startled and whirled in tandem, gaping first at me, and then at the Glock.

Quinn paled. Kerry gasped. Liam took an unsteady step back.

"How did you ..." Bryce started, then trailed off when his gaze landed on my bare wrist. My Xclivity bracelet was inside the kitchen with Darren.

"Surprise, asshole," I said. "Drop the canister and kick it over. The rest of you do the same with the knives."

No one moved. Bryce squared his shoulders like he was still in charge.

My wrist throbbed, and I grimaced. It was white hot, boiling with pain.

Bryce noticed, too.

He lunged for me, moving fast—but not fast enough.

I shot him in the leg, and he went down like a cartoon character, spinning a half circle before hitting the floor. The others recoiled, Liam spouting off a panicked, "Holy shit!"

Quinn knelt with a screech and pressed her hand to the wound. Blood bubbled between her fingers. When she looked up at me, her eyes were blistered in hate. "I'll kill you for this!"

You've already tried, I thought miserably. I gripped the gun harder. "Give me your knife, Quinn." I blinked toward Liam and Kerry. "All of you. And the tear gas."

They kicked them over.

I turned my attention to Bryce. "So, you were going to what, smoke us out? Blind us so you could stab us to death?"

His eyes turned to chips of ice. "What now?"

"Now we go into the kitchen. All of you. Liam, help Bryce up."

"He *can't* stand," Quinn said, her face smeared in shock. "Not like this."

"She's right," Kerry said. "We need to stop the bleeding."

I ignored them and turned toward Liam. "Help him up, or I'll shoot you, too."

Liam shrank back a step and flashed his palms. "Okay, okay, go easy."

"Wait, just give me a minute," Quinn said. She leaned forward and unlaced one of Bryce's shoes then knotted the shoelace around his thigh a few inches above the bullet wound. He grimaced and pounded the floor with a fist.

"Shit, that hurts!"

"I know, baby," Quinn said. "I know. It's okay, I'm right here." She nodded at Liam. By the time he got Bryce to his feet, Bryce's hairline was leaking sweat.

"Move," I ordered.

They pushed through the kitchen doors. Bryce limped between Liam and Quinn with a steady stream of blood leaking from beneath the hem of his linen shorts. Darren stood to the side, near the sink, watching them pass. Kerry hesitated when she reached him. "Darren, I—"

"Is it true?"

"Is what true?"

"That my mother—my *real* mother—was on this ship?"

Her face buckled in mock confusion, then went blank. "I don't know what you're talking about."

His jaw firmed. He took a step closer. "Don't lie to me. For once in your life, will you *please* cut the shit and tell me the fucking truth? Is that so hard to do? Was she on this ship?"

Kerry gave a reluctant tilt of her head followed by a sigh. "Yes."

"And she's dead?"

Another nod.

"How could..." Darren trailed off and gazed over her shoulder, staring at nothing for a long second before looking back. When he spoke, his voice teetered on the edge of a cliff, threatening to plunge into a canyon of grief. "How could you do this to me?"

"I didn't have a choice."

He went rigid. "Of course, you did! Isn't that exactly what you taught me growing up? That my life is the result of the choices I make? That we *always* have a choice?"

Kerry's eyes ticked lower. "Not when it comes to Xclivity."

"You're such a hypocrite. Jesus." The anger melted from his face, the hurt rising now, threading through his voice in undulating waves, his eyes glazing with tears. "Did you ever love me? Did you care for me at all?"

Her face creased, her lips pulling tight. "We gave you a good life. You had everything you needed."

"That's not what I asked."

"He's fading," Quinn said, staring at Bryce. He'd gone pale. Colorless, his eyes unfocused, his chest moving faster, his head wobbling in a struggle to remain upright. "We need to get him to a hospital."

"Olivia, please," Liam said. "He could bleed out."

"What about Alex?" I asked. "Should we get him some help, too? Maybe make a quick call to the Coast Guard? See if they could fish him out of the ocean and give him some CPR? Maybe pick up Chaz and Caprice along the way while they're at it?" I shook my head. "No, Bryce can wait. We're going to turn this ship around and look for the people you tried to murder first. And you better pray we can find them or you're going to have way more to worry about than Bryce." I returned my focus to Kerry. "Now answer the question. Did you love him?"

She ran a hand over her face, sighed. "I wanted to. You were a difficult child, Darren. You were so … different from me. A dreamer who never followed the rules. Xclivity placed you in my life to break me of my selfishness, and I resented you for it. I'm ... sorry."

"Are you?" A small muscle twitched beneath his eye, the anger welling again, slicing through the hurt. "Did you and Dad raise me so you could ..." he looked away and swallowed, looked back. "So you could kill me?"

A flicker of emotion flashed across Kerry's skeletal features—something like regret. It was the first time I'd seen the woman look like an actual human. "No. They didn't tell us what we'd have to do on this trip."

"But you *knew* you'd have to do something, right? Something terrible?"

She paused, swallowed. "Yes."

Darren drug a hand through his hair. "Fuck—who are you? Who am I? I don't even know. But I had a chance to figure it out, and you took that away from me." He was breaking now, coming apart at the seams. "Don't worry, though, *Kerry*. You got your wish. I'm dead to you. And you're dead to me."

He angled across the room toward the large metal door stamped in the center of the far wall and flung it open. Liam stared at the dark room, dazed—a dry storage similar to the one they'd locked us in earlier. "You're not putting us in there."

"That's exactly what we're doing," Darren replied.

"Wait," Bryce said, sucking a jagged breath in through his nose. "Listen, we can work something out, Olivia. There's no need to be rash. We've ... all made mistakes. We—we can fix this. What ..." He swallowed, struggling to get the words out. "What do you want?"

I let loose a shocked laugh. I couldn't help it. I'd studied narcissists before. My podcast was littered with men who believed they were the earth's axis, that the entire world revolved around them. But the fact Bryce thought I'd actually listen to him at this point was ludicrous. Beyond ludicrous. He could rot in the storage room for all I cared. "Seriously? You're bargaining now?"

"We can provide you with as much funding as you need," he continued. "We can turn your podcast into a brand, an entire network! Seriously, think of all the good you could do with that kind of reach, all the people you could save." He glanced at the open door, real fear in his eyes now, his normal self-assuredness gone. "Let's make that happen."

"He's telling the truth," Quinn added. "We can start over."

"Oh my god! Don't you get it? You're not in control anymore, Quinn. Neither are you, Bryce. None of you are! Now, shut up and get inside or I'll shoot every one of you." I looked at my sister as I said it. "Except for you. You're coming with us."

Quinn blinked. "Wait, what? I'm not leaving Bryce."

"Yes, you are."

"I won't. Go ahead and shoot me. I don't care. But I'm not going anywhere without him." She held my gaze, her eyes burning bright with defiance, two blazing green suns. I knew that look, and I believed her. She wouldn't go.

"Okay, fine." I turned the gun on Bryce and curled my finger over the trigger. "I guess I'll have to make the choice for you then."

The fire in her eyes snuffed out. She stepped in front of him and raised her hands. "Wait, *wait*. Don't. Please. I'll come, okay? I'll come."

CHAPTER THIRTY-FIVE

Quinn walked between Darren and I, with Darren in the lead and me following behind. She couldn't run this way, couldn't escape, not that she'd make it far with the barrel of the Glock centered between her shoulder blades.

Or maybe she would.

I still didn't know if I could shoot my sister. Even with the river of rage pouring through my bloodstream, I didn't know if it would be enough to pull the trigger. I wasn't like her. Killing others didn't come naturally to me.

"Where are we going?" she asked.

I didn't answer. I couldn't. The pain was too much to bear. Each step I took set off miniature earthquakes in my wrist, the rubble there clicking and scraping in a way that made me sick. My entire body felt like a demolition site: every inch of it bruised and broken. I wanted to stuff my mouth with a handful of Oxys and wash them down with a bottle of vodka. I wanted to black out and forget every awful memory I'd made over the last few days. I wanted to rewind time and decline Quinn's anthrax-frosted invitation the moment it popped up in my email.

Hey, Via! How are you?
Delete. Delete. Delete.

I put one foot in front of the other. Quinn bobbed in front of me in a walking smear of strawberry-colored hair and graceful movement. Even traumatized, she moved like a model.

We trailed through the atrium and climbed the stairs, the alarms still throbbing with red light every few feet, reminding us that things were no longer normal, that the ship had indeed lost its equilibrium.

So had I. I still couldn't believe Quinn had sent a man to kill me. And when that failed, had tried to do it herself. My sister. My *family*, who was never really my family at all. It was a wound I knew I'd never overcome.

Stop, I told myself. *Don't think about it.*

There would be plenty of time to process everything later, once I got off this boat. But first, we needed to take control of the ship, turn it around, and try to find Alex, Chaz, and Caprice. To do that, we'd need to move fast, which meant we'd need the master key Quinn used to open the security office earlier. That way there wouldn't be any locked doors to contend with.

Quinn glanced back as we entered the corridor leading to her room, her face hanging in a half-moon glimmer over her shoulder, her green eyes sparkling fiercely. "Why are you taking me to my room?"

I said nothing.

"You can't keep them in there forever."

Them when she really meant *him*. A dark web of despair

spread through my chest. All I'd ever wanted was for Quinn to love me like that, or even to like me. Just once. Just for a moment.

"Olivia, Bryce will bleed to death."

She was right. He would, but not as soon as she expected. I wasn't an expert on human biology, but I once interviewed a woman who'd survived multiple stab wounds and lost two liters of her blood before getting help. She'd survived, and so would Bryce most likely. Either way, he would provide me the leverage I needed to get the key.

"It's the next room on the left," I said to Darren.

He looked back at me with a face carrying the dull sheen of pavement, all the light gone. His calm and easy demeanor now tilted toward something darker, courtesy of Xclivity, and I hated them for it.

"They'll find you, you know," Quinn continued. "Even if you make it off the ship, you'll never be able to escape. We're only one small branch. Xclivity is everywhere. You have no idea how powerful some of their members are."

"Just open the door."

She folded her arms over her chest. "Bryce has the key."

I shook my head. "You're wasting time."

"And if I don't?"

"If you don't, we'll stand here until Bryce bleeds out."

Her eyes closed in defeat. She reached into her robe and retrieved the card. The lock chimed and blinked green. We entered the room.

"Hello, Darren. Hello, Olivia. Please, come in."

I froze as Julianna's voice filtered through the air like a wisp of smoke. I couldn't see her. But I *could* see Tim bound to a chair with an electrical cord near the sofa, coils of it digging into his chest and arms. His head lolled to the side, his eyes set deep within their sockets, his face ashen, features worn. Bile burned up my throat. The man looked like he'd aged ten years in a single hour.

My stomach clenched when I saw why.

His fingers flowered from the armrests in two bouquets of broken bones. They splayed in unnatural angles, some snapped to the side, some backward. His fingertips were plump with blood, both thumbs swollen beyond recognition. My wrist looked awful, but Tim's hands looked like the aftermath of an atomic bomb eruption in comparison. I didn't know how the man was still conscious.

"Dad!" Darren gasped, angling toward him.

"Stop," he wheezed. "Don't ... don't come any closer."

Darren paused. Like a wraith, Julianna rose from behind the chair, keeping all but a sliver of her face concealed behind Tim's. She brought a knife to his neck, the blade curving like a scythe, the tip dimpling the skin beneath Tim's Adam's apple. In the dim light of the room, her eyes looked like two chunks of coal.

"Drop the gun," she ordered.

I kept the Glock sighted on Quinn, still vaguely aware of her standing a few feet ahead, but it took everything I had not to swing the gun toward Julianna and fire. This was a woman who tore families apart, who preyed on the vulnerable and weak. This was a woman who ruined lives, and right now, I wanted nothing more than to end hers. All I needed was the chance.

"Tell Olivia to put the gun down, Darren," Julianna said, turning her attention toward him. "I'll spare your father's life in exchange for my daughter's."

"Don't listen to her," Tim said with a grimace. "What we did to you was … wrong, son. I love you. I … didn't know it would come to this."

The words hit Darren like a blowtorch. His face seemed to melt, his mouth wilting, his eyebrows bunching together, his nose quivering. He hadn't looked away from Tim once since entering the room, and he didn't now as he motioned for me to lower the weapon.

Tim's eyes flicked my way. "Don't do it, Oliv—"

"*Quiet!*" Julianna hissed. The tip of the knife pierced Tim's throat, releasing a teardrop of blood that traveled the length of the blade and dripped onto his shirt.

Darren raised his hand, "Stop! Don't hurt him!" He gave me a panicked look, his eyes wide and pleading. "Olivia, lower it, okay? Just for a second."

My heart slammed against my ribs.

Quinn took a step toward me. "He's right, Olivia. It's not too late."

"Stay where you are," I snapped.

"Take the gun from her, Darren," Julianna growled.

"Olivia," he said. "*Please.*"

When I didn't move, Julianna snaked her hand down Tim's

arm, covered his ravaged fingers ... and squeezed. Tim roared, his voice electric with pain, the sound tearing through me like a knife.

"Do it now, Darren. Last chance. Take the gun, or I kill him."

"Okay, *okay.*" Darren edged closer, his palm still raised, like it possessed the power to keep Julianna's hand from plunging the knife into Tim's neck. "Olivia, give it to me."

"Give it to him," Quinn echoed. "Hand it over."

Panic fizzed through my chest. I could feel the situation spinning out of control. The Glock trembled. I glanced at Tim, who was looking back at me with wide, pleading eyes, Julianna whispering next to him, "*Take the gun, take the gun, take the gun,* Darren, take the gun!"

Thwap! Thwap! Thwap!

Rotor blades chewed through the air. A whirring mechanical beast emitting light and sound buzzed past the window. *A helicopter.* I went dizzy with relief. My hasty SOS of an email to Nina in the security office had gone through! A quick bullet-point list of all the shit I'd experienced since we last spoke along with my phone's IMEI and the IP address of the laptop. I had no idea how she'd located *The Athena* but she had, she'd found us. Now we just had to make it upstairs in one piece.

"Run!" Tim roared. He rose like some otherworldly creature, with the chair still strapped to his back. The knife moved with him, and his throat split into a weeping red grin. His voice turned to a wet gurgle as a sheet of blood swept over his chest and drenched his shirt.

"No!" Darren shouted.

Tim thumped down, his eyes rolling into the back of his head. Julianna barreled past him, shrieking as she rushed me with the knife. My hand moved on its own, from Quinn to Julianna, sweeping the Glock in a smooth, level arc as I fired twice. The first bullet missed. The second one didn't.

Julianna's head snapped back in a plume of red mist.

It seemed, for a moment, as if everything went still.

A wail rose. A cry full of anguish. *Quinn.*

I spun toward her in time to see her fingers seize my broken wrist, her mouth stretched wide in an angry scream. A fountain of pain erupted up my arm as Quinn squeezed tighter, the nerves lighting up like I'd dunked them into a vat of hydrofluoric acid. My vision bleached. The Glock fell from my hand.

Before I could move, Quinn snatched it from the floor.

And leveled it at my head.

CHAPTER THIRTY-SIX

"You killed her!" Quinn shrieked. "You *killed* her, you fucking bitch!"

I couldn't speak, couldn't move. My wrist throbbed with impossible agony—a pain so caustic and raw, so unbearable, it felt like my cells themselves were dissolving and turning to ash. All I could do was stand there, reeling, fighting to remain on my feet.

Darren's shoulder brushed mine, his voice trembling as he spoke. For a moment, I'd forgotten he was there. "Quinn, calm down."

"Calm down? *Calm down?*" A mad light swam through her eyes. "Don't you tell me to calm down! She meant everything to me!"

I glanced at Julianna, who now painted the floor in a living chalk outline, one leg bent beneath her in an awkward angle, the other contorted at the hip. Her arms lay at her sides in peaceful contradiction, palms up. But her eyes … they were wide, wide open.

A few feet beyond her, lying in a pool of blood, was Tim.

Darren gazed at him with a tear dribbling off his chin. "So did he."

"That's her fault, too," Quinn said. "All she had to do was give me the gun, and none of this had to happen!"

My head spun in tilt-a-whirls. Her words pulsed in my ears.

"None of this is her fault, and you know that," Darren replied. "Come on, Quinn, put the gun down. It's over."

"Everything is her fault." Her mouth twitched as she glared at him, her face knotted with hate. "All Olivia does is take and take and *take!*"

Her words were darts dipped in poison; I felt every one. "I never wanted to take anything from you," I said, struggling to speak through the forest fire raging in my wrist. "All I wanted was to be your sister."

Even now. Somehow even now.

Something like regret tugged at the corners of Quinn's eyes and pulled the seams of her mouth lower, giving me a nanosecond glimpse of the reconciliation we might have had. And then, as quickly as the look appeared, it vanished, buried beneath a fresh tide of anger. "And all I have for you is hate."

I expected her to shoot me then. I could already feel the bullet. But she didn't. She cocked her head at the ceiling instead, drawn by the muffled sound of rotors. "You must think you're so clever, contacting them. I don't know how you did it, but I know it was you. Not that it matters. You're never getting off this boat now." A smile crept over her face as she said it, something cold in the shape, calculating. "Neither of you."

With one quick movement, she swept the Glock from my chest toward Darren.

And fired.

The room detonated, my ears along with it. Lead hit flesh. Darren jerked and spun to the floor. *Oh, god,* I thought. *No, no, no, no ...*

"*Why?*" I cried.

Quinn's voice poured through the ringing in my ears, sounding distant. "So you know what it's like to lose someone you care about."

"I've *always* known," I shot back, my anger surging past the pain, past the panic and fear and horror swamping my chest and threatening to pull me under. "You aren't the only one who's suffered!"

Her eyes turned to slits. "No. But I've suffered more."

The Glock rose. *Bang!*

A blistering trail of heat tore through my shoulder and sent me staggering backward toward the wall.

Bang! A bullet whizzed past my head and thunked into the wall.

Bang! Another bullet hit wood.

Quinn pressed closer, the bridge of her nose furrowed with rage, her teeth bared. She was toying with me. She was playing—and now I was going to die.

"Goodbye, Via," Quinn said, taking aim at my chest.

Click.

Her eyes narrowed on the weapon, then came back to me, fell back to the gun. *Click. Click. Click.*

No more bullets.

I slammed into her. We went down together. Thrashing,

kicking, biting. My fingers ripping her hair. Her nails clawing my face. Both of us shrieking as our limbs intertwined. Bawling and screeching with pain. My sight came in flashes. Quinn's eyes flaring, her teeth snapping. Spit flying furiously from her lips. I fought to keep her beneath me, fought with everything I had.

But it wasn't enough.

Not with the heat in my wrist cranked to ten like an oven burner. Not with my shoulder bloody and raw. I tried to hold onto her, but Quinn moved like a demon and slithered away. And then she was on top of me, her eyes burning down from behind a skin-stretched mask of hate.

Her knees pinned my arms to the ground.

Her fingers hit my neck. And squeezed.

Her face blurred and became Sean's—and I was back on that forest floor with my heart redlining in my chest somewhere behind my aching lungs. My breath came in oxygen-starved gasps. Bright comets of pain hissed down my arm and erupted in my wrist. Reality burned black at the edges.

Let go, a voice whispered. *It's okay.*

No, you have to fight!

I wanted to, needed to, but I couldn't. I was out of strength. All I could do was lie there and gasp because I knew this was how I would die. Quinn would finally get her wish. I would die at her hands. My sister would kill me.

A warm spray hit my face. I tasted copper.

The pressure released. My vision widened as Quinn's eyes rolled back in her head. A black hilt protruded from her neck. A *knife.* She hung there for a moment, tottering back and forth. Her lips parted like she was about to say something, then she blinked and raised her hand to her neck. When she toppled to the side, Darren stood behind her, fighting for air with great, heaving gasps. Wobbling. Swaying. Bleeding.

But standing. Somehow still standing.

He held out his hand, and I took it, sobbing as he pulled me to my feet, crying because it was too much.

All of it was *too fucking much.*

"Come on," he said, his voice ragged. "We need to get … upstairs."

I tried to speak, and when I found I couldn't, I managed to nod.

We staggered down the hall together, leaning into each other. We moved like a four-legged creature, bearing each other's weight. A fresh wave of agony tore through my shoulder and splintered my wrist. The floor felt like rubber beneath my shoes as it rocked back and forth. I didn't know if it was me or the yacht.

The stairs appeared. The chandelier. Darren stumbled and fell. I helped him back to his feet. Then we were climbing higher, pushing toward the beautiful sound of metal slicing air. Up, up, up, onto the landing and the sight of a helicopter sitting on the helipad outside, washing the deck in bright light. Along the side, printed in between alternating bands of orange and white paint, were four words that filled me with a pure and breathless hope: United States Coast Guard.

Thank you, Nina.

Men leaped from the chopper and ran toward us. Tears fell

from my chin and soaked my shirt. Through the doors they came, their hands cupping my shoulders, their mouths split wide with questions I couldn't answer—too tired to speak.

"Where are you hurt?"

"Are there others on the boat?"

More hands now—arms guiding me outside to the cool brush of wind and the familiar smell of salt. Walking, staggering, coming closer ...

Thwap, thwap, thwap, thwap.

A man in a red jumpsuit helped me into the helicopter, and my heart nearly stopped.

The tears fell harder, but not because of the pain.

Or because of Quinn.

They fell because I couldn't believe what I was seeing. It didn't make sense. I blinked and wiped my eyes, a warm surge of joy flooding my chest. Because there—*right there* in front of me—resting in the center of the helicopter, strapped to an orange rescue board ... was Alex.

CHAPTER THIRTY-SEVEN

One year later

"Hello, Janelle, you're live with Olivia."

"Hi, Olivia! I was wondering, what kind of sentence do you think Bryce Cullen will get after he's convicted?"

A picture flashed to mind, Bryce tooling around the prison yard, looking haggard with his hair no longer styled, trying to blend in and avoid becoming someone's bitch. As much as I wanted that to happen, I doubted it would. I knew federal holding centers were a far cry from the horrors of state prisons, though still awful. Most likely, Bryce was simply bored.

Most murders in the United States are prosecuted under state law, with a few rare exceptions, one of which is death at sea. It turns out the FBI takes the murder of U.S. citizens offshore pretty seriously. And murder was only one of a laundry-list of federal crimes Bryce had been charged with after the Coast Guard pulled him out of the storage room. He'd also racked up a laundry list of crimes including tax evasion, money laundering, fraud, attempted murder, and human trafficking. A strong case, yes. But Bryce had the financial resources to employ a slew of top defense attorneys; I'd seen the rich beat worse.

I leaned into the microphone. "I'm afraid I can't answer that. We're still a long way from a conviction. But the case is solid, so we're hoping for a good outcome. And not just for Bryce, but for all of those who were involved."

Like Liam. He was awaiting his own trial in New York. I hoped he would get life, but I knew he wouldn't. Neither would Kerry. They weren't important enough for the prosecution—a few rungs too low on the corporate ladder. They'd probably wind up at some country club prison in exchange for spilling what little they knew about the organization

I took a drink of water and nodded at Nina. The name John from Kentucky flashed across my screen. "Hi, John, what's your question?"

"Actually, my question is for Alex."

I had to stifle a laugh as Alex stiffened. He wasn't the first guest host we'd had on the podcast, but he was certainly the most nervous. He'd flown in for the week and we'd spent it touring Columbus (what little of it there was to tour) in between catching up over bottles of wine. When he'd first arrived, he'd been quiet and withdrawn, his usual sweet demeanor hidden under a fresh coat of trauma. But then Nina cracked a joke about Liam, and we hadn't stopped laughing since.

Alex cleared his throat. "Hey there, John. Go ahead."

"Yeah, I was—well, I was wondering if you're still single?"

Alex raked his fingers through his curls with a chuckle. "I am, but I don't think I'm ready for another relationship quite yet."

They continued to talk, and my heart swelled as I watched him. I knew Alex shouldn't be here with us; the odds of surviving a plunge into the open ocean were slim at best. Most people who went overboard on cruise ships and yachts were never seen again. So, the fact that he'd survived three hours treading water in the dark with only his legs and a pair of zip-tied hands was incredible. More than incredible. A miracle. There was no other word for it.

Nina cued me. Jennifer from Denver. "Hey there, Jennifer, you're live. What's your question?"

"Thanks for taking my call. I was wondering if you'll ever go on a cruise again?"

I laughed. "No, I don't think so. I'll be sticking to dry land from here on out." I paused, waited for the next caller.

"Hi, Olivia, I'm a long-time listener, first-time caller, and I just want to let you know how much I adore your show. I never miss it."

"Thank you," I said. "What's on your mind?"

"Do you think they'll ever find the other people Xclivity threw overboard?"

I pressed a finger to the bridge of my nose and sighed internally. "No, I'm afraid not." I hated this question. No matter how much I tried to squash it, it always came up. What happened to the bodies of Caprice and Chaz Hanson? What happened to Margaret or the others Julianna and her followers tossed overboard before them? Would they ever be found?

I didn't think so. Even with all her bullshit, Julianna had been right about one thing—the currents surrounding the area they called "Elysium" were strong. A week-long search for Chaz and Caprice by the Coast Guard hadn't yielded any results. I thought of them often, woke at night still hearing their screams. They didn't deserve to die like that, in the middle of the ocean, frightened and cold. But at least they had each other. At least they hadn't died alone like Margaret had.

The thought never brought me much consolation.

I held up a single finger to Nina to indicate the last caller. She nodded and patched in Ethan from New Mexico. "Good morning, Ethan—what's your question?"

Silence hung on the end of the line.

I leaned closer to the mic. "Ethan, are you there?"

"We know where you live," the voice answered. "We'll make you pay."

The hair on the back of my neck rose. Nina killed the call. We would scrub it from the podcast, of course, but these kinds of things were happening more often lately. Calls, mostly, but a few letters as well that we'd turned over to the police. Not that they'd been able to do anything. There were no names on the envelopes, no return addresses. Just vague promises of retribution when I least expected it.

I'd be lying if I didn't admit it worried me. But it also wouldn't stop Nina and I from helping the FBI and law enforcement in any way we could if it meant snuffing out every last vestige of Xclivity. And if they really did want to come for either of us, I'd be ready with more bullets. I'd already purchased another gun.

I took off my headphones, set them on the desk, and stood.

Nina and Alex did the same.

"That was creepy," Alex said, looking worried.

"Forget about it," I replied. "It's nothing."

Nina slung an arm around his shoulders and bumped him with her hip. "You killed it."

One corner of his mouth crooked higher. "You think so?"

"Absolutely," I said. "A born natural."

Nina glanced at me. "You sure you don't want us to come with you?" *Us.* Nina and Alex had really taken to each other. They loved the same music, the same books. They both enjoyed eating sushi and drinking too much sake. Instant friends.

"I'd love for you guys to come," I said, "but this is something I need to do on my own."

Nina detached from Alex and took me by the shoulders. "Call me as soon as you land. You know what happened the last time you traveled alone."

I rolled my eyes. "I'll be fine, Mom."

"You're hopeless." Her lips curled into a smirk.

I stared at her, my partner in crime, and pulled her into a hug. "I love you, you know that?"

"I love you, too, but if you don't call me the second you arrive, Alex and I are jumping on a plane. We'll find you. You know we can."

"I have no doubt," I said, turning to hug Alex. "Will you still be here when I get back?"

He shook his head. "Probably not. Classes start in a week. But you have to promise to visit over fall break."

I leaned in and kissed him on the forehead. "Oh, we will. I promise."

One of his eyebrows arched. "If you don't keep that promise, I'll be forced to sue you."

After returning home to Chicago, Alex had reenrolled at Northwestern, but not to finish his MBA. He'd spent three months studying his ass off for the LSAT and scored in the top two percent nationwide. Like me, his near-death experience had granted him a singular, blinding purpose. He'd taken up Margaret's legacy to dismantle organizations like Xclivity in the courtroom and make them pay. I had no doubt he'd do just that.

CHAPTER THIRTY-EIGHT

Six hours later, I lounged near the baggage claim at the Phoenix Sky Harbor International Airport, watching the passengers from Sacramento search for their luggage. Diego arrived much in Diego fashion, dressed casually in a T-shirt, a pair of shorts, and a black ball cap. I still struggled not to think of him as Darren, though he'd never truly been Darren. Darren was the name given to him by Xclivity, by his abductors, and he'd immediately changed it upon arriving home. He said it was the least he could do to honor his mother.

His name wasn't the only thing that had changed. He now looked older than when I'd first met him, and somehow wiser, his long hair cut short, his round cheeks melted to those of a marathoner's—gaunt and hollow, his entire body stripped of fat. Like me, he'd taken up running to deal with his grief. He ran any chance he got.

When I stood, his face brightened, and I felt mine do the same. We'd seen each other a few times since the cruise, and even hooked up once, but it never felt quite right. After everything we'd been through, he now felt more like a brother to me, and more like family than Quinn ever had. We talked at least twice a week, and at this point, I didn't know how I'd ever navigated life without him.

He neared and gave me a quick hug, pulling back after a moment to look at my hand. "How are you? How's the wrist?"

The wrist. Three surgeries. An army of pins and screws. A bone graft. Countless hours of rehab and doctor consultations, it still didn't feel right, throbbed any time I moved. But my fingers worked, and I still had my hand, so I couldn't complain. The bullet wound to my shoulder had healed right away in comparison, felt like a scratch.

I flexed my fingers and winced. "It's doing great."

"*Right.* You're a terrible liar."

"So, they tell me."

"Okay, Olivia. What are we doing here? Why are we in Arizona?"

"Uh-uh. Not yet."

He crossed his arms. "I took time off work, flew to a different state, all to meet you for some big surprise, and now that I'm here, you still won't tell me what it is?"

"Nope. Sure won't."

He laughed. "Fine. You're impossible. Let me grab my bag."

"I'll get the rental."

We drove. The afternoon sun turned the buildings into pillars of fire, the sky a vibrant blue in contrast. Soon, we were heading north on I 17, breezing through a stark slice of desert manned by a contingent of saguaro. The vista spread away on either side of us, peppered in yucca and mesquite, the road tinged red with dust

We talked on the way. Diego spoke about Kerry and Tim, and how they'd left him with nothing but a name, and how even that didn't belong to him. Since returning home, the feds had seized Kerry and Tim's bank accounts along with Spark Fitness and all the related assets. Unsurprisingly, the franchise had been used as one of many Xclivity money laundering fronts. Like Alex, the abrupt change forced Diego to think about what he really wanted to do with his life.

"I'm thinking about graphic design," he'd told me on one of our many video phone calls. After some encouragement, he'd enrolled in a local community college, said he was doing great. "It's just what I needed to take my mind off things, you know?" He'd grinned as he'd said it, and anyone who'd seen him in that moment would have said he looked genuinely happy. But I knew he wasn't. Grief has a way of clinging to someone; it carries a certain weight.

I felt my grief in the memory of my sister. Could I have saved her? Had there been anything left to save? When I really considered it, I didn't think so. She'd spent years marinating in her hate, telling herself I was the sole reason her life had spiraled out of control. By the time we'd reunited on *The Athena,* our relationship never stood a chance. Still, despite everything she'd done to me, I couldn't bring myself to hate her in return. Life had been unkind to Quinn from the start.

Diego's grief hung in his smile—in the way the corners of his lips never curled as high as when I first met him. I saw it in his eyes, and how they'd transformed from windows to blinds—no longer as clear, no longer bright. Grief threaded through his voice when he spoke of Margaret's letter and what it had meant for him to read her words. He said it had changed his life. "I wish I could have met her. I wish I could have told her I loved her, just once."

"I know you do," I'd say. "I know."

Sometimes life's wounds cut so deep they never fully heal. They become a scar, as much a part of us as the blood in our veins and the oxygen in our lungs. They remind us of what we've lost. And although I could never bring Margaret back, I hoped what I had to show Diego would help ease his pain. I hoped it would help him move on.

Ahead, Sedona cut through the windshield in a sunrise of red and pink rock. Fins and spires, mesas and valleys. With the sun skipping low over the horizon, it felt like we were driving through a water-color dream.

Diego raised his sunglasses. "Wow, this is incredible."

"Isn't it? I don't know if I've ever been somewhere this beautiful before."

"Agreed. I only wish I knew why we were here."

"Soon enough."

He blew out a mouthful of air and slumped back in his seat. "You're killing me."

"We're almost there, I promise."

I scanned my phone, took a right on Thunderbird Drive and then a left on Timber Road, finally parking in front of a southwestern-style home with earth-tone stucco walls and a xeriscape lawn. "We're here," I said. "There's someone I want you to meet."

I got out of the car and Diego followed, eyeing the house warily. "Who?"

I didn't answer, just trailed around the hood and took his hand, then pulled him up the walk toward the door. "Listen, I know you lost a lot to Xclivity, and I know you feel like you're alone. But you're not. A lot of people care about you. *I* care about you."

He grinned. "Are you about to ask me to marry you?"

I rang the doorbell. "Even better."

A moment later, the door opened to reveal a woman with ebony hair and deep, brown eyes. She stood slightly taller than me at five foot seven, with skin as warm as the Sedona sand. Her gaze flicked from me to Diego and hung there, taking him in, her lips parting with a short, gasping breath.

Diego fidgeted and side-eyed me with a look I knew meant, *say something*. I didn't; I simply stood there, staring at the two of them with a smile breaking over my lips. A little girl appeared near the woman's legs. She had the same limpid brown eyes as her mother and the same button nose. Her features reminded me of someone I'd only known for a few days, but who'd impacted my life in a tremendous way.

"Who's that, Mommy?" the girl asked, tugging at the woman's shorts.

"This," the woman said, dabbing at the corners of her eyes, "is your uncle."

Diego took a step back, as if hit with a cattle prod, his mouth hanging agape. A look of wonder crossed his face. He turned to me. "You found her."

My smile broadened. I had, and it had been no easy feat. It turned out I wasn't the only one investigating Xclivity. After the cruise, I discovered the feds were looking into a string of cold-case disappearances similar to Diego's. One of them was Elena's. Her abduction was part of the broader case against Xclivity and she'd been placed in witness protection as a result. It took cashing in a few high-value favors to find out where, and now here we were standing on her doorstep.

"Oh my god," he said, blinking in disbelief.

Tears ran down Elena's cheeks as she laughed. "Hi, brother."

"I can't believe it," he said, stepping forward and pulling her into a hug.

They came together in a tangle of laughter and tears, and I thought of Margaret and all she'd sacrificed to keep her children alive, never once thinking they would discover her existence, much less discover each other. But they had. Here they were, safe, together at last.

My throat thickened as Elena waved an arm toward the door. "Please, come in. We've been expecting you. Dinner is on the table."

"You two go ahead," I said. "You have a lot of catching up to do."

And I had some fresh leads to follow. Evelyn Torrence, twenty-six from New York, had disappeared four months before my trip to Puerto Rico. Her last known point of contact came when she pinged a cell tower near an industrial shipping port in Florida. After that, she'd simply vanished. Her parents were desperate to find her. I thought again of the swamp I'd tumbled into, and the body within. Unfortunately, I had a pretty good idea where she was.

Diego shook his head. "Are you kidding me, Olivia? You reunite me with my sister and then try to leave? No way. You're not going anywhere. You're staying right here where you belong."

"You sure?"

His smile widened, and he took my arm and pulled me inside. "I've never been more certain of anything in my life."

WAIT, BEFORE YOU GO ...

Do you want to read Margaret's letter to Darren? The letter that contains everything she wanted to tell her son in person, but was never able to? The same letter that forever changed his life? Do you want to find out what happens *after* he reads it? Be warned, Xclivity isn't done with him yet.

Sign up for my newsletter and it's yours for free.

Just scan the QR code below and it's all yours. Interacting with my readers is one of my favorite things to do. I'll pop into your email from time to time with insider news, bookish updates, and some funny life stories. That's it. I promise I'll never overwhelm your inbox with anything else.

One more thing. Reviews are an author's lifeblood. It's how we survive. If you enjoyed this book, would you please post a review on Amazon, Goodreads, and/or any other review site you enjoy? It would mean a lot!

Again, thank you so much—I appreciate you, and I'll be back with more books!

ACKNOWLEDGEMENTS

Some books take a tribe to write, and this one was no exception. I have so many incredible people to thank, but the first is YOU.

Thank you for picking up this book and giving it a chance. Without you, this crazy dream of mine wouldn't be possible. I mostly write my novels in the early morning hours, and in margins of my life. It can take years to cobble together a book, so know that I appreciate you reading my work more than you know. I read every single review you write, and I'm constantly wowed by your kindness, feedback, and insight into my stories.

To my wife Jen, your support means the world to me. I love you. To my girls, Harper, Riley, and Adelyn, it's an honor and privilege to be your father. I'm incredibly proud of each one of you and can't wait to see who you become in this world. To my parents, Neal and Becky, I can't thank you enough for your love and support over the years. And there has been A LOT of support. I am who I am because of you. To my sisters, Nicole and Elise, thank you for always being in my corner.

This book was about a cult. I belong to one of my own—a writing cult, that is. I'm profoundly thankful for the input, feedback, and support I received while writing this book from Steph Nelson, Noelle Ihli, and Faith Gardner. I'm not lying when I say that meeting all of you has fundamentally changed the way I approach this crazy business of book writing and shown me what is truly possible. There are no straight lines when it comes to being an author, but there are signs along the way which indicate you are heading in the right direction. Thank you for being my compass.

A shout out to Charles Dunphey. What can I say, man? You've pulled me out of countless plot jams. You've spent hours on the phone, helping me build these worlds. You've picked me up when I've been at my lowest and helped me continue to push on. I appreciate you.

Last but not least, Tina Alberino, thank you for calming me down when my anxiety redlined while writing this story. This book wouldn't be what it is without your patience and input. I'm so fortunate to have you in my corner. You are a brilliant plotter and an idea magician.

Now it's time to get back to writing. I have more novels coming!

ABOUT THE AUTHOR

Caleb Stephens is an award-winning author writing from Denver, Colorado. His novels include *The Girls in the Cabin*, *Feeders*, and *Soul Couriers*. His short story "The Wallpaper Man," was adapted to film by Falconer Film & Media in 2022. When he's not writing, he can be found binging scary movies, watching his kids' soccer games, or playing with his dog, Bodhi. You can join his mailing list and learn more at www.calebstephensauthor.com as well as follow him on Instagram and TikTok @calebstephensauthor.

Read a thrilling excerpt from Caleb Stephens' award-winning psychological thriller The Girls in the Cabin

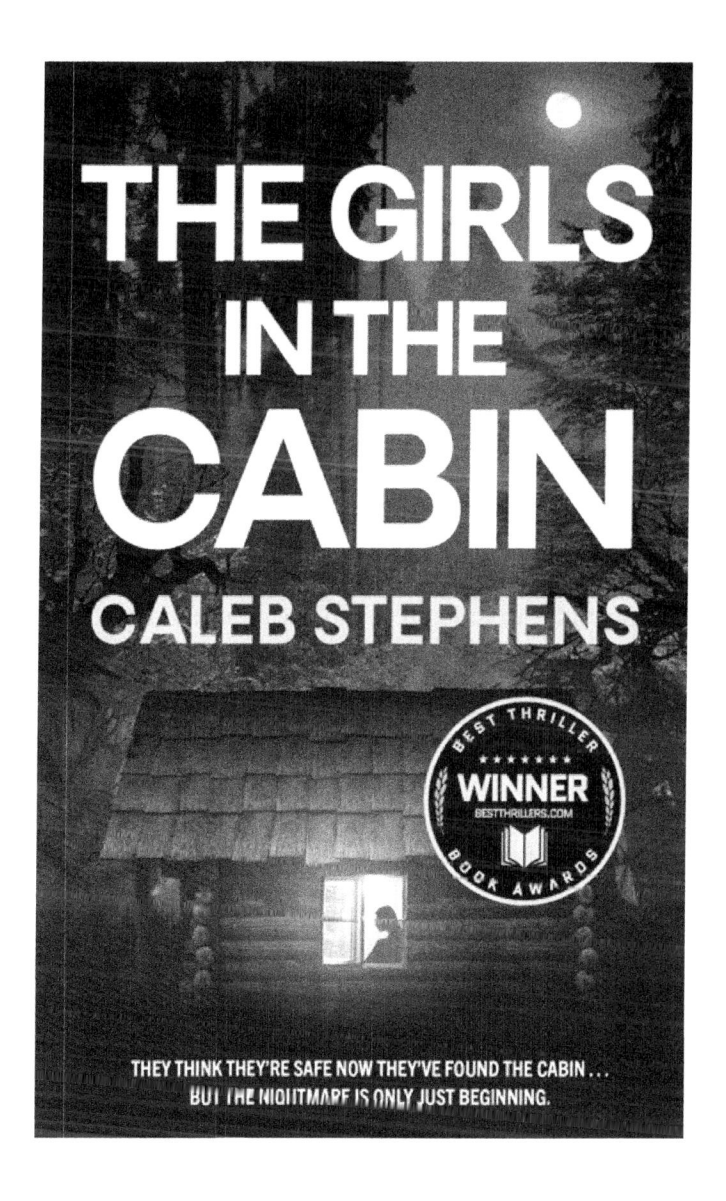

CHAPTER ONE

CLARA
1984

Clara Carver never much liked the Black Place. Even at age nine, a big girl now, she'd never grown used to its rancid smell and the things that would brush across her skin like fallen eyelashes in the dark. She would leap to her feet and smack at her neck or her leg, and sometimes her hand would come away wet with an insect's insides. Sometimes, and more often than not, she would leave the Black Place covered in welts from the ants and blister beetles that lived there, anxious for Mother's calamine lotion to calm her sores.

Father told her the length of time she spent in the Black Place was up to her. If she were to mind her manners and do what he said, she could leave as quickly as a few short hours. If she were to cry and bang and cause a ruckus, time would pass much slower. Father said the things he did to her — the things that made her insides churn and left her whimpering with her arms wrapped around her knees — were a sign of his love for her.

"Clara, never forget how much I love you."

It seemed that his love changed with his moods. When the corn came in thick and sweet, and money was flush, Father would take Clara for ice cream at the malt shop in Meeker, along with Mother. He would laugh and tell stories of the harvest, and how hard the men worked to bring it in. Mother would lace her fingers together and smile at him, and to anyone who passed, they seemed a normal enough family.

There were other times, though, when Father came home smelling of liquor and dragged Clara from whatever she was doing, out through the backyard and into the fields toward the Black Place. Sometimes, Father would force Mother to join him. She never resisted, but she didn't seem to enjoy it much, and Clara guessed she did what he wanted because she preferred those things to a belt or his fists in her stomach.

Clara only resisted once at age six. She'd been playing in her room with her favorite doll, Mabel, who had a head full of lemon yarn hair, when Father told her to come. She said no. It was late, and she couldn't bear the thought of leaving Mabel all alone for the night. When Father grabbed her, Clara clawed and scratched and kicked and bit. As a result, Father left her in the Black Place for two days. When Clara returned to her room, it was to Mabel lying torn in half with her cotton insides strewn over the pink comforter. Clara cried for a week, and, after that, she decided she would cry no more.

She learned to endure the Black Place. She forced herself to find comfort in the small places Father couldn't touch. She imagined a park with bright green grass and other children who would chase her up and down slides and push her on blue bucket swings.

She pictured places other than the dust-caked farm with its rusted buildings and abandoned tractor equipment, places she'd seen in magazines and read about in books. Places like France with its gleaming metal cities and sun-speckled beaches, the sand as white as snow. She told herself, someday, she would escape the farm and go there.

But not today. Today was worse than most. Her stomach hurt, and sharp cramps tore through her abdomen like shards of glass. She craved light and air. She needed to escape the sweltering dark and reeking stench of the Black Place. It was as if something were swelling within her, a creature inside she could no longer control. It burst up her throat, and she climbed the steps to the hatch door and clawed and scraped and screamed for someone — for anyone — to free her. She smashed her fists against the iron hatch until her knuckles bled. Clara didn't care if her shouts brought the wrath of Father. She only wanted out.

But no one came, and she was about to return to her cot when she heard something click. She cupped a hand against a seam of light as the hatch squealed open, half-expecting to see the familiar outline of Mother's cruel scowl or Father's hard, brown eyes. Instead, she saw a girl not much older than herself with soft, white skin and a waterfall of raven-black hair. She wore a warm smile and a dress the color of the summer sky.

"Hello," the girl said. "I heard you knocking. Would you like to come out?"

Clara nodded and knew she had finally found a friend.

CHAPTER TWO

KAYLA
DAY ONE

I climb a jutting slab of rock and hold Dad's phone skyward, tap it and hope for a signal or a text, anything to prove the outside world still exists. After three days of backpacking through nowhere, Colorado, I'm not sure it does.

I'm so pissed at Dad for dragging us out here. Camping somewhere new every night sucks, Dad snoring away in the tent like a broken tractor engine on one side and Emma kicking me on the other. If I had my phone, maybe I could distract myself. But no, Dad made me leave it in the car, even when I begged and begged. "Sorry, kiddo, but we need to spend some time together as a family." What a load of crap. We stopped being a family the minute Mom died. Now we're just three strangers who live together.

Besides, camping was Mom's thing. Not his. He's only doing it because he thinks he has to — because Mom always talked about backpacking in Colorado someday. He's driving me crazy, asking me all these questions about boys and school and volleyball like he cares, which he doesn't. Not really. All he's ever cared about is his work because it gets him away from me and Emma and all of our drama. Or it used to, anyway. Now, with Mom gone, he's stuck with us.

But whatever; it's not like I can do anything about it. And, I have to admit, Colorado is pretty. There are lakes everywhere, stamped in perfect blue circles in between all the fir and pine. And the aspen trees, wow, are the leaves amazing — all these oranges and reds sparkling for as far as you can see. When we hike above the tree line, I can almost lose myself in the scenery. I say "almost" because the moment I do, I can practically feel Mom standing next to me, whispering in my ear.

Isn't it so beautiful, Kit Kat?

Everything has been so shitty since she died. I can't remember the last time I felt happy. About anything, really. It would help if I could talk to someone, but Dad is oblivious, and Mimi is never around anymore. Even if she were, she doesn't get me the way Mom did. I can't tell her about the stuff with Ethan and what a dick he was to ditch me right after we hooked up. It was my first time, and it couldn't have been worse. He won't even look at me now. Mom always told me to wait, that my first time should be special, but that if I did go through with it, I should tell her. And I would have. I totally would have. She wanted to be there to support me. Now there's no one to do that except Dad.

Dad. Ugh, he thinks everything is just fine because I hang out with Bree and Abby from time to time and get decent grades. He has no idea how much I hate my pasty white legs and skeleton arms, or that my chest belongs to someone in middle school, not that anyone notices. I'm pretty much invisible at Brookline High

School. Or I was before Mom died, anyway. Now everyone looks at me like I'm damaged goods:

She's the one whose mom died, right?

God, she looks so sad all the time...

Oh, poor thing, that must be so hard on her. Cancer, I hear.

At first, I thought Mom would beat it. She'd sit there and tell me so — "I'm going to beat this, Kayla. I promise." — and I was dumb enough to believe her because she seemed so strong. What a joke. She never stood a chance.

I settle onto the rock and stare at Dad's phone, the dumb thing, then click on the photo icon. A picture appears, one of Bernie mid-bark, chasing Emma around the backyard with her sundress flared behind her like a cape. It's easy to tell the picture is B.C. (Before Cancer) because she's got this big smile splashed on her face. A real one, with the corners of her eyes crinkled. In the A.C. pictures, Emma's smiles are gone, or if they're there, they're totally fake.

My finger hovers over the screen, and I tell myself not to do it, not to swipe because I know what comes next. I do it anyway. It's a selfie of me and Mom at Canobie Lake, Mom in her swimsuit right after her diagnosis, looking happy, normal even, with her face still full and round. (I can beat this!) I swipe again, fall now, the leaves changing, Public Park alive with color. Mom's hair is gone in this one, her head wrapped in a cherry silk scarf. I hated it when she lost her hair. It felt so mean. Like, how could God take something so beautiful after all he'd put her through, the very thing she loved the most?

I keep scrolling, and my throat swells when I reach the hospital pictures. The first is of Emma nestled next to Mom on the bed, Mom giving the camera a cheery, fake thumbs-up. (Maybe I'll beat this?) Then one of me plopped in a chair beside her, crying. She has her hand to my chin, both of us staring at each other and being honest for once: there is no beating this, not this time. I remember looking at her and thinking, Don't you do it. Don't you dare leave me. I can't handle it. But I knew she would, and there was nothing — absolutely nothing — I could do about it.

"That's one of my favorites."

I nearly drop the phone. Dad stands behind me with his arms crossed and his face flushed red from the climb. For a second, I think he's about to blow up on me for leaving Emma by herself back at camp, but instead, he settles onto the rock and pats my leg.

"She's so beautiful in that picture, don't you think?"

I glance at it, annoyed. Mom wasn't the only one he thought was beautiful.

"You look just like her, you know."

"That's what you always say." And he does. All the time. It drives me nuts. It's why I avoid mirrors. Every time I pass one, I see Mom staring back. Her auburn hair. Her lake-green eyes. The lips that are, in my opinion, a little too thin, set above a neck that's definitely a little too long.

"You know I said no phones on this trip, Kit Kat."

"Yeah, and I left mine in the car." Kit Kat. Mom's nickname for me since I was five. I used to love it. Now I can't stand it, especially when he says it.

"Hand it over," he says.

I toss it into his lap. "Fine. It's not like it works up here, anyway."

"Look, just hang in there one more day. You can call all your friends tomorrow when we're back in the car, okay?"

"Whatever," I mumble.

He falls silent, and we sit there for an awkward moment, watching the clouds blow off the mountains. I know what he's thinking, because I'm thinking it, too: I wish we could go back. Back to when cancer wasn't a thing and Mom was still alive. We all wish it. Especially Emma. She thinks if she just doesn't talk, doesn't say anything, it will somehow change things and bring Mom back. But it won't. Nothing will. She's gone, and no matter how quiet Emma is, or how badly Dad wants to fix everything, or how angry I get, things will never be the same.

He squeezes my knee. "We'd better get back before Emma jumps in the lake."

She won't. She doesn't do anything these days but sit around, looking sad while she colors.

"Besides," he says, pointing at the clouds, "rain's on the way. We need to set up the tent."

I move to stand, but he keeps his hand on my knee a moment longer, his eyes serious like he's about to have one of his "Dad" talks.

"What?" I ask, hoping to get it over with. I can't handle his lies, how he says he cares and how sorry he is for everything. Blah, blah, blah.

I groan, and he shuts his mouth, suddenly looking angry. My eyes heat up again, but I won't cry. Not here. Not anywhere. Especially in front of him. After the last year, I'm all cried out.

With a sigh, I stand and head for the trail before he can stop me.

CHAPTER THREE

CHRIS

We set back toward camp with leaves sprinkled around us in scatters of scarlet and gold. Ancient strands of blue spruce rise toward a gray sky, marbled and thick with the promise of rain. I can already smell the ozone dissolving in the air, blending with the sweet tang of pine sap and earth.

Kayla leads, flattening the dense mountain grass as she threads her way down the slope. She slows and steps gingerly over a fallen log, and I think for the thousandth time that she moves like Lexi. The way she centers her weight on the balls of her feet with each step, the way she swings her arms . . . it's almost enough to convince me I'm walking behind my dead wife and not my daughter. It's so damn frustrating. Kayla talks like her, smiles like her, does everything just like her, this living echo of Lexi; just enough proof to convince me that, yes Chris, she was here and, yes Chris, you did have that perfect life once.

That other life . . .

And Kayla is so damn frustrating. She shut me out the minute

Lexi died, and no matter what I do, she won't let me back in. Not that I've ever fully understood what makes her tick, or what, exactly, it is she's thinking when she looks at me with her mother's eyes. I could at least figure out Lexi from time to time. Not Kayla. She was born beautifully pissed off — this red-faced, fist-balled infant ready to grab life by the throat. I never knew what might set her off. I still don't. Only Lexi did. She was the key to Kayla's puzzle, the one who cooled her flame, and now, with Lexi gone, I'm locked out.

"Never have a girl, Christopher. Do it, and you're in for a world of hurt." My father's words after my sister got knocked up at sixteen. A world of hurt. The Suicide Blog. I found it sandwiched in Kayla's browser history. Detailed instructions printed in cheerful, blue font. I sat there, sick, eyes glazed, as I scanned it: when, exactly, to step in front of a moving train to prevent the engineer from braking; the exact number of painkillers to swallow, listed by milligram according to body type; how to jump, just so, when hanging yourself to ensure the rope properly snaps your neck. I imagined Kayla, clear as day, floating in a tub of cool, pink water with her skin turned as white as the porcelain around her. It made my stomach clench, that image. It made me sick.

She bit my head off when I confronted her about it: "God, Dad, it's for a school paper. Don't I get any privacy?" Then I was staring at the backside of her door, thinking, Jesus, only fifteen years old, and my little girl already wants to kill herself. I have to do something.

"Something" turned into backpacking Colorado's Flat Tops Wilderness. Lexi had begged me to take this very trip a year before her diagnosis. I'd groaned and bitched about it, too consumed with an upcoming board presentation to care. We were in the middle of a deadline — the lead bank in a huge corporate divestiture from which Gorman & Gorman would profit nicely. I was running the deal. It was my ticket, our ticket, Lexi and I, to a better life. Then Lexi stumbled out of the shower with her hair wet and dripping and smashed my hand to her breast.

"Do you feel it? Do you?"

I did. A lump that sucked the moisture from my mouth. I remember tracing my fingertip over the mound, thinking, surely not, right? Cancer happened to other people. Not us. Cancer was a threat on par with global warming and plastic oceans. Always there, but out there somewhere else. Terrible, but not our problem. We were good. We were right where we needed to be. Fine, even. We'd always been just that — fine.

She was gone in six months.

I swallow hard and curse myself for the memory and the instant hot ache of it. A piece of the past I can never recover, only relive over and over without changing a goddamn thing. And there are so many things I would change. But right now isn't the time for indulging my grief. No, I need to focus on breaking the move to the girls. I have to stay clear-headed.

It won't be easy. I can picture how Kayla will melt down when I tell her about Denver. She'll complain about leaving her friends and Lexi's parents. Tears will spill. She'll whine about how much she hates me, and how her mother would have never, ever, done something like this to her, even though it was Lexi who'd spurred our move from New York to Boston, who'd done this exact thing to Kayla when she was nine. But Kayla will get over it, and it's not Kayla who worries me most. It's Emma.

Boston is all she's ever known. To her, Boston is Lexi. It's why we have to move. She needs space to heal, space to speak again. Jesus, I still can't believe it. Nine months without hearing a single word from my little girl. God, how I miss the sound of her voice, of her laugh. I need that laugh right now. We all do.

The thought pushes me forward a little faster, and I catch up with Kayla and loop an arm around her shoulders as we break from the trees. She stiffens and squirms from my grip, and I wonder, briefly, why I even try anymore.

"Hey, why don't you cook us dinner tonight?" I say.

"You mean heat up the soup?"

"Well, sure, but after, we can have s'mores."

She rolls her eyes. "God, Dad, I'm not ten. And it's going to rain."

"We'll have time if we hurry. Emma would like some s'mores, don't you think?" I look for her as I say it, something tugging at me, a blank space by the packs where I left her coloring a few minutes earlier. "Kayla . . . where's your sister?"

Her eyes narrow and she scans the lake, the water turned to slate and rippling with the wind. Her lips tighten, and right then, in that exact moment, I know my daughter is gone.

Printed in Great Britain
by Amazon